Works by S.M. Perlow

Vampires and the Life of Erin Rose

Novels

Choosing a Master

Alone

Lion

Hope

War

Short Stories

Alice Stood Up

—

The Grand Crucible

Novels

Golden Dragons, Gilded Age

—

Other Works

Short Stories

The Girl Who Was Always Single

HOPE

VAMPIRES AND THE LIFE OF ERIN ROSE

S.M. Perlow

Bealion Publishing

A Bealion Publishing Book

Editor: Lynn O'Dell, Red Adept Editing Services
Cover design: Streetlight Graphics
Formatting: Polgarus Studio

smperlow.com—updates, social media links, and more information about the story

ISBN: 978-0-9992858-3-1

1.0.4-p1

1

After my rescue from Alexander's compound in October of 2009, I spent three months traveling across the country with Zhilan and Grant, before returning home to Virginia in January. Nights flew by while I saw new cities, met new Sanguans, and trained and sparred with Zhilan.

November 21, 2009

A leak from the police to a local news station was the only reason the video from earlier that night became public. In my hotel room in Austin, Texas, I found a high-quality version on a tabloid website. By then, Massimo Sartori was in the hospital, listed in critical condition. The second generation Italian-American ran the nation's largest defense company, which had already announced its intention to sue the television channel that broadcast the video. It hardly mattered. A lawsuit could never completely suppress something already spread so far and wide on the web. I closed the article about the company's reaction.

In the next tab, while the video continued to buffer over

the slow wireless connection, I scrolled down to read. Massimo had been on his way home from Los Angeles when his plane had trouble with its landing gear. The airplane had to circle for two hours before touching down at Dulles, ten minutes after sunset. David, Massimo's thirty-four-year-old son, and Raymond Santiago, the company's marketing director, had flown in hours earlier, then waited for Massimo. In the limousine from the airport, Raymond sat across from the two Sartoris, shooting the video on his phone.

The web page's player finally finished loading and began with David facing his father, speaking. "Twenty years and what is this, the third time I've been on a highway after sundown? Or anywhere but a guarded hotel, office, or—"

"You shouldn't have waited for me," Massimo interrupted, without turning from the window.

"I was worried. No one would tell me anything about your plane." David looked out his window. "And I'm not complaining. *Caleb* can have the night."

"The night grows darker, not lighter," Massimo said. "Those twins… sometimes I wonder about it all. I wonder about the choices I've made for us."

"Dad—"

Babump. The scene jolted, probably from the limo hitting a bump.

"—we'll be fine," David finished.

"Tonight? Sure," Massimo said.

David shot his attention to Raymond. "Are you recording this?"

Raymond kept the phone steady. "Yes."

David's brow furrowed. "Why?"

"I'll edit it. I promise. I just want my wife to believe that I was out after sunset with you two."

"Ha! Do me a favor and delete that one. We'll take another you can show her."

Boom! The camera shook. *Boom!* Bright flames burst out the right side window.

The phone fell to the left on the seat, where it captured cars veering outside the far window.

Thunk! Massimo's head hit the glass. David fell into him. Raymond's legs came into the camera's view.

The phone caught glimpses of the three bodies tumbling in midair, and rising flames, smoke, and wreckage outside, until—*crunch!*—the Sartoris and Raymond hit the upside down roof, and the phone settled with its lens blocked.

After a shudder, the camera once again recorded bodies rolling over, while the highway outside did the same. *Crunch!* The three passengers hit the roof again and the screen went blank. The video ended.

I left the website and clicked through the coverage at washingtonpost.com. Witnesses reported that four cars ahead, a huge male Sanguan, shirtless, pale white, and wearing tattered jeans, ran onto the highway and flipped over a navy Corvette. Eight vehicles were caught in the accident. The Sanguan darted into the resulting blaze, then stood motionless until flames reduced him to ash.

I learned the next night that seven people died, including Raymond. Eleven were injured, two critically. Massimo ended up in a coma, with a fractured hip and severe internal bleeding. David broke his collarbone and arm, but was expected to make a full recovery.

November 23, 2009

The detective fired twice before retreating behind the corner of the wall in the steel mill. His shirt was covered in blood, his partner, long dead. Danny, sitting to my right, had already seen the movie, so as I bit into his wrist, and his eyes closed, I didn't worry he would miss anything. I took care to avoid his memories of the film's ending. The redhead to Danny's right sipped on her sangria, while she, and Grant next to her, stared at the chase on screen.

The theater in Austin was special in that every other row of seats had been removed and replaced with a narrow wooden bar. Waiters served humans food and beverages during the film, and my kind drank freely on those willing. I had met Danny earlier at a bar, and he had suggested the movie. He was really cute, and I hadn't been to a theater in months.

We were watching a rare big-budget film completely devoid of vampires. As the movie neared its conclusion, the absence seemed a stunningly minor detail. The human serial killer, on the run with police closing in, might as well have been a crazed immortal. Instead of fangs, he used knives. The killer's cuts had offered his victims none of the pleasure of a vampire bite, but in the end, as with so many bites, a heart ceased to beat.

What I had hoped would be a brief escape from reality was

instead reinforcing my bleak opinion of the harsh world. So many Sanguans were evil—Alexander had been, as had the one who caused the Sartoris' horrible car crash. Sanguans who killed each time they drank were evil. The leaders of the Spectavi condemned Sanguans to death unjustly and controlled the actions of their flock with laboratory made synthetic blood. Maybe "evil" wasn't the word for the Spectavi because they had long been allied with humans, and aimed to help them, but "good" didn't seem to be correct either.

In spite of the constant threat from vampires, plenty of people committed horrible crimes against other people. And in the well-reviewed film that was drawing to a close, in an imagined world devoid of blood drinkers, a serial killer was the chosen villain.

Night or day, fact or fiction, mortal or immortal, evil, or at least some darkness, was everywhere.

Danny put down his beer and ate a cold french fry from his plate. When he finished chewing, I sipped from his wrist again, thankful I had learned to stop drinking before killing.

December 7, 2009

Me: You're certain these messages are private?

Victoria: Yes. They aren't on Eure's network.

On my laptop, I clicked through picture after picture, in article after article from the night before, of Caterine and Ariane—tall, slender, and pale as ever, wearing flowing black gowns and sitting between spires on the ledge atop their late brother's cathedral in Chartres. I continued my text message conversation with Victoria on my phone.

Me: Before last night, had you seen Caterine and Ariane recently?

I watched a video from Chartres of the identical twin beauties holding each other's right wrists, sipping in unison.

"Drink from me!" a man yelled from below.

They stopped their sucking. "Soon," Caterine called down, her gown and long hair blowing in the wind.

Ariane licked her lips.

"No, me!" another man yelled.

"Me!" came from a woman.

The twins stood and got back to their drinking. They'd share each other's hunger when they next awoke, an increased hunger, the price of vampires feeding from one another for longer than a few seconds. I had never experienced such a thirst, but had no doubt the pair would make quick work of however many people they needed to satisfy theirs.

Victoria: I hadn't seen them for a while.

Police sirens sounded in the video. The twins stopped their sipping and smiled for the cameras.

"Soon," Ariane called.

They raced off the cathedral's roof. Predictably, excited fans of the spectacle made up most of the online comments.

December 15, 2009

"Your eyes are just as green as mine, you know," I said, refuting Zhilan's comment from the first time we met.

"Yes. I know." Wearing her red robe, Zhilan tapped her

bokken against the foam mat. "Are you ready?" The eighteenth-century Chinese vampire's youthful, normally pleasant face was decidedly agitated.

"What's the rush?" I adjusted the belt at the waist of my black robe. We stood across from each other, alone in a gym in Palo Alto, California, at one of her friends' places. "Can't I savor yesterday for a little longer?" We hadn't been alone the night before when I had finally scored a solid hit against her. Grant and Houjin had seen my wooden katana smack her arm squarely and send her flying. The thin vampire stood two inches shorter than I did, and had a little less reach, but aside from that one hit, her speed continued to give me trouble.

"Yesterday is over." Zhilan came at me.

Crack!-crack! Our bokken met, and I retreated a step.

December 16, 2009

In San Francisco, Houjin led Zhilan and me into a Sanguan-owned, human and vampire apartment building. The place was dirty, old, and pretty dreary, but supposedly safe for the young adults who sought it out for the cheap rent and for the opportunity to be near immortals. The few Sanguans on each floor had easy access to willing prey.

We walked into an elevator. The silver doors closed, and Houjin pressed his pale thumb against the bare wall panel below the controls. We descended to the basement level, and after the *beep*, the LED floor indicator went blank, and we kept going.

Born in the thirteenth century, Houjin had learned a great deal while working with Sanguan scientists over the years in labs like the one where we were headed. Nevertheless, he focused on strategy and guiding their work instead of directly contributing to it.

When the elevator finally stopped, it opened to a metal door a few feet away. Zhilan and I followed Houjin into a large, poorly lit room. A mess of lamps, papers, and computers covered the two long tables. The same disorganization, plus microscopes, test tubes, and other scientific equipment, was spread over counters along the walls. Two Sanguans sat at the counter to the right; one peered through a microscope, and the other typed on a laptop.

"Erin," Houjin said. "Meet Omar and Nigel." He gestured at each as he said their names.

The two swiveled in their low-backed office chairs.

Omar asked, "Has Vera, the great scientist, come to teach us a thing or two?"

"Vera's long gone. I'm no scientist anymore." I had picked up a couple of chemistry textbooks, but found the material dry and, at times, practically incomprehensible. Perhaps years of study would allow me to relearn the subject, but the knowledge used to alter synthetic blood in attempts to heal Caterine and Ariane when they were prisoners was nowhere to be found. I assumed the physical, muscular aspects of sword fighting had caused that skill to stick with me, ready to be unlocked through instruction and practice.

"What a shame," Omar said.

"Omar is working on a supplement he hopes might

lessen our aversion to silver," Houjin explained.

"How's it going?" I asked.

Omar rolled up his sleeve to reveal a line of black circles up his arm, each smaller than a penny. "Not especially well tonight."

Houjin motioned to the other vampire. "Nigel is trying to uncover exactly how the Spectavi engineered their synthetic to cause specific changes, like forgetting being forced to become a vampire. Then, there's the question of how they made those changes permanent."

"How's *that* going?" I asked.

Nigel glanced at Omar. "Considerably better."

December 25, 2009

"Merry Christmas," Zhilan said.

A Sanguan clerk handed me a polished metal case the size of a large hardcover book. The small Portland shop was chock full of swords, knives, guns, explosives, and an array of other weapons, so I couldn't wait to see what the case contained.

I frowned at Zhilan. "But I didn't get you anything."

"Don't worry. Open it."

I undid the clasp at the bottom and lifted the hinged lid to find a long, thin black handle, about an inch wide, set in gray foam. To its right, straps were wrapped tightly around a narrow strip of leather. I picked up the handle and found two buttons near my thumb. Pressing one did nothing. I slid the other down, and a folding blade shot out, then locked into place.

"It's vampire-forged, Japanese steel, seven inches long," Zhilan said. "Long enough for just about any neck you will come across. The handle is aluminum. I know how you love your sword, but this will be more practical on some occasions."

"It's incredible. Thank you." I waved the knife in front of me a few times. The aluminum was slightly longer than the blade, making the whole thing quite long, depending on where I held it. One side of the handle had two recessed, four-pointed star shapes. The knife weighed nothing to me and fit the size of my hand perfectly. I folded the blade closed and noticed small symbols etched vertically at the end, opposite the two buttons.

Zhilan explained, "Chinese. They mean, 'Look to the future.'"

"I love it." I ran my thumb over the characters. "Can we go practice?"

———————

Wearing blue boxers and a t-shirt, I lay on the couch of my hotel room with my laptop, across from my coffin for the day. More and more often, I spent daytime dressed in my clothes from the preceding night. Unlike mortals, I rested soundly whether perfectly comfortable or not. Nevertheless, on occasions when I had a long time before that rest would come, I did sometimes change.

Zhilan and I had practiced with wooden knives for hours. The reason for all the sparring and training to fight faster and more precisely was because one bad move in battle could cost me a limb or be the end of me all together. I had plenty to learn with the short weapon, but had quickly become decent.

A specially designed holster accompanied the gift. Two leather straps wrapped securely around my thigh. Another strip of leather ran perpendicular to them, with a small pocket for the bottom of the knife. Halfway up the vertical strap, a raised, star-shaped metal protrusion matched a notch in the handle. Another protrusion was at the strap's top. To secure the knife to the holster, I slid it into the pocket, then brought the handle down over the two protrusions, which locked the knife in place.

I planned to wear the device on my left thigh, so I could comfortably reach across my body and push the top release button on the handle. I couldn't wait to use it, or even just to bring it out with me.

Penguins slid out of an igloo on a flashing banner ad on yahoo.com. I typed "Nicolas Duchart" into the search box. Edmond's brother had supposedly been responsible for Caterine and Ariane's transformation from human into the first vampires, but no one, including any of the Sanguans I had met during my travels, had ever heard of him. I had run the same query, over and over, on every search engine I could find, but ran it again anyway.

The results met my expectations—lots of Nicolases, some Ducharts, but no Nicolas Duchart. As with the twins, information on their brother, Nicolas, had apparently been scrubbed from the internet or had never been posted in the first place. I wondered if the twins ever planned to reveal the nature of their origin or their family name, or if they had reason to keep those secret.

January 7, 2010

"Bye, Grandpa." I hit End. We had spoken for fifteen minutes after he called to wish me a happy birthday. It would have been my twenty-third. Yet I had been Erin for less than three years and a vampire for less than one. In the long run, especially after he was gone, I wondered which day I would celebrate.

January 12, 2010

Me: Were you in Argentina when they destroyed the factory?

Victoria: Yes, but it didn't matter. The twins brought a larger force than we could handle. We're increasing our defenses at our other synthetic plants around the world.

Me: Do you think it's right to use synthetic blood to control the thoughts of Spectavi?

Victoria: It was a hard choice, but a necessary means to an end. You're young, but I've witnessed hundreds of years of human suffering at the hands of Sanguans. The Spectavi all want to take strong action against Sanguans, but building consensus about the best way to help has always been hard. The politics were frustrating and time consuming until we began doing things this way.

Me: What if the twins tell everyone? Their fame might give them credibility, and there's no way all will agree with your rationalization.

Victoria: That's why we're trying to stop them.

January 24, 2010

I lifted my fangs out of his neck where I usually bit and swallowed Luke's hot blood. I kissed his cheek, then rolled off his broad, bare chest to lay on my back. "Gwen really doesn't like that you see me."

Jonathan, his band's drummer, wasn't home. His was the other of the two small bedrooms in the cozy apartment at the bottom of Adams Morgan's main street of bars, clubs, and restaurants in D.C. Gwen was the bassist and Luke's ex-girlfriend.

Luke joined me in staring up at the ceiling. "It doesn't matter what she thinks."

"She thinks it's dangerous. She doesn't trust me."

We turned to face each other.

"She's just jealous." He wrapped his arm around me.

We kissed. His tongue ran over one of my fangs, and I tasted fresh blood.

January 25, 2010

The new Spectavi leader, Reinald, a product of eighth-century France, was different, but proving no less ruthless than Edmond. For a long time, Edmond strove to be known as the leader of Eure, the business, and downplayed his role as the ruler of the Spectavi, at war to wipe out the Sanguans. Reinald seemed to prefer the opposite. He gave minimal attention to Eure's corporate board, which oversaw a group of senior Spectavi who managed thousands of mortal employees around the globe. He only weighed in on the most important business decisions and only appeared at the most high-profile public events. He spent far more time with his war council: Victoria, his chief scientist William, his second-in-command Konrad, the priest Pietro, and a handful of others. Most of those Spectavi leaders had met Vera, though of course, I didn't remember that at all. According to Victoria, there had been no special call for revenge against me over Edmond's death, because in addition to her portraying me as a young, unimportant Sanguan, most who knew that Edmond had wiped my mind and sent me away considered it absurdly risky for him to have taken me back as he had.

In the weeks after Eure's security cameras had been rolled out to all of D.C., Sanguans had destroyed stoplight after stoplight in an effort to cripple the system. Instead of participating, Grant moved south to Alexandria, Virginia, which was a good thing because the Spectavi later rounded up the Sanguans who had caused the mayhem. Reinald had both ordered the operation to be carried out by his obedient army of young Spectavi clad in gray fatigues with assault rifles and swords, and fought individual vampires, blade to blade.

While being interviewed about their crackdown by local media, the Spectavi let slip that their camera system had been completely unaffected by Sanguan attacks. Grant and I got in touch with Sagar, the vampire we had kidnapped from Eure and starved of synthetic blood until he remembered being forced into becoming a Spectavi. He confirmed that most of our intelligence about the cameras was accurate—they were always on and their video, processed in real time, tracked Sanguans—and also explained the Spectavi's boastful claim. The cameras had been hidden and never in the stoplights. Because of that, my ex-boyfriend, Todd, was especially important to the Spectavi. Sagar had seen plans and maps, but Todd had gone out and finalized installations on sites all over the city. Aside from knowing the intricacies of the software that ran the system, Todd knew the location of every camera.

D.C. was changing. Except for between four and six in the morning, Sanguans were having an extremely difficult time getting away with *any* crime—whether they took a life or not. I found it uncomfortable to be in the city, which, doubtless, was the Spectavi's plan all along. Complaints from civil rights groups were dying out as the streets got safer and safer. Everyone cheered at the capture and execution of a few older Sanguans who had been too stubborn to leave the city. I doubted most people would have cared that the crimes they had been accused of were fabrications.

Very few Sanguans remained residents of the nation's capital, and we all feared that the next surveillance installation would be in Northern Virginia. When I suggested going after Todd, Zhilan persuaded me it would be unwise. Even if we managed to convince him that the Spectavi had brainwashed him, if we didn't strike against the Spectavi and cameras in D.C., little would have been gained. Unfortunately, we couldn't sustain such a large-scale campaign. Significantly outnumbered and with the vast majority of humans on our enemy's side, we'd eventually lose, and the system would be rebuilt. I would rescue Todd someday, but while I hated admitting it, the time wasn't right.

I checked my phone—*11:59*—one minute to go. Dressed in my typical black attire for such occasions—a tight, long-sleeved shirt with a high rounded neck, athletic pants, flat shoes, my katana across my back, and my knife strapped to the outside of my thigh—I peered around a tree at Alexander's dimly lit military compound. Zhilan and Grant were both nearby. I had tagged along on other missions, but had never had as much responsibility on one.

I checked again—*11:59*. While some Sanguans had been openly angry with Zhilan and the others for assisting Victoria in killing Alexander, most didn't mind. His rivals were thrilled to see him go. Others condemned Alexander's love of torture, and nearly all found it perfectly reasonable that Zhilan would do whatever necessary to save her friend. Plus, Sanguans often fought Sanguans. When Zhilan had gotten word that three-hundred-year-old Silas, who had taken over for Alexander, was plotting revenge against us, we decided to strike first.

11:59. Atop the concrete wall, a Sanguan guard in green fatigues sat with one hand resting lazily on his stationary machine gun, while he studied the cell phone in his other hand. *11:59.* I remembered vividly my steel prison in that compound—my wrists bound at my sides, my feet pinned together at the coffin's base, my struggles to break free, the bites, the darkness... it could have ended so much worse.

They had cut my long chestnut hair so that it didn't reach my shoulders, and after the initial shock, I had decided to keep it that way. *11:59*. The guard took his cell in both hands and used his thumbs to type. *11:59*. Was my phone broken?

12:00. I secured my phone on my belt and raced from the woods. I leapt at the middle of the compound wall and silently kicked off it, aiming for the sturdiest nearby tree. When my shoes touched bark, I grabbed my knife and pushed the release button. While the blade unfolded, I kicked off again, sending myself flipping forward toward the machine gun. The guard was struggling to get to his feet when my knife blade sliced through his neck. I caught his falling head and body and gently placed both near the big gun.

I jumped down and headed to the front gate. Zhilan stood there, wiping blood off her straight black *jian* onto her pant leg. She sheathed the sword in the scabbard on her back. I considered the possibility that she had attacked the guard on the opposite side of the compound early in order to get to our meeting place first, but that didn't sound like her. She nodded at me, then sped to the right.

With my knife out, I made my way past an unmanned jeep to the nearest small building to the left. The dark green steel door was locked, but easily forced open by my shoulder. A dangling fluorescent light flickered in the disturbing room. I made my way between a line of vacant cages and a wall covered with chains, racks, and other blood-splattered torture devices. In the last cage, a gaunt, bitten man had been dead for a while, possibly neglected after Alexander's gang fell into disarray. While we had confirmed some had returned to the base, perhaps they lost interest in the toys in that room.

I ran back outside, checked the time, and didn't notice anyone out on patrol. Deeper into the compound, the next building looked exactly like the last one. Finding the door unlocked, I crept into a bright hallway with heavy metal music blaring from a dark room at the end of it. I quietly made my way down the hall, stopping to peer through a door window to a small room full of weapons—mostly guns. The silver knob was locked, and I chose to leave it. The next door was ajar, and I went halfway in, but found nothing except a few computer workstations. I continued toward the music.

With my back against the end of the hallway wall, I used the front camera of my phone to see around the corner. Aided by a tiny lamp that glowed blue, a vampire studied a map spread over a large table. I recognized him as one who had frequently plotted with Alexander when I had been captive. I put away my phone and considered my options, from among all Zhilan had taught me.

I took a small white pellet from a pouch on my belt and threw it into the room, to the right of the table.

Phwof! A burst of light left a small cloud of smoke.

I rushed the distracted Sanguan and slashed at his neck with my knife. He avoided the swipe and punched my stomach, launching me into the wall a few feet away. He drew a gun, but I pushed myself off the concrete and kicked it out of his hand before he could fire. I ducked under a punch, then blocked another with my left arm and slashed down at his right hand.

"Agh!" Blood gushed from his wrist where his hand had been, then the flow slowed significantly. He raced for the hall.

Determined to be faster, I darted the same way and drove him into the wall. He pushed back, while I stabbed my knife straight into the side of his neck.

I held him there, bleeding. "You're all bastards."

"Gra-a…" He struggled. "Grrr…"

The blood from his wound slowed to a trickle, so I rotated my blade. Fresh liquid poured from his neck. I kept turning, blood kept spilling, and his eyelids drifted closed. His resistance ended. In a swift motion, I slid the knife across and severed his head. His body slumped to the ground, and I wiped my knife on my leg before putting away the weapon.

I ran outside and met Zhilan in front of the large building where I had been tortured.

"You're late," she said.

"Sorry."

"Any trouble?"

"Nope." I checked the time on my phone. "I'm *one* minute late."

"Late is late." She smiled. "Come on."

I followed her through the unlocked door and down the long, drab hall with fake stone siding. Dim light bled around the corner from the cavernous throne room.

A chain rattled. We expected many of the vampires who

still lived at Alexander's to be out for the night, but assumed at least Silas would be around. His death would further cripple the gang and, hopefully, send the message that it would be unwise to come after Zhilan and me.

Zhilan silently pulled her sword from its scabbard, and I retrieved my katana, Tomori, from mine. I twirled the leather-wrapped handle between my fingers at my side, as I had seen Ariane do in that very building. End over end, the slightly curved, inch-wide, twenty-eight-inch-long shiny steel blade spun. Zhilan must have noticed because she stood up straight, looked back, and rolled her eyes. I stopped my spinning.

Zhilan shook her head, then sped around the corner.

I followed as quickly as I could. "Ahh!" A small dagger dug into my side. I pulled it out and threw it at the Sanguan who had thrown it. She avoided the knife and threw another as traces of silver that had melted off the first dagger caused my wound to throb. Her second knife hit my shoulder, and I pulled it out, but not fast enough to avoid another source of pain.

Silas's two straight swords clashed with Zhilan's blade near the metal throne. At the walls, two muscular, barely dressed men and four skinny women in various colors of underwear stood with their wrists chained above them. I raced at my assailant—the taller of the two who had drunk from the human, Keith, to torment me while I starved in that room. I swung my blade, but she darted away and hurled another dagger. I batted the small missile away with my sword, like hitting a baseball. She threw a fourth, and I did the same.

"Grah!" Silas growled as one of his blades clattered to the ground.

My foe drew a large knife from her hip, glanced at the entranceway, then charged me. I stood my ground and parried some blows, while avoiding others. She cut and stabbed quickly, and if she had held a sword and wielded it with similar skill, it might have been a fairer contest. But with the short knife, she didn't stand a chance.

She jabbed with her blade, and as I stepped aside—*fschwt!*—my sword sliced clean through her midsection. Her legs crumpled to the ground, then her other half hit concrete, and blood poured.

"Traitors!" Silas screamed. He bled from his right side and swung his blade with both hands.

Zhilan used a single hand on her sword and seemed quicker than her larger opponent. She might have been stronger, as well.

I rushed into the middle of their battle. "Ye!" I yelped, when Silas slashed through the outside of my arm.

Zhilan shot me a look of warning and—*tyn!*—blocked his next swing. My wound healed, while I shifted half a step away and focused on being more careful.

Tyn—I blocked a strike. *Tyn*—Zhilan blocked. Silas raced for the door, but Zhilan beat him there. I caught up and swung at his back—*tyn*—Silas met it. *Tyn*—he blocked a blow from Zhilan. *Fschwt*—I cut across his leg.

"Ahh!" He dropped to one knee.

Fschwt!—Zhilan sliced his body in half. The newest leader of Alexander's gang bled at our feet.

Zhilan grabbed her phone. "Grant, now." She ran to the prisoners chained to the wall on the right. I went the other way and cut the chains above a man's head.

"Thank you," he said.

I didn't respond. He wasn't Keith, and the other man in the room wasn't, either. I wished we had come sooner, despite the fact that Keith had probably not been allowed to live long after the night his blood had revived me.

The freed man followed close while I sliced the chains from a woman who fell onto me.

"Help her," I said and passed her to him.

Zhilan motioned to the entrance. "Hurry."

The man lifted the woman and staggered out the door. The others followed, and I trailed, watching for vampires. At the exit, Grant helped the freed prisoners into a dark green van with three rows of bench seats. Those inside had already wrapped themselves in blankets.

After the last of them, Zhilan sat at the end of the bench near the side door, and I hopped into the front passenger seat. Grant took the wheel, sped us around a few turns, and out the gated entrance, onto a dirt road that cut into the woods.

"Who are you?" one of the men asked.

I twisted in my seat to look at him. "We're not all monsters, like they were."

Ten minutes later, we left the van full of people at a hospital emergency room.

January 26, 2010

Victoria: Good job last night.

Me: Thanks. How did you hear?

Victoria: News of Silas's death is spreading. His gang is finished.

Me: Good. Can I ask you a question about Caterine and Ariane?

Victoria: Of course.

Me: Is the story of where they came from true—that they were Edmond's sisters and that the Devil made them vampires?

Victoria: That is the story Edmond told me.

Me: What did his brother have to do with it?

Victoria: His brother?

Me: Nicolas. Ariane mentioned he was responsible, not her or Caterine.

Victoria: The first I learned of Nicolas was when I drank from you in Edmond's basement. I had never heard of him before and have not since.

February 7, 2010

Massimo Sartori died in the hospital. He had come out of his coma two days earlier. I saw the news on my phone, in between rounds of sparring with Zhilan in her basement gym. I had read about the family at length after the car accident.

David took the reins of Sartori Equipment Corporation— Sarcorp, the company his grandfather founded in 1921. For decades, Massimo and David had refused to go out after sundown. Worth billions, they traveled by day, never together, and spent considerable funds to keep themselves protected from vampires at night. They weren't the only ones who lived that way, but they were two of the richest.

David was well regarded at Sarcorp, where he had been working his entire life, so most expected the transition to his leadership to be a smooth one.

Massimo's other son, twenty-seven-year-old Caleb, had a strained relationship with his father and brother and did not share their aversion to nighttime.

February 20, 2010

After midnight, a few miles from my home in Arlington, Virginia, I strolled on a sidewalk lined with snow-dusted shrubs. I was seeing Luke a few times a week, loving each visit, but couldn't see him every night. I feared he'd grow weak and dependent if I drank his blood so often. I had witnessed my old friend Kristi become distracted at work, constantly in a daze remembering her last bite from Christopher or imagining the ones sure to come with the setting sun. As a mortal girl, I had been ensnared by Edmond the same way.

At a brick row house, I stopped in front of a window. Inside, young men and women chatted, carrying drinks around the living room and listening to eighties rock music. I found myself a little jealous of them. I was truly excited about who and what I had become—no gift could compare with immortality. I loved what I could do with a blade, and the blood... well, the blood was incredible.

But those ten people seemed so carefree—unburdened by a past full of tragedy and cruelty and unconcerned with the ongoing war that was my future. Their lives must have been so different from mine.

The front door opened. A short, blond-haired girl wearing a blue wool coat backed out halfway. "Come on, Zack!"

A car drove by, and I retreated to the end of the block. A young man—I assumed the summoned Zack—walked out to where the girl stood on the porch and kissed her cheek. They headed away from me on the sidewalk.

I followed at mortal speed, my high-heeled boots making the same sound on the concrete as the girl's. Zack stopped, and then the girl did. They turned to me, and I halted. Zack put his arm around the girl, and they started marching briskly.

I matched their pace. Why not have a taste? I wouldn't kill them.

The couple rounded the corner, and a few seconds later, I did the same. The boy looked cute enough. She'd scream while I drank from him, but I'd be long gone before help came. He glanced back again, then grabbed the girl's wrist and pulled her a quick step forward.

Faster than they could see, I raced around to get in front of him, and when he ran into me, I held him and bit his neck above his sweater collar. His grip on the girl's wrist loosened, then his fingers slipped off of her arm as the familiar heat and flame inside me built. A car passed on the opposite side of the street, its driver either oblivious to what went on or uncaring.

Zack and June had been celebrating a friend's birthday. Their first stops had been a Mexican restaurant for happy hour, followed by a heated rooftop bar. Then they went to the house where I had seen them to play card games and listen to music. Some of them had graduated, and others attended George Washington University, where Zack and June were juniors.

June watched me intently while I sipped. She hadn't moved or made a peep.

All of the friends were having a great time. Zack and June had left to catch a cab. At the sight of me, Zack had been immediately terrified.

I withdrew my fangs, and Zack stumbled when I let go.

"Are you okay?" June asked.

"Yes." He collected himself, grabbed her wrist, and tried to pull her to him, but she shook her arm free.

Her blue eyes looked up at me. "You won't hurt me, either?"

I smiled. "No, I swear." Nothing I had glimpsed from Zack had hinted at June's reaction.

"June!" he yelled.

"I'll be fine." She stepped toward me.

I brought her closer and leaned down to her lovely neck. I guessed the taste would be sweet, but the little girl's blood turned out not to be especially so. Hers burned warmer than his.

June had been curious about vampire bites for a long time. She understood Sanguans were dangerous, but couldn't help wondering.

Zack pushed at me with both hands. "June!"

I held him at arm's length and continued drinking.

June loved Zack and didn't know if he felt the same way. I searched Zack's memories—he liked her a lot, but wasn't sure about "love." Her blood was so hot!

I stopped drinking, and June slowly opened her eyes. Zack prepared to steady her.

She didn't need the help. "I'm June."

"I'm Erin."

"Let's go!" Zack urged. He pulled her wrist and managed to get her moving away from me.

June stopped and looked back.

"I'll never hurt you. Or Zack," I told her.

He pulled harder, and June had to resume following. She glanced back repeatedly until out of sight.

————————

Three nights later, I called June. She wanted to meet me by herself, but I asked her to try to convince Zack to come. Initially, the request was for their sake. I didn't think June seeing me on her own would have been healthy for their relationship. Later, I realized that half the couple would have been far less interesting than the whole.

We met outside a jazz lounge downtown, away from campus. The public setting allayed some of Zack's fears, and he figured the distance from their school would reduce the likelihood of any of his friends running into us. June appeared downright giddy while we made our way through the sparse crowd to a back corner booth.

They sat down on the far side, and as soon as I sat opposite them, June popped up and slid onto my bench. She leaned into me. While the band improvised across the lounge, I didn't hesitate to dig my fangs into her delicate neck and suck her fiery blood. Since the moment we had parted, she had longed to see me again. It had taken a while, but she had convinced Zack to trust me, telling him, "She *knew* they could." I felt her fib—she *hoped* with all her heart it would be safe to see me, night after night, but she didn't *know* anything. I withdrew my fangs from the English major, and she slumped back, taking a long, deep breath.

June opened her eyes and nodded at Zack. He pushed up his sleeve and brought his wrist toward me. I took it gently and leaned forward. When I sipped, I learned that while he remained scared, he had also imagined another of my bites. On top of that, as wrong as it felt to him, seeing June with me turned him on. Zack was eager to be alone with her later.

I stopped drinking, and the pre-med student inspected the fang marks.

"I should go." I turned to June, who gave a pouty look. "I'll see you soon?"

"Yes!" She got up, sat back down beside Zack, and rested her head on his shoulder.

Zack gave a half smile.

As I left, June called over the music, "Bye, Erin!"

March 5, 2010

Me: Was there any indication they planned to attack your factory in Moscow?

Victoria: No, they weren't even there.

Me: Where were they?

Victoria: I chased them all over Cairo that night.

Me: What were they doing in Cairo?

Victoria: I don't know.

Me: What would stop the twins, or anyone, from altering the synthetic blood to issue their own orders to Spectavi?

Victoria: We have processes in place to ensure that does not happen.

March 23, 2010

A little after four, under an overcast sky, I sat with my legs off the end of a dock in Alexandria, with sail boats tied up on both sides. I wore black pants and hadn't bothered with a coat over my gray, short-sleeved shirt. My knife hung off my belt on my left hip.

Hours earlier, five Sanguans had murdered thirty people at a fancy restaurant in New York City for no apparent reason. Spectavi responded by taking out four of the Sanguans. Their pursuit of the fifth dominated the news. The attack had been especially blatant and gruesome, but I had other vampires on my mind.

So far, the twins hadn't done anything to expose the secret of how Spectavi leaders used their synthetic blood.

Aside from destroying a few production facilities and showing up in Chartres, the pair had actually kept a surprisingly low profile.

Zhilan found my fear that Caterine and Ariane might alter the synthetic for their own purposes legitimate. The blood was produced in factories all over the world. Single-serve cans and bottles were shipped by the caseload to Eure's offices and Spectavi outposts. Some drank it there, and others picked up what they'd need for the upcoming month. The number of factories meant no single point of failure would disrupt the overall supply.

At the same time, the spread-out distribution network offered Sanguans plenty of targets to compromise the system. The twins hadn't indicated anything, but my gut told me they were up to something beyond merely destroying those factories. Their absence from a few attacks added circumstantial evidence to support my instinct. Unfortunately, since the attacks they had skipped were *at factories*, that evidence led away from them being concerned with the synthetic blood, leaving me nowhere.

I got up and headed off the dock, onto a narrow asphalt path toward Old Town. Who was Nicolas? I hated not knowing the whole truth. I couldn't figure out how, but I had to consider the possibility that whatever the twins were up to had something to do with him. Even more farfetched—could Nicolas still be alive?

Two blocks from the river, I heard a growl, followed by a scream somewhere not far ahead. Considering the time, I had an idea of the cause. Just as I decided to go another way, a man called out, "Help! Please!"

The tone struck me as more desperate than usual. I sprinted toward the voice and found a short Sanguan holding a young, blond-haired man against the brick wall outside a parking deck, a block to my right. Visible under a single yellow light hanging high above him, the man's face was covered in white makeup and dark eye shadow. Upon recognizing the vampire, I slowed to a stop across the street from the pair.

The man spotted me over Snake's shoulder. "Please! Help me!"

Snake turned to look. "You?" The scrawny creature who had thrown my human body against a bathroom wall and broken two of my fingers at the club Night remained as deformed as he had been then. His burnt face hadn't healed and long, crooked fangs distracted from his other jagged teeth. "What do *you* want?"

Blood ran down the bitten man's neck while he struggled.

"Let him go," I called.

"Ha! I don't think so. My fun with Blaine is only beginning."

I moved toward him. "Let him go."

"Why?" Snake growled. "That damn cross tattoo! Do you reckon yourself some kind of saint to these pathetic humans?"

"When I kill you, I don't want Blaine getting in the way." I pulled my knife off my belt and rushed at Snake. I unfolded the blade and swung at the arm that held Blaine. Just before

I made contact, Snake let go, slashed up with a switchblade, and caught my cheek. I swung at that arm, but too late, and he got my other cheek.

Blood slid down both sides of my face, while Snake bobbed from side to side to disguise the aim of his next attack. Blaine made a run for it and disappeared around the corner of the garage.

Snake stabbed high and hit only air. "You're just as pathetic as before." He grinned. "I'll cut off fingers this time, instead of breaking them."

He stabbed deep into my abdomen. I grabbed his hand over the handle and held the knife there, perfectly still. While blood spilled out of me, I sliced up through his left shoulder, and his arm fell to the ground. He fought to free his knife and remaining hand from my stomach, while I reached around his back and stabbed into his heart.

"I'm not pathetic," I said softly.

"Aaaggh," Snake groaned and struggled, then leaned closer, trying to bite me.

I slid my knife up from his heart, diagonally through his skull. Most of his head fell to the ground. "And I'm no saint." I dropped his body and pulled his knife from me. Blood poured for a few seconds, and then slowed.

Blaine returned from around the corner. "Thank you."

I clipped my knife to my belt. "You shouldn't still be out."

"I know. I lost track of time. I was headed home."

"Where's home?"

"An apartment, a mile that way." He pointed north, toward D.C.

The wound in my side had stopped bleeding. "I'm going that way. I'll walk with you." I felt my cheeks. One cut hadn't gone away completely.

"Have a drink first," Blaine offered. "It's the least I can do."

His attire told me what kind of place he had been at earlier, and his matter-of-fact demeanor suggested he had been around his share of immortals. I drank, and as my wounds finished healing, I felt so satisfied. Ending Snake's miserable life had been easy and reminded me anew how powerful I had become.

Blaine frequented Sanguan clubs and bars, and that wasn't the first time he had accidentally stayed out after four. He was often very careless.

Vwhoosh—boom! The inferno inside demanded fuel!

I ripped my fangs out of Blaine. I held him up and worried about his limp body for a moment, before he suddenly inhaled.

"Wow," he said softly.

I let him go and inspected the knife cut in my ruined shirt, before starting off in the direction he'd indicated. Blaine yapped on and on the whole way, and thoughts of his cruel attacker slipped from my mind. Blaine worked as a waiter at a classy American-style restaurant, and aspired to be a standup comedian. I recalled his act from memories that had come with his blood. Some of it was pretty good. Other parts, not so much. As we strolled, his comfort around me and general goofiness amused me.

2

The bouncer at the club on Wilson Boulevard in Ballston called to let me know Caleb Sartori had shown up. Half an hour later, I took my time the last few blocks to the club and drew plenty of attention in my short leather skirt and white halter top. My hope was that Caleb would be just as interested.

I passed a group of hunky guys and was tempted, but let them be. Skipping a night of drinking had become slightly more bearable, though not because I had been a vampire for seven months. While it would be a while before my cravings diminished noticeably, suffering at Alexander's had taught me I could live in pain and hunger for many nights. Regardless, I almost never went that route. Most of the time, I visited someone I knew or went to a club or bar filled with those eager to be bitten. An aching, thirsty body crying out to be fed didn't interest me, but all I experienced when drinking interested me plenty.

Even before meeting Blaine a month back, I had started seeing Luke less. Luke worked as a bartender and needed his energy to write new songs, practice with his band, and perform well at shows if they were ever going to make it big. Drinking his blood, I saw visions of their hard rock all over the radio and internet and Luke belting out vocals to enormous, packed arenas of captivated fans. He wanted to be a rock star so badly, and I loved it. The struggle to stay away from him some nights would have been significantly more painful without Zack, June, and Blaine.

The third time he and June met me, Zack asked how long I had been a vampire. My answer of "less than a year" floored them, and Zack's typical nervousness briefly resurfaced. June didn't care, and ultimately, neither did Zack. His question brought us closer. They realized our situation was new and strange for me, just as it was for them.

I loved feeling all they had since each of our previous meetings—their friendships and budding love for each other. I even enjoyed exploring memories of the student clubs they participated in, their schoolwork, and the dreaded cafeteria they ate in less and less as college went on. Their lives brimmed with one experience after another that I had never had.

Most of Blaine's customers seemed to find him as amusing as I did. He told jokes, usually resulting in a good laugh. He often practically sleepwalked through shifts after staying out at clubs until four or later. He also ate the occasional french fry off plates before serving them.

I reached the club, thanked the bouncer, and headed to the back, where Caleb sat in the middle of a large, half-circle booth against the far wall. Since his father and older brother's car accident, the more I read about Caleb online, the more he intrigued me. He had always clashed with both family members, and unlike David, Caleb held only a mid-level position at Sarcorp, which, based on reports of his infrequent attendance, he didn't take very seriously. Both Sartori sons had dark hair and were athletically built. Caleb looked great in his black dress shirt that night.

After months of investigating, discussing, and speculating, I had uncovered nothing about Nicolas or anything secret his sisters might have been up to. I wasn't even certain those mysteries were real and worth my concern. And if they were, Nicolas still seemed a ghost from millenniums past.

Caleb, on the other hand, was no apparition. He might help answer another question I couldn't seem to figure out—why his brother and father were deathly afraid of going out after sundown. People with their kind of money should have been able to afford ample security wherever they went, not only when holed up in mansions and hotels. After nights of dissecting the situation from every angle, I concluded that using Caleb to learn about his brother would not be especially risky. It might even be fun. Caleb had a reputation of not merely *going out*, but going out big, throwing his money around and surrounding himself with Sanguans at the trendiest clubs.

To Caleb's left sat a large man in a suit, but no tie, a young woman in a tight blue dress farther down, and another woman in red beside her. A fierce-faced female vampire and a second man sat to Caleb's right.

I made my way through the crowd over to Caleb, but

stopped to stare, along with everyone else in his group, when the Sanguan at the table leaned over and bit into the neck of the man to her right. She sipped, sucked, and sucked harder, then pulled out her fangs.

With a blood-red mouth, she shoved her meal against the back of the seat. Hoots, hollers, and raised glasses came from everyone, except Caleb. He handed a wad of cash to the vampire, who took it and pushed the man off the bench and onto the floor. She left the booth while the others laughed.

The man got up off the floor as I approached the table. All eyes came to me.

"After you," the man said.

I slid across the booth to sit next to Caleb, and the man sat down on the other side of me.

"Caleb Sartori," he said, extending his hand.

I shook it. "Erin Rose."

Caleb pointed past me. "This is Giovanni." He went around the table from his left. "Mitch, Rachel, and Krystal."

I nodded to them, and Caleb continued, "I don't know that Giovanni is ready for another bite."

"I'm fine," Giovanni shot back. Everyone else laughed.

"You pay to watch?" I asked Caleb.

"Sanguans need money, like everyone else, and my friends like to be bitten without fearing for their lives. I provide a service."

A broad-chested vampire came out of the crowd.

"Andre!" Krystal—the one in red—called to him. She scooted off the bench and threw herself into hugging him. He kissed her neck and whispered into her ear. Grinning, she held his hand and sat down. Everyone shifted over, and I ended up squeezed between Caleb and Giovanni. Andre sat on the end next to Krystal.

Andre looked at me. "And you are?"

"Erin."

"Hm." He shrugged.

Krystal said, "Andre, where have you be—"

Andre's fangs sliced into the far side of her neck. Her eyes rolled up before they closed, then her head rested against the top of the seatback. Her mouth opened, but no sound came.

Rachel frowned while intently watching the vampire drink. Mitch and Giovanni sipped champagne, taking in the show. Caleb checked his phone and poured himself another glass of the bubbly.

Andre swallowed, then kissed Krystal near where he had bitten.

"*Anndree…*" Krystal almost moaned while her eyes remained closed. He bit into the other side of her neck, and her chest heaved.

I noticed Facebook open on Caleb's phone and quietly asked, "You're not interested?"

He glanced at the show for a moment. "I've seen it before." He looked at me. "You, I haven't. You might be worth watching."

"I'm not here to be watched." I leaned closer to him. "I'm here for you."

Mitch pulled a huge silver pistol from inside his jacket and had it pointed at me just before Giovanni did. Rachel stared. Caleb hadn't moved. The music intensified. Andre withdrew his fangs from Krystal and faced me. Krystal kept her head back, gulped, and seemed unable to catch her breath.

"Calm down, guys." Caleb reached into his pants pocket and pulled out more cash. He handed the money to Andre.

The Sanguan took it. "You need any help, Caleb?"

Caleb turned to me. "You tell me, Erin."

"You're fine," I said, then looked around the table. "Everyone's fine." I scooted toward Giovanni, who stood to let me out, but kept his pistol trained on my face. "I hope to see you again, Caleb. You look like you could use a change of pace."

I walked away from the table, confident that if they fired, the bullet or two that might hit me while I ran would be of no concern.

———————————

An hour before sunrise, mostly hidden from view by a high wooden fence, I practiced with Tomori in my backyard. I cut high, spun, ducked, and slashed low, catching the tips of a few grass blades. My phone chimed on the round cedar table. On my way over, I saw 'Facebook' in the subject of the email notification. I hadn't used the account in months, but I chuckled and accepted Caleb's friend request.

He posted on my wall almost immediately. *You weren't too hard to track down.*

I laid my sword on the table, deleted his post, and sent him a private message. *Neither were you.*

He took the hint and responded privately. *Why did you come to the club?*

I've read about you. I wanted to see for myself.

Now that you have, what do you think?

I composed my answer right away, but considered it for a minute before hitting Send. *You seem bored.* His earlier messages had been quick, but none came after that. I sent another. *Meet me tomorrow night?* I had a number of assurances ready like, "I swear I won't hurt you," and "You don't need to fear me. I promise."

After the Wizards game. At Blue Lounge?

I had prepared my list for nothing. *See you then.*

Outside Caleb's luxury box at Verizon Center the following night, a doorman spoke on his cell. "She says her name is Erin… okay." The man swung a card beside the door to unlock it, then opened it for me.

Wearing a charcoal skirt and black sleeveless top, I went inside and walked past a U-shaped countertop and two beige cloth chairs.

Caleb, in jeans and an untucked white dress shirt, stood alone among six leather seats. "Didn't want to wait?"

"I wanted to see LeBron James, actually." It hadn't been hard to locate Caleb's family's box, and after waking, I had gotten there as early as possible.

"The second half's just starting. Please, have a seat."

"Thank you." I took the chair to his right.

Caleb sat down and looked out at the court. "He's got twenty so far, six assists and five rebounds."

"Cool." The scoreboard showed the Wizards losing by five.

"Big basketball fan?" Caleb asked.

"Not really. I saw the Wizards were playing the Cavaliers. It was either sit at my computer alone or meet you early and see LeBron. You and LeBron won."

He nodded. The Wizards inbounded the ball.

Dull, radiating pain from my midsection reminded me I hadn't fed. "I guess you've been around enough Sanguans that you're not scared of me?"

"If you wanted to hurt me, you could have at the club. Gio and Mitch are fast, but they're not faster than you. You look human in your Facebook picture, and it's not from that long ago. You haven't posted much, though. I'm intrigued."

"It's a long story."

James stole the ball, raced down court, and slammed home a crowd-pleasing dunk.

"I'm sorry about your father," I said. "Is that why you were a little uninterested at the club?"

He turned away from the game to look at me. "You're not going to bite me and find out for yourself?"

"The thought had crossed my mind."

His moment of amusement quickly faded. "It was my father's time, I guess. That's what he would have said."

The Wizards knocked down a three-pointer to cut their deficit to four. The Cavs quickly hit a layup and pushed the lead back to six.

"So why'd you come looking for me?" Caleb asked. "And am I right that you haven't been a vampire for long?"

"It's been about seven months." I didn't see the harm in telling him. "You've been all over the news. I did a little digging, and you intrigued me, too."

"I doubt you'll find me that interesting."

In spite of my original goal—getting to the bottom of David's mystery—I *was* interested. "So if it's not your father, why so glum?"

He waved his hands in front of him. "Ah, it doesn't matter."

"Please? You're making me even more curious."

Caleb looked toward the court, where players huddled during a timeout. He took a deep breath. "My father was a man of tremendous faith. So is David. Much more than me. I never got it and still don't. I see sadness and pain everywhere. My life's been easy, but I see so many others who are poor or sick or dying."

"Yeah."

He turned to me. "And then there's your kind. No offense, but most of you are pretty terrible."

"I know." I smiled a little. "I'm not, but I know."

"My father always assured me there was a reason for all the pain, the suffering, and the immortals. God had a reason. I didn't understand it, and his words never really moved me. But near the end, after the car accident, when my father woke up from his coma and whispered to David, those words *did* shake me. With death at hand, it sounded like his faith was failing." Caleb shook his head. "Years ago, I started going to Sanguan clubs to see what I could learn about why vampires exist, to try to understand *some* of the evil in a world that's supposedly a good God's creation. I haven't found many satisfying answers, and after the way things went with my father, everything makes even less sense. But my friends like the clubs, and staying home won't reveal anything, so I keep going."

I had never read about that side of him. "I don't understand any of it either. Least of all why vampires exist."

The Wizards inbounded the ball.

Caleb ignored the court. "I figured you wouldn't have those kinds of answers, once I guessed that you were very young."

"I know how we came to be, though."

He perked up. "Really?"

I found myself eager to cheer him up. "Most of it."

"Was it the Devil? God? Something else?"

"It could be dangerous for you to know, if word gets out that you do."

"Why?"

I decided against explaining the twins' connection to the Spectavi, in case another drank from him. "It just could." I pressed a fang into my lip and pondered. "Will you keep it a secret?"

"Yes."

"I'll tell you if you let me drink from you."

"Sure," he said, without hesitating.

I probably would have gone for it anyway, but asking permission felt good. "The twins were humans in France fifteen hundred years ago."

His eyes widened. "Caterine and Ariane?"

"Uh huh." I had phrased it that way on purpose and enjoyed his reaction. I told him the story Edmond had told me, glossing over many of the details. "The twins grew ill, and for three years, remained sick and bedridden. They prayed to Jesus and God, but no answer came. One day, they prayed to the Devil instead, and *he* did answer. He offered them power and immortal life, and in return, they would have a great hunger they had to feed. The sisters accepted his terms, and later discovered that the hunger was actually a thirst for blood. The twins have hated God and his mortal creations ever since."

Caleb appeared awestruck. "So it is true."

"What is?" My aching had intensified all over my body since describing the twins' ancient hunger.

"I've read that story before. I've heard and read a lot of different stories, but that one I saw in a book at Georgetown. In Riggs Library. I went for work and figured it had as much chance of being true as any of the others."

"Was there anything about their brother?" I asked, careful not to name Nicolas.

"Brother? Not that I noticed."

The crowd roared as the Wizards scored to take the lead.

Caleb rolled his sleeve. "Go for it."

I took hold of his well-toned wrist, and my heart picked up its pace while his pulse did the same. I had expected to see numerous fang marks, and while he could have had them somewhere else, the skin I brought to my mouth was unscathed. When my fangs pierced his flesh, I shut my eyes to focus on the blood. He hadn't been bitten in over a year, but used to be all the time when at clubs.

I grew warm, then hot. So did Caleb. He thought *I* was hot.

I dug my fangs deeper, but only sipped. I understood how his brother had always been his father's priority. David had to get straight As. David was to run the company. David couldn't go out at night because of vampires. Caleb was an afterthought. His mother had left them when he was very young, and Caleb blamed his father. She couldn't stand their father's steadfast refusal to be out after sundown.

The crowd cheered again, and I watched Caleb, lost in my bite, while I journeyed through his dark emotions.

He was jealous of his older brother, mostly for all the time he got to spend with their father. "It's for the company's sake," and "Sarcorp" were the answers Massimo usually gave about why David had to be so careful. Caleb used to think there was more to it, but had stopped wondering after years of frustration and the same answers.

Caleb resented his father more than he did his brother. All David did was what his father asked. David excelled at work and was a genuine, driven man. Caleb couldn't fault his brother for that, and he did love David.

Caleb's heart had leapt when I mentioned the story of the twins, which he had seen drawings of in Riggs Library four months back. I glimpsed images of pages depicting the tale—some he remembered clearer than others. A few notes had made their way into his files at Sarcrop, though he was certain no one would ever inquire about them. While my account of the twins hadn't settled his ultimate curiosity about God and His plan for the world, Caleb relished the concrete information I did supply. We had that thirst for answers in common.

Through Caleb's eyes, I saw his father dying in his hospital bed. Caleb sat against the wall, but he wouldn't have been there had his brother not insisted on it. David, healed from his injuries, stayed bedside after Massimo had come out of his coma.

The weakened man whispered to his eldest son, "I fear for us all. I've done all He's ever asked." Massimo coughed. "I did as He asked, and it drove your mother away. Now, here I am. What if I was wrong about everything?"

"It'll be all right, Dad," David assured him.

"Will it?" Massimo wheezed. "The world grows darker… I see it—heavy and dense. I feel it crushing me, crushing my bones."

Later that day, Massimo mumbled in his sleep, "He can do it… he's ready…"

At night, awake, Massimo stared up at David. "It's up to you now. Don't forget. It's up to you."

An hour later, Massimo struggled for breath after breath, and Caleb prepared himself for each to be his father's last. Eventually, one was.

I stopped drinking and withdrew my fangs. "Your father was terrified of our kind."

Caleb gulped and wiped his sweaty forehead while leaning back in his chair. "Yes."

"You should talk to your brother." I recalled a memory of Caleb's where he and David discussed the car accident and the Sanguan murders at the restaurant in New York, and how powerless the humans in both cases had been. "He seems to be having a hard time with your father's death."

"He is."

I stood up. "Keep the twins' story a secret."

"I will."

I leaned down and kissed his warm cheek. "Bye, Caleb."

3

After leaving Caleb, I researched Riggs Library on my cell, then headed straight for Georgetown University. Riggs, located in the south tower of medieval-styled Healy Hall, had been Georgetown's main library until 1970. Since then, Lauinger Library held that title, but the original still contained rare collections and was used as a reception space. That it was located in the tower accounted for its almost preposterously small size. The multiple levels of books, accessible by winding staircases, helped, but it was no wonder Lauinger had been built.

An unoccupied security guard's car was parked to the side of the front gates of the campus. Past the entrance, on a diagonal brick path across the lawn to Riggs, a student stared at me as we passed each other. I doubted he guessed that I was as curious about him as he was about me. The scattering of other students didn't notice me, didn't realize I was a vampire, or simply ignored me.

Inside Healy, I followed signs for the library. After walking up three flights of stairs, I found myself before a brightly lit, empty lobby. Muffled voices came from beyond a set of golden doors to my right. As I stepped forward, one of the doors opened. I raced to the far side of the room and stood motionless next to a potted plant. A couple headed down the stairs I had just used. Their cocktail attire and the conversations I heard with the door open gave the impression a reception was being held.

I rushed to the library door and peered through the window. Perhaps I'd dart in, unnoticed, when the next person exited.

"Can I help you, Sanguan child?"

I spun to see a tall, angular priest—the white in his collar left no doubt. How did he know? I considered my options.

"Your cross says 'Spectavi,' but your hiding says you are not." He raised his eyebrows. "What are you doing here?"

I didn't want to run away, and he couldn't hurt me. Attacking a priest seemed like an awful idea… until I imagined experiencing his devotion to the Lord for myself. What would a priest's blood taste like? "I'm looking for something. A book."

"All right. What about?"

"Vampires, believe it or not. A friend mentioned a book here."

He nodded. "We have a few."

He reached past me and pulled open the door. People inside gave inquisitive looks until the priest appeared behind me.

"This way," he said. Conversations resumed while the priest headed for the far corner of the room. He glanced back at me. "You're lucky. Riggs isn't usually open so late."

While the pictures had captured the old library's small size and cramped feeling, they hadn't really done the place justice. Bright lights illuminated golden, cast-iron columns and railings on its three floors. Blue and gold coats of arms topped decorated pillars. It was quite beautiful.

We went up a winding staircase, then between short bookshelves to the back wall. The priest pointed at a bottom shelf. "This is what we have." He looked me in the eye. "These books contain stories and legends, and perhaps facts. Only one as old as the tales themselves might know which is which. I do not believe you fit that description."

"I don't."

"It's good you're curious and that you've come to investigate. Most I've known of your kind do not care to spend their nights learning. Nevertheless, do not forget that these books were written by other creatures born of this earth."

I nodded.

"We've gone to great lengths to preserve them and did not display the books until the passing of Edmond Duchart, who would have destroyed them, even the one with censored drawings on its few remaining pages." He checked the hands on his old wristwatch. "I trust you will replace the books when finished and take care when handling them?"

"I will."

"Are the people at the reception safe if I leave you with them?"

"They are. I swear."

"No need to swear. Stay as long as you wish. The library

doesn't open until after sunrise tomorrow, and I don't expect to see you then."

I cracked a small smile. "Thank you."

He nodded, then went back the way we had come.

When he was out of sight, I crouched to look at the bottom shelf. At the end, a short, old book with a brown, inch-wide binding read simply, *I*, in yellow. To its right, thicker, taller, and ebony, was *Figli del Diavolo*. A very thin book came next, and after that, a huge book: *Dutch Economic Journal*. Others like the journal continued to the end of the shelf. The vampire collection was small indeed.

The conversations below dwindled in number. I pulled *I* off the shelf and ran my hand over its well-worn cover. The binding creaked when I carefully opened to the first, thick beige page. The title was repeated in handwritten black. The lower right read, "1408."

The following page had three short lines, centered. The first two, in matching script, I couldn't make out. The bottom, in a thinner handwriting read, "The Twins." I googled on my cell for a French-to-English translator and typed in the first line. "The" came back, but the second word wasn't found. The second line might have been Italian, and like the French, used an old spelling that wasn't part of the current translator. The modern English must have been added later.

The binding creaked again when I turned to reveal a full-page drawing done in black lines of varying weight. Under a large sun, two tall women smiled, holding hands with two men. Caterine and Ariane's images had been faithfully produced.

I sat all the way down and leaned backward to rest against a bookshelf. I turned to the next drawing. Specks and splotches marked the women's skin. They held their stomachs as though in pain, while reaching out for the two men, who had their backs to them. The following page was divided into four sections, each with the twins in narrow beds. A large cross hung on the wall above them. Snow blanketed the ground in one section, and bare trees filled another. One or both of the sisters prayed in each drawing. As the seasons progressed, the twins appeared sicker, with darker shaded and increasingly marked skin.

On the next page, a small cottage stood all alone in a field in the distance. The path leading to it from town had a huge tree trunk across it with a paper note with a skull pinned to it.

Judging by empty space in the book binding, a few pages were missing. Most of the left side of the next full page had been colored over in solid black. In what remained visible, the twins lay in bed, wide-eyed, focused on that obscured area. No cross hung between their beds. In its place, an inverted pentagram had been drawn inside a circle. It could have been Nicolas in the black. Or the Devil. Or both. Looking through the page from the reverse side didn't reveal any of what was hidden.

In the next drawing, the twins stood beside their beds, apparently healed, staring down at a lower half of the page that had been blackened. Then came a drawing of the twins terrorizing townsfolk, eating flesh and drinking blood.

The library lights went off, and a door closed. All was silent.

So Nicolas could have been there, but had been covered in the drawings—which was hardly new information. The missing sections meant there was more to the story.

Moonlight shone through tall windows, and with my vampire eyesight, I could see well. Another set of three titles included *The Search*, in English. Pages were missing before a drawing that appeared to be of Caterine and Ariane, both looking very strange. Hovering over a pile of bloody bodies, each twin had large, bat-like wings spread behind them. Flames wrapped around the pair from their necks down to their toes, except the fire didn't seem to be inflicting pain.

The following page's English title was, *The Capture*. Many more pages were missing after that one. The next drawing showed a group of vampires surrounding the twins, who were again depicted as their normal vampire selves. The most prominent captor wore armor and resembled Edmond. He stood, fangs out, holding a huge sword over his head. A cross had been drawn in the sky near the moon. On the last page of the book that remained, the twins, nailed and chained to upright crosses, bled profusely from their wounds.

Obviously, Caterine and Ariane had escaped, somehow. I closed the book. Before their escape, there had been a search. I flipped back to that section. Who had searched, and for what? I stared at the picture of the twins with wings and flames all around them, wondering what it meant. I had never heard of such a thing, but could Caterine and Ariane assume that form? Did *they* do the searching? Did Nicolas? It seemed logical that at some point at least one other volume, *II,* had existed. Perhaps it still existed somewhere. I carefully replaced the book on the shelf.

The thin book, *Fighting Vampires! by P.J. Smithenson,* had only ten pages or so. The light blue, glossy plastic cover wasn't worn at all. Upon seeing the faded, machine printed letters on the first page, I realized the cover had been added later. The book was actually a pamphlet. The entire first page was an advertisement for *P.J.'s Holy Water,* a small bottle with a cross on its front and a label that read, "Be the last person they want to bite!" The next page had a drawing of a grotesque-looking vampire with pronounced fangs recoiling away from a woman's neck. The caption read, "P.J.'s Holy Water: Vampires hate it!"

I guessed it was a nineteenth-century work and turned the page. "If you're short on P.J.'s Holy Water, a stake through the heart is sure to kill a vampire." A long stake and a mallet were drawn. *Real* holy water had no special effect on me, so I highly doubted P.J.'s did. And while a stake driven into my heart would hurt—a lot, most likely—I didn't think it would kill me. A lesser immortal, perhaps, but Edmond's ancient blood had made me extremely resilient. I pictured, as I often did, the boiling blood dripping from his coffin—the blood itself had proven resilient.

Flawed guidance for P.J.'s poor customers filled the rest of the pamphlet. Garlic was said to deter vampires—it wouldn't. Sanguans were supposed to fear crosses—I had one tattooed on my neck. Extreme cold was supposed to slow me—the temperature had been below zero in Spokane, and I hadn't noticed any ill effects. P.J. did get two things correct when mentioning that direct sunlight and fire could be lethal. The last page read, "P.J.'s Holy Water: Let 'em bite someone else!" I put the pamphlet back on the shelf.

The jet-black binding of *Figli del Diavolo* felt slicker than expected. Unlike *Fighting Vampires!*, the machine-printed type on the title page hadn't faded at all. I guessed *Diavolo* was Italian for "Devil," then used the translation website to figure out the whole thing—*Children of the Devil.* The next page had a short block of text at its center, which I carefully typed into the same site. The result read:

Hope blinds.

Hope emboldens.

Hope twists.

When enough live and enough have died, hope will bring the red rain, and Hell will be on Earth.

—Rome 1883

Page after page of small typed text and an occasional drawing or diagram followed. I translated one heading to be "Celebrating the Son's Death." In the corresponding drawing, a naked man lay on a stone table, his legs together and his arms stretched out to his sides. A male vampire drank from the upturned palm of the man's right hand and a female vampire fed from the left. Another pair drank from the feet. The largest vampire, another male, bit into the side of the chest on the right, where the holy lance was said to have pierced Jesus while on the cross.

I resumed turning pages and found lots of pentagrams, vampires feeding, and no shortage of blood. There were also a few images of Baphomet, the human-bodied, goat-headed creature I had seen a statue of at the club Night. I flipped back to the introductory paragraph.

Hope blinds.

Hope emboldens.

Hope twists.

When enough live and enough have died, hope will bring the red rain, and Hell will be on Earth.

Hope? Everyone hoped. I hoped to confront the twins and imagined slicing them apart with Tomori. I hoped I would discover Nicolas's story. I hoped to live a long, long time.

I closed the book and put it back, then slid out *I* and found the pictures of the twins with blackened sections. I flipped between the two. What had Nicolas done? And what had the search afterward been for?

Using my cell phone, I took pictures of each drawing in the book, then replaced the volume as instructed. On my way out, I spent a few moments taking in the artistry of the library in the moonlight.

A little after one the following night, I lay flat on a bench in Crystal City, with my arms dangling at my sides. Just as I noticed an interesting crater in the full moon, a long limousine with tinted windows stopped on the street to my left. Exactly how I expected her to arrive.

I sat up and watched Victoria emerge from the rear door. Near the collar of her long leather coat, her black chain necklace was a predictable sight, with the red cross that hung off it hidden behind her top. The lack of wind left her long hair straight behind her. "How have you been?" the eight-hundred-year-old Spectavi warrior asked.

"Fine," I replied. It continued to astonish me that her pretty German face had become so welcoming. Her imposing height, powerful physique, and calm demeanor had once seemed so monstrous to me, but since she had saved me from Alexander and counted me among her daughters, her presence had become undeniably comforting.

She sat beside me. "Fine?"

"Much better than last time." Six months had passed since we had met in person on the night after that rescue.

"Good. I've been glad to see you absent from any police reports."

I half-smiled.

"So, you want to know about this supposed brother of Edmond's? Nicolas?" she asked.

"Yes." I had emailed her after my trip to the library, and she had suggested meeting since she happened to be in town.

"Unfortunately, I have nothing to tell you."

"Really?"

Victoria spoke as matter-of-factly as ever. "I asked some of the oldest vampires in the world, and none knew Edmond to have a brother."

"How could that be?"

"Edmond. You saw that book, the blacked-out drawings. Edmond probably had that done hundreds of years ago, or others did it in fear of him. He spent centuries wiping away any reference to his family being responsible for our kind.

While they did not mention Nicolas, the twins occasionally attempted to spread the "rumor" of their family name, but Edmond was always ready to squelch it anew."

"Why haven't they spread it this time?"

Victoria shrugged. "Who knows? They did it to anger Edmond mostly. With him gone, maybe they won't bother. Or perhaps they wait for a particular moment."

My guess was the latter. "Do you think it's strange they weren't part of the last two attacks on your factories?"

"Not really. They spent so long captive that I'm not surprised they're being careful."

"Or they're up to something else."

"Possibly." Weariness had crept into Victoria's voice.

"The book I told you about mentioned a search. Do you know what it was for?"

She shook her head. "I stopped at Riggs on my way here. Judging by the book's arrangement, the search likely occurred soon after their transformation, long before my time. Edmond never spoke of it."

I recalled the drawing from that section. "They looked truly demonic in that picture—wrapped in flame, with wings. They can't... take that form, can they?"

"No." Victoria sounded sure. "I have never seen or heard of a vampire with wings. I've hunted Caterine and Ariane long enough that I would know if they had that power."

"Then what does it mean?"

"It's just a drawing, Erin."

"Maybe. Could it have to do with Nicolas somehow?"

"Whenever I asked about his sisters, Edmond answered

with the same story that he told you. He also described the twins as humans, fondly, and as young vampires, less fondly. But of his sisters having wings, or of Nicolas, he never spoke."

I shook my head. "Forget the wings. There has to be *some* record of Nicolas, somewhere."

"If there is, I have not found it."

I slouched. By the time Edmond made Victoria a vampire, he was already seven hundred years old, if all I had been told was true. Did it hurt Victoria that he had kept the secret from her? She was so stoic, though. Perhaps such things didn't matter to her. "Who might have known about Nicolas, or who might Edmond have told before you met him?"

"At one time, perhaps quite a few," she said. "Edmond was one of the first, and he made many others to help fight his sisters. Surely, some he told. But most have not survived the long years of our war. Those who have, the ones I spoke to, were not forthcoming with information."

So someone did know, but if Victoria couldn't get them to talk, surely I couldn't. "Can't you use the synthetic blood to make them tell you?"

"Like me, those old Spectavi aren't drinking that blood." She raised an eyebrow. "There is one who might know, and if he did, might tell me. However, like every time I've looked for him in the last three hundred years, I found no trace."

I sat up straight. "Who?"

"Ahmose. A fledgling of Edmond's who lost his appetite for our war in the fourteenth century."

"What happened to him?"

"He decided he would do nothing except watch the world change. I last saw him in the seventeenth century in France. Even then, hundreds of years after he had stopped fighting, Edmond was furious with him. I did not agree with Ahmose's choice, but I also didn't care that he had made it. It was different for Edmond because Ahmose had been one of his favorites."

"So where could he be? Are you sure he's still alive?"

"He may be alive; he may not be. I searched for him occasionally, mostly out of boredom, but never found anything concrete, save for one thing."

"What?"

"He liked to isolate himself from the world, twenty years at a time. He'd start by guessing at what would happen; then, when the years had passed, he would see how he did. Edmond found it absurd, but Ahmose didn't let that bother him. Unfortunately for you, if Ahmose is sticking to that schedule, he'll stay hidden until 2020. Something tells me you aren't interested in waiting ten years for that."

I was in far better control of myself than when I had first become a vampire, but my reputation clearly preceded me. "So where do I look? If you couldn't find him, how can I?"

"He's from Egypt, originally, but we usually crossed paths in Europe. I would start in France or England. And you are correct; you probably won't find him. But I questioned Spectavi. You'll be talking to Sanguans. If you want information about Nicolas or a forgotten search from the Dark Ages, finding Ahmose is your best bet."

I thought about it for a moment. "How old is he?"

"Edmond made him a vampire in the seventh century."

"Would he be in a city or out in some remote corner of the continent?"

"I don't know."

"Does he always hide in the same place?"

"I don't know." Victoria got up. "Will you start your search soon?"

"Of course." I had a hunch what she expected me to say next, but said it anyway. "I'm not good at being patient."

She did seem amused. "You never were. Good luck, Erin."

"You, too."

She returned to her limo while I wondered what Zhilan would think of me going to Europe.

4

I opened my eyes to the underside of my black coffin lid the next night. Near the hinges on the left, my sword rested on two metal hooks with my knife to its right. I pushed open the lid, sat up on the dark gray, satin mattress, and stretched my neck from side to side. My throat was parched, but I'd deal with that later.

On my silver laptop at my desk, the *Shattered Nights Newsletter* announced the band's show in Richmond, in two weeks. Luke had already told me about it, but unfortunately, I planned on being in Europe by then. Another email contained a coupon for fifteen percent off at a local Thai restaurant. I clicked *Unsubscribe*, and as usual, a white error page loaded. The fried rice in the email looked annoyingly colorful, including the pork, egg, and scallions.

My RSS feeds in the next tab included a few Google Alerts. The news articles and blog posts mentioning Caterine and Ariane didn't look like anything new. Among the alerts for "Eure," an article detailed Reinald's successful leadership of the company since Edmond's death. Profits were up.

The list of tabloid posts about "Sartori" was most

interesting. Seven covered an appearance by David outside the Kennedy Center the night before. I clicked to the first article with a video.

On his way in to see the National Symphony Orchestra, David was stopped by a young reporter with a camera. Instead of rushing past her, David confidently declared himself "thrilled to finally see a concert here that isn't a matinee."

A vampire in a tuxedo darted into view behind David. Others nearby shifted their attention to the immortal. David turned to see the source of the commotion and jumped back. Everyone else laughed. The Spectavi was just there to see the concert. David muttered to himself while hurrying inside. The other articles showed the same video, most with a joke or two about David's reaction and speculation on how long it would be before he returned to his old life of hiding in the sun.

I got changed and headed upstairs to my living room, where I had yet to hang a thing on the walls. My front door automatically locked behind me as I went out into the cloudy night.

After a four-block walk through my residential neighborhood of old homes mixed with new, I made my way up a hill and down the street to Zhilan's.

Tao opened the door. "Good evening, Erin. Zhilan is out back."

"Thanks, Tao." He meant the deck, which offered an impressive view of downtown D.C. Zhilan and I had spent hours out there talking and, occasionally, meditating. While

I struggled to relax and focus, with her guidance, I had enjoyed the occasional tranquil moment.

Tao led the way to the kitchen, which he used far more than Zhilan. There, he opened a sliding door.

"Old President Hughes is set in his ways," a male voice outside said. "His whole career, from Pennsylvania to the Senate to the top, he's endorsed the Spectavi."

To my surprise, the wooden armchair with a white cushion that I normally sat on was occupied by a Chinese Sanguan.

"Erin, this is Renshu," Zhilan said from her identical chair. She wore her loose pink satin robe.

Renshu stood and nodded to me. "I've heard a lot about you, Erin. It's nice to finally meet you." He was the younger of Zhilan's two living fledglings—the one she kept in touch with. She told me she had made him an immortal in 1901, when he was thirty-eight. She had considered him very wise and practical for a mortal and had fallen in love, largely because he combined those traits with an eagerness to act when circumstances demanded it. As vampires, the two had lived and traveled together for decades until, when they both knew time had subtly dimmed the spark between them, Renshu made the decision to go his own way. Zhilan had sounded as though she missed him while telling some of her stories.

"And I've heard about you. Nice to meet you." I sat on a wooden bench in front of Zhilan's garden. "What brings you to Virginia?"

Renshu took his seat. "The Spectavi have made Beijing

an uncomfortable place to live. Reinald is here, so I decided I should be, as well."

I glanced at the skyline. "D.C.'s probably not much better, and hopefully Virginia isn't next."

Zhilan said, "We were discussing our disappointment that the twins have not taken advantage of their fame to expose how the Spectavi use their synthetic blood."

"You think it's time we say something?" I asked.

Renshu answered, "We were thinking, 'show,' not 'tell.'"

"What do you mean?"

Zhilan explained, "If we cannot aim to destroy all the synthetic—and I maintain that thousands of suddenly hungry blood drinkers would be chaos—the Spectavi must stop using it for control. If we could accomplish that, we might receive just treatment from them. Of course, they have no reason to change how they operate. Houjin's idea is to convince the humans to pressure the Spectavi to change."

That made some sense. Other Sanguans were bent on violence or oppressing humanity, but I fought out of necessity. What my Sanguan friends and I really sought from the Spectavi was fairness under the law. That young Spectavi might not be thinking for themselves further muddied the situation.

Zhilan continued, "But no one will believe us if we tell them. Not the president, not congress, not the vast majority of Americans. However, if we modify some of the synthetic and use it to publicly influence a group of Spectavi's decisions, humans won't be able to ignore how wrong what the Spectavi leaders are doing is. Additionally, the tremendous threat inherent in the Spectavi's system—your fear of how the twins might use the synthetic—will become clear."

I wanted to be more excited about Zhilan's plan. "Victoria told me they were prepared to stop anything like what you propose."

Zhilan waved her hand. "She's overconfident. They cannot even defend their factories."

True, but I had another question. "How do you think the Spectavi will react?"

"I doubt most will," Renshu said. "They either will not believe what we have done or be programmed not to believe it."

"So how do we do it?"

Zhilan leaned forward. "Houjin tells me Nigel is near to being able to do exactly as we hope with the synthetic. He will want to test his modifications on a Spectavi, and for that, he wants samples from a recent batch of the synthetic. Would you like to help us get some?"

"Of course," I said, offended she would ask and not assume. She was too polite.

Renshu smiled. "She did say you were ever eager."

When Zhilan smiled, I realized that she might have led me on as a show for her fledgling.

She asked, "Erin, what is the occasion for tonight's visit?"

"Nicolas. I spoke to Victoria, and she hasn't been able to find anything about him, but she had a suggestion of who might tell his story. Have either of you heard of a vampire named Ahmose?"

Renshu shook his head.

"One of Edmond's," Zhilan said. "His name means 'Child of the moon.' I have never met him. I assume she does not know where he is."

"Right. She thinks he might be in Europe. She said he might be hiding, in seclusion until 2020, when he'll reappear and take stock of how the world's changed in the last twenty years."

"It sounds like he does not want to be found," Renshu concluded. "Are you sure you can trust Victoria?"

"Yes." I looked at Zhilan.

She nodded. Her comfort level with Victoria didn't match mine, but Zhilan agreed that for as long as I had been a vampire, the old Spectavi had only had my best interests in mind.

Renshu asked, "Why is Nicolas so important?"

"Because *I* set those twins free," I said. "And nobody knows for sure what they're up to. It seems strange to me that the twins weren't at the last few attacks on the Spectavi synthetic plants. Victoria thinks they're being careful, but I don't buy it. The alternative is that they're up to something else. I found a book with blacked-out images of the twins' transformation. It must have been Nicolas that was hidden." I turned to Zhilan. "The same book contained a drawing of the twins with wings, seemingly empowered by flames enveloping their bodies. I don't know what it means, and I don't know if it has anything to do with Nicolas, but I hate all the uncertainty around Caterine and Ariane."

"Then you should search for Ahmose," Zhilan said.

"Really?" I blurted.

Zhilan smiled. "Yes. It will be good for you to be on your own for a while. You are ready." Her expression became contemplative. "It could also be very bad if you are reckless." We surely recalled many of the same things. "It could be disastrous."

"I'll be careful," I promised.

"You'd better." She relaxed. "Meet Hayden in London to start. We can discuss where you might go from there."

"Okay." I made a point of responding evenly, like someone who *was* ready for such a mission.

Zhilan shifted gears again. "Now, back to stealing some synthetic. I have a plan."

The clock on Luke's nightstand read *5:46*. Worn out from the last few hours, he slept next to me. Red dots made up the familiar bite mark on his neck and the fresh one at the side of his bare chest. As I often did, I had licked blood from both wounds until they stopped bleeding—we both loved it. Other splotches had gotten on his bed, but the sheets were black, which helped.

I turned all the way onto my side and watched Luke's chest rise and fall. Zhilan had declared me "ready." After all the poor choices I had made in my life, my initial excitement at her approval had faded into worry that I struggled to dismiss.

5:47—I knew myself well enough to know I wouldn't change my mind about Europe. I kissed Luke's cheek, then propped my head on my hand. "I have to go."

His eyes cracked open. "Already?"

"Yeah. And I could be gone for a while."

He blinked a few times and forced his eyes wider. "Gone? Where?"

"England. Europe. I don't know exactly."

He put his arm under his head. "Why?"

"It's complicated. It's better if you don't know."

"Okay."

I appreciated him not asking more. A detail was his reward. "I need to track down an old vampire."

"How long will you be gone?"

"I don't know." That uncertainty added to my nervousness.

He frowned. "I'll miss you."

I began to choke up, but wasn't in the mood. Moving at vampire speed, in an instant, I sat on top of him. He smiled and held my hips. I leaned down to his chest, and his grip relaxed as I kissed one fang mark and then the other. I bit into the wound again and knew from his mind just how much he would miss me.

———————————

Two hours after sundown, on the tarmac at Manassas Regional Airport in Virginia, my short hair blew in the wind while I followed Grant, Zhilan, and Renshu to the small, single-engine plane. My sword was already onboard. Grant, who stubbornly wore blue jeans instead of black pants like the rest of us, had compared me to a child having their special blanket taken away when they packed my weapon.

John Womack came halfway out of the side entrance to the plane. "Zhilan, hello. Welcome, all."

Zhilan reached the door's built-in staircase. "Hello, John. Thank you again."

John waved a hand. "I'm always happy to help." He stood aside as we boarded.

Aside from rare, special cases, vampires were never allowed to fly on normal commercial airlines because the risk of one taking control of a plane and crashing it was simply too great. It didn't matter that night—commercial wouldn't have worked. To steal a case of synthetic blood being transported by truck, we were headed east of Memphis, Tennessee. Out there, we wouldn't be the most obvious suspects. Once we had the synthetic, Grant would take it to the lab in Palo Alto, while the rest of us flew back to Virginia.

As far as the FAA and anyone else knew, John was headed to one of his beverage bottling plants for an inspection. And the inspection really would take place, but he wouldn't have been going if not for us. John had known Zhilan for over thirty years and was sympathetic to our cause against the Spectavi.

Toward the back of the narrow plane, I took a cushy leather seat on the side opposite Grant and Renshu. John and Zhilan ended up across from each other farther up.

I peeked behind me and saw a long black case. As the plane began taxiing, I got up, opened its latches, and lifted the lid to find Tomori lying next to Zhilan and Renshu's swords. I brought the sheathed blade to my seat and leaned it against the wall.

"Wait." Grant interrupted his conversation with Renshu and turned to me. "Really?"

I rolled my head left on my seatback to see him. "Really." From my belt, I grabbed my phone and pulled my headphones out of a small pouch. Soft, electronic trance music played through the white earbuds, and I closed my eyes. The plane sped up, and visions of sparring with Zhilan came to mind, followed by memories of our raid on Alexander's compound.

We lifted off, and my thoughts shifted to June and Zack. They had recently flown to Florida for a long weekend. It was new for me to have so many memories from people I truly cared for. The fact that they weren't *my* memories was occasionally disappointing, but mostly marvelous and fascinating.

———————

Thirty-five miles northeast of Memphis, I lay in the bed of a rusty old pickup truck, staring at the partly cloudy sky. A field of tall grass was to the left with two-lane Route 14 to the right. Grant lay beside me with a long, green rocket launcher separating us. I held my unsheathed sword in my gloved right hand and waited for a truck carrying packaged Spectavi synthetic. The setup was a little weird.

I faced Grant and whispered, "How's Alice?"

"Fine." He smiled. "How's Luke?"

"Fine." Great. I had managed to make the situation even more awkward.

Grant changed the subject. "So, you're starting in London?"

"Yeah, I'm going to meet Hayden." I hadn't seen him for months, since a few days after he had fought valiantly against Caterine and Ariane in Alexander's throne room.

"Good. Just be careful over there, okay?"

I glared at him.

"All right, all right." Grant got the message. "Do you think you'll find him?"

"Hayden?"

"No, Ahmose."

"Yes... I don't know." I had considered it repeatedly. "Since Victoria couldn't, I'm a little worried, but I have to think I will, or else why bother going, you know?"

"Makes sense."

"Do *you* think I'll find him?" I heard a vehicle approaching.

"Sure." Grant checked his watch. "They're a little early."

It sounded like a truck, and the noise was getting louder.

"Not yet." Grant took hold of the rocket launcher. "Not yet."

I gripped my sword tight.

Grant leapt out of the pickup, and I got to my feet. He fired the instant he landed on the road in front of the long, boxy silver truck. A Spectavi with a katana came flying through the slanted windshield of the vehicle and slashed down at Grant, through denim and his thigh. I raced to them, while the front of the truck exploded, flames consumed the driver, and the truck stopped.

Tyn! My blade met Grant's assailant's, while Grant dropped the rocket launcher, limped backward, and pulled out a handgun. He fired, but missed.

I ducked under a cut from the Spectavi. "Get out of here, Grant!"

He wasted another shot. Three Spectavi came around from behind the truck. One fired an assault rifle and two drew swords. Grant and I rushed away from each other. The Spectavi I had been fighting went after Grant, into the dark field. The other three focused on me.

"Ah!" A bullet hit my thigh. *Tyn*. My blade met the second Spectavi's sword. I leaned low to avoid a cut from the third vampire. "Ungh." Another bullet hit my right side, and painful silver seeped into my leg. The first Spectavi kept firing.

Our black SUV finally arrived. Zhilan leapt from the left rear door while Renshu continued driving to the truck, where he'd run in and grab the synthetic blood. With the diversion Zhilan caused, I spun and cut at one of the three Spectavi—*tyn*—he barely blocked it. *Fshwt!* I sliced his body in two. Zhilan engaged the other sword fighter, and I rushed the Spectavi with the rifle, chasing him in the opposite direction Grant had gone.

I would have been faster than he was, but my wounded leg slowed me in the tall grass. The Spectavi made the mistake of turning to fire. He missed, and I shortened the gap between us. He stopped to take a better shot and succeeded in hitting my left side, but it was still a mistake. I lunged and sliced off his head before he could resume fleeing. While I caught my breath, my thigh stung, but not nearly as badly as the two throbbing wounds in my midsection.

BOOM! The Spectavi truck exploded, and flames engulfed it. *Boom!* Our SUV slid away and burned. I ran back to the road.

"Renshu!" Zhilan screamed. With a few quick, powerful cuts of her blade, she finished off her opponent. I reached her and stood, watching the blaze.

"Renshu!" she called.

Grant emerged from the field with a blood-red mouth. The Spectavi who had been chasing him was nowhere to be seen. Our plan had been to blow up the truck once we had stolen the synthetic. Renshu had carried the explosives with him.

Zhilan sheathed her sword and raced into the fire, disappearing for a few long seconds, before carrying out a limp body. With flames flickering out in her hair, she knelt and carefully placed burned Renshu on the asphalt beside me. The whites of his brown eyes remained bright, but his light skin had been charred nearly black. His facial features were hardly recognizable. His fingers let go of a large silver case. I sheathed my sword and crouched as Grant did.

Renshu wheezed, struggling to pull air into his lungs. "I'm... s-sorry."

Zhilan pushed up her sleeve, bit a crude gash into her pale wrist, and brought her arm over his mouth. With the first drops, the pain on his face lessened. He bit in, gulped down more, and his breathing relaxed. Zhilan began taking quicker breaths. She shut her eyes and used her other hand to force her open wound to stay over Renshu's mouth. His skin lightened slightly. She bit her lip, and blood trickled down her chin.

"Gah!" Zhilan tore her wrist away.

Renshu looked better, but far darker than he should have been. Discolored patches and streaks marked his skin.

"My dearest Zhilan," Renshu said hoarsely, though he breathed more easily. "Your sweet blood has saved me again."

"Are you in pain?" she asked.

"Yes." Renshu winced while slowly rising.

We all joined him standing. Zhilan had described how the pain and scars from a fire one survived could linger. I had never witnessed the affects in person.

"Can I help?" I pushed up my sleeve and held out my wrist.

Renshu grimaced. "You are sweet as well, young one. Unfortunately, vampire blood can only do so much."

Grant added, "Human blood is needed to heal the worst burns and wounds."

Very conscious of the bullet holes in my side, I let my sleeve cover my arm. Grant turned his back to us and brought his phone to his ear. I picked up the silver case.

Zhilan put her arm around Renshu. "At least we got what we came for."

Grant got off the phone and pointed into the field. "Eight miles that way. John will send someone to drive you to the airport, and I'll split off then."

Faint sirens sounded and distant blue and red lights flashed. Grant sped off, and we all followed.

On the plane, there were no pairs of connected seats, so Renshu sat on the floor, and Zhilan rested her head on his shoulder. My wounds had partially healed, but because of the silver, they ached and likely wouldn't be completely gone until the following night.

"Another Spectavi stayed in the truck," Renshu explained as we taxied. "He got the jump on me, but I thought I had taken care of him. I don't know where he found the strength to set off the explosives."

We took off, and I put on my headphones to listen to Shattered Nights. I skipped to my favorite song, *Ember,* and closed my eyes.

5

"This is going to be it for a while," I told June and Zack. We sat in a booth at a run-down bar a few blocks from their campus.

As expected, June appeared worried. "What do you mean?" Zack had a similar glum face, but I was fairly certain a lot of it stemmed from anticipation of how my absence would disappoint his girlfriend.

"I have to go to Europe. I don't know for how long. It could be weeks... or months."

With watery eyes, June came over to my side of the table and hugged me. I held her and bit into that delicate neck I adored. June was so upset. I drank slowly and tried to calm her fears that I would never return. My efforts had no effect, and she remained scared that I'd be defeated in battle or fall victim to some ancient's trickery. I sucked harder, and the fire within me intensified. June and Zack didn't understand my strength. The flames flared higher! June and Zack had never seen me with Tomori.

I withdrew my fangs and leaned her out of our embrace. June's eyes opened, and she fell into me. She clutched me tightly until I gently pushed her back and turned my attention to Zack.

That drink was less intense—a difference I appreciated, as usual. He'd miss my visits, but worried more about how June would cope.

I addressed one of his fears as soon as I let go of his wrist. "Don't you two go out looking for another vampire while I'm gone. It wouldn't be safe. One of my human friends was murdered by a Sanguan she thought she could trust." That wasn't exactly true, as Christopher hadn't done the killing, but the simplified explanation would work best for June. "Don't trust any others. Okay, June?"

"Yes. Okay."

"Good." I nudged her. She joined Zack on the other side of the booth. "I'll miss you guys."

"We'll miss you," Zack said.

"Be safe. Good luck with everything. I'll see you soon." I got up and left the bar.

———————————

In my basement, my backpack was nearly full. I had almost bought a larger one because the weight wouldn't matter to me, but while shopping, I tried some on and found the smaller one less cumbersome. Besides, I didn't sweat, so I could sometimes wear the same clothes repeatedly.

I packed two types of outfits—things to wear to fight or practice in and things to wear out to bars or clubs. Unsure where my search for Ahmose would lead, those activities seemed most likely. I'd wear my boots on the plane, and had also included a few other pairs of shoes. My laptop fit easily. I figured I would often leave my sword wherever I was staying, but could wear it on my back with the backpack over it if necessary. A store clerk had changed my service plan so my cell phone would work overseas.

When picking out a few pairs of simple earrings to stow in an inside pocket, I glanced at the platinum cross necklace from Edmond that hung from a nail above my desk and shuddered.

"Turns out, you *should* listen to your parrot," Blaine finished his joke.

I smiled, sitting across from him at a small table outside the restaurant where he worked. The place had emptied for the night.

"You're not laughing," he said.

I gave a sympathetic look. "It's just... I know all your jokes. You know?"

"Oh, yeah."

"Do you want me to pretend I don't?"

He lit up. "Yeah!"

"Oh." I hadn't expected him to say yes, but why not? "Well, sure. I'll try."

"Thanks."

"Tell me another before I go."

Blaine was pretty bummed I would be gone, and I would certainly miss him. Since the excitement of our first meeting, I had thoroughly enjoyed our relaxing encounters.

_____

An hour before sunrise, Tao was driving me to Dulles Airport. I sat alone in the back seat of Zhilan's Mercedes. Saying goodbye to her hadn't taken long. Only twice did she remind me to be careful, and when assuring her I would, I tried my best to accept the advice graciously.

Zhilan remained skeptical that Nicolas mattered and gave even less consideration to the peculiar drawing of the twins. While I feared what they would be like, able to fly and unharmed by fire, Zhilan felt those powers were nothing more than the product of an imaginative historian.

Nevertheless, she had listed places for me to seek information in England, France, Italy, Germany, and a few other countries. I'd likely travel by train some, which would be a first for me outside of D.C.'s subway system. Zhilan didn't expect language to be a major issue because if they didn't know English initially, most vampires eventually found learning it worthwhile. I had emailed myself the names of the bars and clubs she mentioned, so the list would be saved online should anything happen to my laptop or phone.

Zhilan had also arranged for me to stay in an apartment in England upon arrival. She suggested I seek out the oldest Sanguans who would talk to me. Europe was huge, and searching every town, city, and country blindly could take ages. Her two hundred and seventy years of experience had taught her that old vampires often kept tabs on the whereabouts and activities of other ancients. Ahmose was very old.

Most shockingly, Zhilan transferred ten million dollars to my bank account. She said it wasn't a loan and that I should have the money 'just in case.' She had never kept her extreme wealth a secret. Long-standing laws severely limited the amount of stock immortals could hold in public companies, but vampires were allowed to invest in mutual funds and other diversified products. Like all the old ones with any sense, Zhilan had invested heavily and watched her fortune grow. At her suggestion, I invested thirty percent of what she had given me.

Renshu had looked a bit better. I hadn't pressed for details, but he indicated that the pain from his burns persisted. Hopefully, additional blood would heal him before long. In spite of his injuries, he and Zhilan seemed very happy to be spending time together again.

A Facebook message from Caleb arrived as we neared the airport. *How are you? Can you meet me tonight? Or talk?*

Caleb… He had turned out to be nothing like the playboy portrayed in the media. Our conversations and all I had read in his blood revealed a darker, far more contemplative man. While his family cowered from anything vampire, Caleb, to varying degrees over his life, risked venturing into the world of immortals because he truly craved answers.

Wishing he had written earlier, I responded, *I'm fine. Headed out of town. I'll be in touch when I get back.*

My flight to Heathrow was one of a few regular routes operated by an airline catering to Sanguans. At most, three passengers would be aboard the small Gulfstream V. We'd

S.M. PERLOW

all start in our coffins for the daytime takeoff and would remain that way for most of the flight. The sun would set half an hour before we landed in England.

Sleeping in a hangar for a few hours before being 'shipped' somewhere didn't thrill me, but for such a long flight at that time of year, it was one of the few options. Being awake at the end was supposed to make it feel less strange, and the airline had a solid reputation for safety.

A mile from the main terminals, Tao stopped the car outside the hangar. "Good luck, Erin."

"Thanks." I got out, shut the door, and noticed a lone Spectavi guard at the entrance. With my backpack over my shoulder, my knife hanging off my belt, and my sword in hand, I walked to the plane.

I boarded and made my way down the aisle of the narrow aircraft. The first two small cabins on the right were occupied, so I pushed in the folding door of the last one. A white coffin ran the length of the room. A blue leather seat beside it on one end and a small sink on the other filled the rest of the cramped space. The single small window was covered. I shut and locked the door, knowing full well that either of the other passengers had the strength to break in.

6

Half an hour from Heathrow, I sat up in my coffin. I reached over and unlatched, then slid open the thick window cover to see my first European sky—the same darkness as back home. I got out of the coffin, closed the lid, and sat on top to watch the rest of the flight.

With a blade in my hand, I knew what to do. I was getting better all the time, and for the most part, my skill matched my confidence. In D.C. and everywhere Zhilan and I had traveled, nothing over the last few months had scared me. But as the plane descended, for the first time in a long time, I was about to be alone. I had assured Zhilan I would see her again, and it hit me how much *I* was responsible for making that happen. Whatever came up, *she* would be fine for however long my search took. But would I? In my mind, I heard with perfect, horrible clarity the sounds and sensation of my fingernails scratching against my steel prison at Alexander's. I recalled sitting at Victoria's arena in a daze while Edmond sipped from me, over and over. When the time came, would I add to my list of poor choices and not be so fortunate with the outcome?

With a bump and a lurch, the wheels touched down. We taxied to an isolated hangar where two Spectavi stood guard. Three limousines, including the one Zhilan had arranged for me, waited just outside. The other two Sanguans got off the plane first and into their rides without ever acknowledging me.

"Ms. Rose," the driver said, holding the limo door.

"Yes," I answered. "Hello." I threw my things across the seat and slid in next to them.

The driver didn't say anything on the trip to Islington. The GPS on my phone told me we were looping around London to take the highway, instead of the most direct route. Traveling on the left side of the road seemed bizarre.

Removed from the busiest tourist spots, Islington was supposed to be quieter. After forty-five minutes of driving through light rain, the limo stopped at the end of a row of narrow, three- and four-floor, connected brick homes. Zhilan and a few others maintained an apartment in the four-story building on the end, and it was mine to use for however long I needed.

I stepped out, and the limo drove off. Another row of brick buildings was behind me. Some tall trees with wide, leafy crowns lined the street. Visiting cities across America, I had seen plenty of similar areas. Nothing major was drastically different, but in addition to *knowing* I was on another continent, all the little things—the cars, the street signs, the architectural accents—made me feel out of place. I figured the sensation would be impossible to drive away completely, as I continuously moved to new cities and countries.

To the right of the brown door of Zhilan's building, I slid up a dirty white panel and pressed my thumb on the pad. With a click, the door opened. According to Zhilan, most of the humans who lived in the building also opted to use the reader, instead of a key. Up three floors of concrete staircase, at the end of the dimly lit, carpeted hall, I pressed my thumb to the scanner to open the apartment's red door.

A plain coffin lay in the corner of the living room. A small kitchen contained old appliances. The bathroom and the rest of the furnishings matched the dated theme. The whole place was very clean, and two windows offered views of drizzling rain hitting the street.

It made sense that the apartment was designed for utility, not luxury. A fancy hotel in a prime location would work for the latter, and the extra few miles to downtown were no trouble as fast as I could run.

Hunger growled from my stomach out to my arms and my legs, and then my fingers and toes. Perhaps I'd find a tasty drink at the pub when meeting Hayden. My black trench coat seemed appropriate for the dreary weather. I clipped my knife to my belt, left my sword in the coffin, and headed out.

With an hour to cover less than two miles, I didn't run and found myself glad to have begun in London. The cars drove on the wrong side of the road, and the unfamiliar streets felt older, but people spoke English, and that was huge.

The rain picked up. I ducked into a convenience store, picked out a small umbrella, and brought it to the counter.

Whaoooo-whaoo. A siren sounded outside, and I froze, thinking I hadn't done anything wrong.

"Three fifty," the old man at the cash register announced.

A silver police car drove by, with blue lights on its roof. I retrieved my wallet from my coat pocket and handed over my credit card. The printer grinded, producing my receipt. Back outside, I opened the umbrella and continued to the pub, in the opposite direction the police car had gone.

Zhilan had confirmed what I understood of the Spectavi in most of Europe. Their relationships with governments were generally similar to those in America. In addition, London already had an established citywide camera network. Unlike the real-time system in Washington, D.C., London's cameras were primarily used for reviewing crimes that had already been committed. Even so, I would have to be careful. If I had to feed out on the street, waiting until four a.m. seemed prudent—the legal window lasted until six in England, the same as in the U.S.

Also like home, most mortals didn't seem to notice I wasn't one of them, and the ones who did only realized when close. In those cases, the vast majority made an effort to steer clear and avoid eye contact. Most vampires kept to themselves, while others looked to be sizing me up, just as I did them. The Spectavi reeked of synthetic, exactly like the ones in America.

A small green sign hanging off a building a block ahead read, "O'Reilly's." I was early, but once there, I collapsed my umbrella and headed right in. The dark, narrow pub extended unexpectedly deep. An unattended microphone and guitar stood near the entrance. A black wooden bar ran most of the length of the room. Like the booths across from it, the bar was about half full. I hung my coat and umbrella below it after choosing a stool at the end.

A fiddle and drum played from overhead speakers. Two stools to my right, a young man sat down, folded his sport coat over the bar, and got the female bartender's attention. "Guinness."

"Me too," his friend said to the Sanguan, taking the stool to his right. The men glanced at me and then spoke quietly to each other. One of them would do, I decided, perhaps the nearest with brown hair.

Aside from the bartender, I noticed two other Sanguans—both males, sitting in booths. One was with a woman, who was smoking a cigarette. The other had squeezed onto the end of a bench and chatted eagerly with a group of men and women. The place appeared reasonably civilized.

"You need anything?" the bartender called to me on her way over.

"No," I answered. "I'm waiting for someone. Actually, I'm looking for someone, too."

"Who?"

I considered whether it made sense to be cavalier and just start asking around, then decided I would never learn anything without trying. "Do you know a vampire named Ahmose?"

"Ahmose?" She thought for a moment. "Nope, never heard of him. Sorry."

"No problem. Thanks anyway." I did *not* think launching into questions about Nicolas or the twins in such a public place would have been prudent.

The bartender went to help a customer on the other end of the pub, and I got my phone from my coat. No new emails—the sun hadn't yet set in Virginia. The front door opened, and Hayden entered, wearing jeans and a coal-colored blazer over a pale green shirt. For the last few months, he had been all over Europe, keeping tabs on the twins' activities. It was comforting to see the spiky-haired Texan's familiar face.

He took the barstool between the two men and me. "That's some knife."

"Yes, it is."

"Good flight?"

"It was fine."

He nodded. "How's the search going so far?"

I pointed at the bartender. "*She* doesn't know where Ahmose is. Do you?"

"No."

"Then I'm oh-for-two."

The men next to Hayden scooted their stools away from him. My lips grew parched.

Hayden said, "I'm afraid I have mostly bad news for you. I asked around London—a few older Sanguans. One knew the name Ahmose, but nothing other than that he was Edmond's fledgling."

My search had just begun, but hearing that certainly disappointed me. In any rational analysis, my odds of finding Ahmose were remote, and it hadn't taken long for Hayden to reinforce that fact.

"And then there's Duncan," he said. "When I mentioned Ahmose over the phone, he asked why I was interested. Your name came up, and he insisted on meeting you in person. I hope tonight is good for you."

"Sure." Maybe I had been disappointed too quickly. "That's why I'm here."

Hayden looked to his right. "And you two? Is tonight good for you?"

"What?" the man nearest him asked, while putting down his half-empty beer mug. Hayden moved around to the stool on the far side of the second guy.

I casually slid over to where Hayden had been sitting and eyed the thick neck above the shirt collar next to me.

Hayden put his hand on the back of the man nearest to him. "My friend and I are thirsty. How about a drink?"

"Uh…" the one near me said.

I placed my hand on his tense shoulder. "It'll be fine. That's why you're here, isn't it?"

He didn't blink. "Yeah."

Hayden bit, and I slid my hand across my meal's shoulder and down his arm, then gently pulled him close. My fangs sliced into the skin below his ear. His blood filled my mouth and then quenched my thirst all over my body. The two were there for a bite, except they were supposed to be meeting other Sanguans. He and his friend had discussed us and disagreed about what to do if we approached. They guessed I would be friendly, but neither trusted Hayden. I drank, and among memories of a life that had been shaped by an English upbringing, I enjoyed finding differences. The American War of Independence in 1776 had been a revolt, not a revolution. A queen reigned—if only as a figurehead. Football was played with the feet.

I withdrew my fangs, swallowed the last of his blood, and held him until he reached out to the bar for support.

Hayden had already finished drinking. "Two more beers for our friends." He threw a bill onto the table. "Thank you, gentlemen."

Neither responded. Hayden got up, so I collected my things and followed him.

———————————

Duncan was Scottish, over five hundred years old, and lived in a mansion an hour southwest in Windlesham. Hayden drove the straight route out of London in his new Sterling Gray Ford Mustang. He noted the specific color before mentioning that he had left his 1967 version in the States. Duncan, who'd had a falling out with the Spectavi hundreds of years earlier, could be a little "intense," Hayden explained. Hayden had become a vampire in the nineteenth century, so in addition to the possibility that other Sanguans would outnumber us at Duncan's, we were also far younger than the old Scot.

Light rain fell along the unfamiliar route, from crowded city, out through residential neighborhoods, to a three-lane highway.

"What do you think the twins are up to?" I asked, feeling odd turning to a right-side driver seat.

"More than we know, I fear."

"Yeah." I pulled out my phone and brought up the pictures from the library book, *I.*

He glanced over. "Are those the ones you emailed?"

"Yes."

"That was a long time ago." He peeked at the picture of the twins with wings. "You really think, after so long, those two are concerned with anything from back then?"

"Maybe." It disappointed me that his initial agreement about their true intentions didn't extend to my theory that their current plans might have to do with their origins.

Hayden changed lanes. "Can I ask you a question?"

"Sure."

"Why the cross tattoo? I asked Zhilan and Grant, and they said to ask you."

"I used to have a bite scar there. The tattoo covered it. At the moment, it's a reminder that there *is* good in the world, at battle with the same evil that makes us immortal. I hope there is, anyway."

Hayden focused on my neck. "A reminder for whom?"

"Me. Others can see what they want."

He nodded.

"My turn," I said. "Why Europe? How does a soldier from Texas become Houjin's agent so far from home?"

His eyes shifted my way, then back to the road. "Zhilan told you about the Alamo?"

"Only a little." Whenever it was possible for me to hear a firsthand account, she preferred I find my answers that way. It usually meant waiting longer, but the stories ended up being richer, once I had.

"I was mortal when the battle began and immortal when leaving the mission once it was over. The two hundred of us might not have won, but men versus men, if Santa Anna hadn't broken his agreement with the Spectavi to keep vampires out of the fight, we might have held on long enough for reinforcements to arrive."

He shook his head. "Or we might not have, but damn I wish I knew. After that, Texans had their revenge, not far away or long after. I spent years hunting the Sanguans from the Alamo, including my maker. I learned to fight and got to see the world along the way. I love Texas, and as it turns out, I also love Europe."

"Wow."

"I'll tell you the whole story another time."

Eventually, a few miles off the highway, we pulled up to a closed black gate with brick columns at the sides. Bright lights hung off each. The gate slowly swung inward until we could pass. I had kept my expectations low, but as we drove through Duncan's grassy courtyard, toward his dark, imposing home, I grew very eager. Why did he want to see me? What did he know?

We parked most of the way around the circular drive, behind two motorcycles and an old, pale blue sedan. I got out and rushed to the covered porch in front of Duncan's large wooden door.

Hayden turned the car off and joined me. He gently grasped my shoulder. "Relax."

I nearly shot back, "I know," but instead answered, "Okay."

He let me go and prepared to knock, when the door was opened by a slim, willowy Sanguan wearing a short silver dress. "Duncan is expecting you," she said. "Come in."

We entered a small foyer with a black marble floor. Numerous narrow hallways led from it.

She shut the door behind us. "Follow me." She walked slowly on her thin high heels.

The next room was dark with a projected movie playing silently on the wall to my left. A man sat on a couch with a can of beer in one hand and his other arm around a woman. They both wore big headphones and intently watched as an exploding building in the film lit the room momentarily. To my right, a wine glass stood on a vacant bar, next to an uncorked bottle and another pair of wireless headphones.

We made our way into a brighter, hexagonal room. The vampire leading went to her left, and I stepped around Hayden. A vampire, presumably Duncan, sat at a desk, holding a young woman with a mohawk and numerous piercings, drinking from her neck. In addition to a clock, penholder, and laptop on the precisely arranged desk, on the front of it, a low stand held a short sword horizontally.

Duncan finished with the girl and motioned to the door. The girl passed us, blank-faced. I watched her go to the movie room, put on headphones, and pour a glass of wine.

"They come and go as they please," Duncan announced. "I ask them not to tell their friends, so the place isn't overrun." He walked around his desk. "Nadine on the other hand… I don't know if I could bear it if *she* ever left." He wrapped his arm around the vampire who had led us in and bit into her neck.

Nadine kissed his cheek. "I'll never leave you." She chomped into his neck.

Watching and listening to their soft sucking and swallowing, I felt like a child. I knew the joy of drinking dense, luscious vampire blood and the horror of being drained by another immortal, but had to imagine what Duncan and Nadine were experiencing. The thirst they would wake to the following night would be intense, I had been told. And they could quench it by drinking from each other again—but only temporarily. The true cure was always human blood.

They slid out of their embrace, and the wound in Nadine's neck closed. She licked all the way around her mouth to clean the last of his blood and, without a word, strolled out of the room.

Duncan asked, "Perhaps *you* would like to stay for a while, young one?"

"No, thanks." I fought off an urge to reach for my knife by crossing my arms.

He shrugged, then returned to his desk chair. "How can I help you, then?"

"Hayden told me you had information about Ahmose."

"On the contrary, I have very little. I told him that it would be wise of you to speak with me on the matter."

Hayden appeared annoyed. "Fine. We're here. What *do* you know?"

Duncan remained calm. "I last saw him in London, where

he was on his way from meeting with Queen Elizabeth I."

I reached for my phone.

"Late sixteenth century," Duncan added. "He's not in London now, however. If he were, I'd know about it. And I would be shocked if he were in the United Kingdom at all."

"That's helpful. Thank you," I said, relaxing. The news also came as a huge disappointment. Another ancient didn't know Ahmose's whereabouts. "What was he up to when you met him?"

"Meetings. Discussions. He was constantly busy, absorbing whatever information he could," Duncan answered. "He was days away from returning to seclusion."

Hayden asked, "Why didn't you tell me that on the phone?"

Duncan focused on me. "I wanted to meet Erin. I wanted to meet the one who succeeded where so many of us failed. Erin, it is *you* who deserves *my* thanks."

He wasn't the first to thank me for Edmond's demise. I reused a prior response. "I had some help."

He gave a sly smile. "Yes, you certainly did."

I moved on. "What do you know about how his sisters came to be the first of our kind?"

"What everyone knows. They grew sick and called out to anyone who would listen for help. God, Satan, pagan gods, spirits. It was the Devil who answered their prayers. Why?"

"Just curious." Duncan hadn't been so hospitable that he deserved all the details.

He brought a finger to his lips. "Have you seen the news from Belgravia?"

"What news?" Hayden asked.

Duncan spun his laptop to face us. "It's within the hour." With the sound muted, a female reporter spoke in front of a large brick home in London. Police car lights flashed behind her. We watched while Duncan explained, "Twelve Sanguans were killed in a Spectavi raid. One woman and a man were rescued from the house. Spectavi demonstratively brought shackles, chains, and a whip out for the cameras when they hustled the two *victims* into police cars."

Hayden pulled out his phone and started to text.

Duncan continued, "The thing is, I recognized the woman they 'rescued.' She's MI5."

"Figures." I gritted my teeth. The Spectavi planting an agent was worse than them using complete fabrications to justify their actions. Instead of typical reports of murders in the usual channels, the staged spectacle would give everyone in the media plenty to run with for a while. I had always believed those stories as a mortal.

"Yes, it does figure." Duncan turned the computer back around. "Best of luck with your search, Erin."

I nodded, and Hayden followed me out of the house. Light rain hit me on the way to the car. After Hayden sat behind the wheel and shut the door, I asked, "Do you believe him about Ahmose?"

"Why not?" He started the car. "Duncan hated Edmond, and he hates the Spectavi. You will have to be careful whom you talk to, and whom you trust, but when I asked around, most were interested because of Ahmose's ties to Edmond. Even with Edmond dead, many were eager to help you find one of his own and deprive him of his desire to stay hidden."

7

The grains of wood in the coffin lid felt closer together than back home. My coffin in Virginia was oak. An older vampire might have known what type of wood my temporary one was made of, but all *I* knew was that it wasn't the same. I opened the lid and climbed out.

Hayden had gone on to Belgium, and I had no set plans to meet anyone. In spite of Duncan's firm opinion, I had decided to investigate on my own in London. I probably wouldn't stay long, but it felt wrong to leave having spoken personally to so few.

I showered in the old tub, then got dressed. My outfit—knee-length gray skirt, boots, and black turtleneck—reminded me of when I had gone out searching for information about the life I couldn't remember. It hadn't quite been a year since the last of those days, but everything had changed. Under my skirt, I strapped my small pouch wallet to the outside of my right thigh, then my knife to my left—things were very different.

Ominous clouds filled the sky, but no rain was forecast. I left the apartment and, not in a rush, walked block after block, south from Islington to central London.

Outside Saint Paul's Cathedral, I stopped. I hadn't traveled all the way across the Atlantic to sightsee, and if I ever wanted to, would have time to return for that kind of trip. Then, a bit awestruck, I realized that if I did live for hundreds of years, I might outlast the stone construction. I pulled out my phone, launched the camera app, and took a few pictures of the brightly lit dome.

At two clubs, the bartenders were no help. None had heard of Ahmose, and when pressed, all of them suggested seeking out Duncan for information. I crossed Tower Bridge on foot and found a quiet pub on the other side of the Thames. That bartender didn't help, either, but a Sanguan from Norwich overheard me and suggested paying a visit to an old vampire named Udolf Gloster in Southampton, a little less than two hours outside London. Short of concrete information, that was exactly the kind of lead I had been looking for. Before leaving the pub, I found a handsome young man who was a little shy, but ultimately eager to satisfy my thirst.

I chose to hold off on Southampton for a night and made my way through the South Bank. At a lounge not far from the huge London Eye Ferris Wheel, the bouncer pointed me in the direction of a sharply dressed vampire sitting in a back booth with two women. The vampire was not forthcoming with information and kept asking who had sent me. His reluctance hinted that he knew something, so I broke down and revealed being friends with Hayden. The name rang a bell, and mentioning Zhilan convinced him. The Sanguan told me to meet with Duncan, and upon hearing that I already had, he suggested Udolf. While my question about reaching Udolf by phone was met with laughter, he did give me an address.

I crossed the river again and stopped to take a picture of Big Ben. Seconds later, a group of four Spectavi rounded the corner. They passed me with only a glance. After that, I sat in huge Hyde Park for over an hour, catching up on the news on my phone. Reliable details about Udolf were nowhere to be found online, so I emailed Zhilan to see if she had any and also to check how Renshu was doing.

Learning of Udolf was, indeed, a positive development, but after Duncan had revealed so little, it was hard to be overly optimistic. I headed to my apartment a few hours before sunrise to fire up my laptop and figure out how to get to Southampton.

While at a car rental agency the following night, I received a text from Caleb.

Erin, sorry to bother you, but please call me if you can.

He wasn't the type to cause a fuss for no reason, so I decided to call once outside the city.

I threw my sword and backpack into my silver hatchback. The female clerk had given Tomori a long look, but never said anything about it. When I shut the door, I spotted a vampire strolling on the sidewalk across the street. His hands were in his pockets, and white headphone wires ran to inside his black coat. He had brown hair and reminded me of the Sanguan from O'Reilly's who had been talking with the group in the booth. What were the odds of us crossing paths twice? When he turned the corner, I checked the time on my phone. Then, I thought of Caleb and decided against following the vampire.

Brring... brring... brring...

Caleb answered, "Erin, hello."

"Hi. Is everything okay?"

"I don't know. Thanks for calling. Do you have a few minutes to talk?"

I clicked the volume control on the wire running from my headphones so I could hear him better. "Yeah. I'm an hour and a half from Southampton, trying to get used to sitting on the right side of the car and driving on the left side of the road."

"Ah, yes. Good luck with that."

"Thanks. What's up?"

"Well, it's my brother. He's been acting differently lately, and... I'm worried about him."

"He's had a rough few months. That wreck was pretty horrible."

"I know. I know. It's... for example, he has bodyguards now, four Sanguans. They seem reasonable, but he went from having nothing to do with vampires to surrounding himself with them."

The question about Sanguans explained why he had called *me*, and the choice of bodyguards was not unprecedented. "I don't trust the Spectavi," I said. "And I could see why David might not want anyone associated with Eure around. He probably has company secrets he doesn't want a competitor to see."

"I thought of that. It makes sense. Eure *does* do business in defense."

"Right," I agreed.

"Okay, then there was three days ago. David was on the phone when I met him for dinner. I sat down, and he finished the conversation. He had been arguing, and it sounded like he lost. When I asked, he said it was Fernand Bisset. I googled the name later, but there were too many different results to know which one he had been talking to. When I asked what they had been discussing, David was evasive and changed the subject to Sanguans. It was the usual stuff: Sanguans are terrible, and the Spectavi aren't doing enough, but there's nothing anyone can do about the situation. Then David asked me, 'What if there *was* something we could do? Just... what if? How much would you risk to change the world for the better?'"

"Wow."

"Yeah. I was shocked. I told him I didn't know and asked what he meant. He brushed aside my question, refusing to explain, and we talked about Sarcorp for the rest of the meal. What do you think he meant?"

"I think... well, I don't know." I really wanted to be helpful, but didn't have a clue.

"Me neither. But I'm worried."

"It sounds like your brother could use someone to talk

to. After all that happened, he's worried about vampires more than ever. Your father's gone, and he's running a huge company all of a sudden. It's good you're there for him." I decided to slip in something I had glimpsed in Caleb's blood. "I know you love him."

"Yeah," Caleb said.

"I guess my only advice is to continue to be there for him. Talk to him. Maybe he'll tell you what's really on his mind."

"Maybe... and you're right. He was so close to my dad. He's been through more than I can imagine."

"Exactly."

"Thanks, Erin. Thanks for listening to all this."

"You're welcome. Keep me posted how things are going, okay?"

"I will. So what are you doing in England?"

I almost launched into the whole story. I had plenty of time in the car, and Caleb would surely have been fascinated. But I stopped myself. It seemed unwise to share those details with someone who frequented Sanguan clubs. "It's a long story."

"Sure. Sure... well, I'll let you get back to it. Thanks again."

"No problem."

I threw my phone and headphones to the passenger seat, turned the radio louder, and hit *Seek* to find a station.

The opposite side of the road felt more natural by the end of the drive to the port city of Southampton. My actual destination was Totton and Eling, a significantly smaller town a few miles away. I lowered the radio when my phone lit up with an email from Zhilan.

Udolf is old. He used to be loyal to the Spectavi, but hasn't been for centuries. Renshu is in a little less pain each night. Good luck.

According to the address I had been given, Udolf lived on the outskirts of town. Darkness gradually faded to pitch black as the thin trees lining the road became denser. After a long stretch with no light except the glow from my car, dull yellow shone from a window in the woods. I checked my GPS. The blue dot representing my location blinked faithfully, but with no cell service, it blinked over a blank grid instead of a map. The window seemed like my best bet.

I slowed and found a gravel path that might have been a driveway. With overhanging branches scraping the top of my car, I pulled in just far enough to be off the road. Two windows of a small house were noticeable through the woods. I turned off the engine and checked my phone—still no service. I grabbed my knife from the driver's seat, clipped it to my belt, and got out of the car.

I closed the door and, standing still, heard nothing but insects. Forest surrounded the brick single-story house. Ducking under branches, I tried to take light, quiet steps on the gravel. More rocks alongside a row of dead shrubs made a path to the front door. I approached cautiously, then stepped onto the stone slab that served as a porch. I knocked twice.

Bugs chirped.

I tried again.

A door inside closed, and footsteps creaked on an old wood floor. My hand clutched my knife, before I forced myself to let go.

The door opened, and a stocky, almost ivory vampire stood before me, wearing faded jeans and a loose tan t-shirt. "Can I help you?"

"I'm... I'm here to see Udolf." I scolded myself for sounding so feeble.

"I am Udolf. Please, come in." He stepped aside to reveal a surprisingly well-lit living room. On a large beige area rug, a worn brown couch sat to the left of a matching recliner. The first TV antenna I had seen in a while sprouted from an old boxy set. Three table lamps gave off the yellow light. A small kitchen was to the right.

Udolf closed the door behind me, and I realized that the filthy windows were what made the place appear so dim from the outside.

Udolf motioned toward the living room. "Have a seat, please."

I sat on the end of the couch and was thankful when Udolf opted for the recliner.

"You are young." He leaned back with his hands on his legs. "Of course, to say one of our kind is young can mean so many things. I am guessing you are extremely young."

"Why's that?"

"Most would introduce themselves when showing up uninvited on another's doorstep."

"I'm sorry! I'm Erin Rose."

"It is nice to meet you, Erin."

"I'm sorry to show up like this. I was told you didn't have a phone."

Udolf raised an eyebrow. "Told by whom?"

"Other Sanguans." What should I say? I decided to give their names if pressed, but since he had me thinking of manners, perhaps it would have been impolite to reveal those who had suggested I meet him. "A few in London mentioned you. I'm looking for another vampire, and they said you might be able to help."

"So it has nothing to do with the knife at your side?"

I shook my head vigorously. "Oh, no, not at all." My knife had raised suspicions before, but I had decided to take it where I pleased, regardless, preferring to fight my way out of any trouble it caused than be caught in trouble without it.

"Good. I have no interest in hand-to-hand combat." Out in the woods, across from an old Sanguan I didn't know, that made two of us. "So, how can I help you?"

"Do you know a vampire named Ahmose?"

Udolf's lips might have turned up, or I might have imagined it. "I do."

Perhaps my trip had been worthwhile. "Do you where he is?"

"No."

Or maybe it was a waste. "When did you last see him?"

Udolf pondered for a moment. "More than five hundred years ago if I'm not mistaken."

I slumped into the couch.

"I am not certain he is alive. Why are you looking for the crazy historian?"

"Crazy" was a new adjective for him, but it did fit how others had described him. "You knew Edmond?"

"Of course."

"And you know about his sisters?"

"Caterine and Ariane?"

"Yes. I'm looking for details about what changed them into the first vampires." I liked to phrase it that way in case anyone ever refuted the facts and mentioned a different origin story.

Like everyone else, Udolf didn't find anything wrong with my statement. "But their tale has already been told."

"Have you ever met them?"

"Yes. But we never conversed, if that's what you are asking."

"Well, I haven't spoken to them either, but I've listened to them some. Before they killed Edmond, he argued with them about their brother Nicolas's role in their transformation. No one has ever heard of Nicolas, not even Victoria." I immediately regretted mentioning her.

"So you are Vera?"

I nodded.

"And you think Edmond's Ahmose might be willing to tell the story?"

"Yes."

"Does Nicolas matter?"

"Maybe. Maybe not. I just hate that those two are out there and there's a part of their story no one knows, or is willing to tell."

"I see," Udolf said. "I'm sorry to say that I know nothing of Ahmose's whereabouts or of Nicolas. Have you spoken to Duncan in Windlesham? I could arrange a meeting if you'd like."

"Yes, I met with him. After he couldn't help, others suggested I come to you. Why?"

"Hmm?"

"Why was I told to come see you?"

"Those who sent you were wise to do so. This home may not look like much, but it serves me well. You are young, impulsive, and on the move. Duncan and I are not, nor is Ahmose most likely. If Ahmose were in England, one of us would know."

I got to my feet. "Well, thank you for your time."

"You are so impatient. You should ask me if there's *anything* I know that could help. I am over seven hundred years old."

I sat down again and considered rephrasing his suggested question before deciding that wasn't the point. "Is there anything else you know that could help me?"

"Perhaps. If I share what I know, will you tell me your story?"

"What do you mean?"

"Rumors have reached me of the girl Vera and the Sanguan Erin Rose. I did not care for Edmond and would enjoy hearing of your life and a firsthand account of his demise."

It was so personal, but what would it really cost me to tell him?

He added, "I will keep the story a secret, if that helps."

It did. "All right."

"There are very old books chronicling some of our history hidden from the Spectavi in Plymouth and Liverpool," Udolf said. "I will inform their keepers you are coming to inspect them. I haven't read them in hundreds of years and doubt they will help you find Ahmose, but perhaps Nicolas is mentioned."

On the map of England I pictured, those two cities weren't nearby. "Who wrote them?"

"Old Spectavi, actually, those who thought our history was too important to lose, in spite of Edmond's desire to control the narrative."

"What are the books called?"

He shrugged. "It's been so long…" He might have read disappointment on my face. "If that's not what you hoped to hear, you need not tell me your story. My intent was not to trick you, and those books might help."

The information didn't thrill me. How useful could the books be if he didn't even recall their titles? But I liked Udolf. He seemed genuine. A quick glance at a wall clock confirmed we had a while before sunrise. I had fed earlier, and he probably didn't have to. I needed to continue my search, but aside from that, had nothing pressing to do. I felt it more as my nights went on—that forever lay before me, and I didn't have to rush.

After asking Udolf to promise, again, that he wouldn't repeat it, I began my tale with the key events of my early years, based on what Victoria had told me and I had glimpsed in my Grandfather's blood. In the middle of a sad part of the story, I let a smile slip, and Udolf prodded me until I shared the memory that caused it.

Twenty-two years earlier, in my grandparents' kitchen, my young mother looked so exasperated with one-year-old me. "Vera Isabella, you have to eat *something*." I clenched my mouth shut and pushed away the spoon full of puréed carrots.

Udolf smiled warmly.

I finished up with Vera and moved on to the first day I could remember as Erin. Udolf asked questions that reminded me of important details I had forgotten to mention. The ancient Sanguan reacted dramatically to some of the twists and turns. In spite of the centuries he had known Edmond, Udolf was repulsed to hear the specifics of how cruel Edmond had been to me.

When I finished, Udolf told me he had been born in England in 1283 and had become a vampire at the age of thirty-one after being badly wounded in the Battle of Bannockburn in Scotland. He fought so valiantly that the Spectavi offered him the chance to join their ranks, and on his deathbed, he accepted.

Years later, he made Duncan a vampire, and in the mid-seventeenth century, Edmond and Duncan both loved the same woman. When she chose to be with Duncan, Edmond drank her dry. Both Udolf and Duncan turned their backs on the Spectavi and had called England home ever since.

When I prepared to leave for town to find a room for the day, Udolf offered an old coffin he had in his basement. My first instinct was to politely decline, but it ultimately sounded better than the grimy hotel he described in Totton and Eling. I brought the rest of my things in from the car and slept with my sword, as usual.

After sunset the next evening, Udolf wrote down the addresses in Plymouth and Liverpool for me. I tried to appear thankful, but he might have realized I was less than thrilled to be leaving with nothing other than the location of some books. When I started my car, he came out and gave me the name of an old French Sanguan. Udolf had no idea if the vampire had information about Ahmose, but I appreciated the tip. Udolf said to stop by whenever in the area. I suggested the same if he made it to Virginia. I knew it might be ages before I saw him again, *if* I ever did, and the beginning of a friendship hadn't been my goal, but it was something.

8

On and off rain during the three-hour drive to Plymouth annoyed me. The city on the south coast of England was west of Udolf's, while Liverpool lay far to the north, and Dover, where Zhilan had suggested I cross the Channel to France, to the east. That ultimate destination got farther away as each mile ticked by on the digital odometer. Using my phone while I drove proved difficult, so I exited the highway halfway to Plymouth. Two turns later, on a quiet street, I shut off the engine, but left the radio playing.

I had a message from Victoria:

Did you have anything to do with Memphis?

She had never mentioned any of my missions with Zhilan aside from our attack on Silas.

I typed, *No*, but then deleted the response before sending it. Instead, I emailed Zhilan the question that had prompted me to pull off in the first place. I told her what Udolf had said and asked if she thought visiting Liverpool made sense. I figured it probably did, but a sanity check before the long ride couldn't hurt. I started to ask for advice on how to respond to Victoria's question, but stopped. The whole point of flying to Tennessee had been to disguise who had destroyed the truck and stolen the synthetic blood. I sent the email to Zhilan with only the question about Liverpool, then wrote back to Victoria, *No, what happened?*

The radio powered down to preserve the car's battery. Light rain peppered the windshield. I checked the news and my alerts—nothing interesting about the twins. I wondered if it would have been simplest to locate them and ask what they were planning, or at least ask about Nicolas and the strange drawing of the pair in the book. I considered how I would fare in a fight with them. Against both, I had no illusions of being able to win. But I had improved dramatically since our last encounter. One on one, could I take Caterine? Ariane acted even more aggressively than her sister did. Could I use that against her?

I started the car. Mighty Victoria struggled against those two demons. Driving to find old books didn't excite me, but seeking out the sisters could have been suicide.

In Plymouth, at twelve-thirty, the antique dealer's door rattled from my soft knock on its glass. Rain continued beyond the tiny awning. After a few moments with no answer, I retreated to my car. I drove two miles between rows of houses and stores—many soft pastel colored, others new brick, none especially tall. The route to one of the nicer hotels for vampires took me along the water. There was plenty of parking in the lot in front of the six-story white building, and I brought my minimal belongings with me to check in. The brightly lit lobby filled with modern furniture and a few plants could have been in any hotel.

"Can I help you?" the receptionist across the counter asked. He had been a middle-aged man, but I figured him as a young Sanguan.

"I need a room."

"Just today?"

"Probably."

"One twenty-five now, and if you stay longer, we'll bill you daily."

"Fine." I handed him my credit card, a little disappointed by the high price, but more glad not to be staying in some dive. He charged my card, and I signed his paperwork.

"Key or print?" he asked.

"Print." Those places went to great lengths to keep credit card and fingerprint information private, but many vampires paid cash and always opted for a key. Zhilan had explained certain times and places for taking the extra precautions.

The receptionist pushed a glass pad toward me, and I pressed my thumb onto it. "You're all set," he said. "Room 416. The elevator is to the right."

I took the staircase beside it, then walked down the red-and-black-carpeted hallway.

"*Mmm…*" It sounded like a girl in Room 404.

I hadn't fed.

"*More…*" the girl urged.

I moved on and, six doors down, pressed my thumb to the small pad next to the handle. The screen illuminated, and with a *click*, the door unlocked.

A flat-screen television hung on the wall across from a black couch with thick cushions. I checked inside the coffin—white cotton lining, which looked fresh and clean. The room had no window. On one hand, I would have preferred one with a thick shade that let in no light when closed. On the other hand, not having a window reminded me of my basement, which must have been the point.

I checked my phone—not yet two. TV didn't interest me. Thirsty and tired of ignoring it, I dropped my things and left.

I headed back near the antique shop because I hadn't driven past anywhere more promising. The first pub I tried was completely empty, except for the bored bartender watching television. The second had a few human patrons, so after speaking to that bartender—who had no information about Ahmose—I settled into a booth near the back that offered a good view of potential prey.

Zhilan wrote, saying I *should* go to Liverpool and for me to be patient.

The pub door opened, and a Sanguan in a black overcoat entered–the one I had seen when renting my car and possibly at O'Reilly's before that. He sat at the bar between two men working their way through beers.

It could have been a coincidence, but I doubted it, so far from London. I wished my booth were more secluded, but didn't want to draw attention by moving. Surely, he had already spotted me, anyway, as I always noticed other immortals nearby. He leaned away from the bar and looked around, but not directly at me. After a second, he got up and walked out the front door.

I had to follow him. I still hadn't fed, but that didn't matter. My aching deepened. My thirst *did* matter, but would have to wait. In an instant, I was at the door. I opened it and raced across the street. I spun around and, far to the left, the vampire stood, staring at me.

I rushed at him, and he darted to the other side of the street, stopping with his hands in his pockets in front of an old restaurant on the corner.

"What do you want?" I called.

A man came out of the restaurant, took a look at me and the other vampire, and hurried back inside.

The Sanguan smiled, then jumped and landed on the flat roof of the restaurant.

I raced across the street and leapt to where he stood. He was on the other side of the roof by the time I landed. I yelled, "Who are you? Why are you following me?"

"*You* are following *me*." He ran and jumped the short distance to the roof behind him. I followed, and when he paused on top of the next building, I kept charging at him. He fled to another roof, and by the time I got there, he had jumped down to the street.

He raced up a block and then right. I lost sight of him. I wasn't used to being slower than those who ran from me. My gifts from Edmond's ancient blood were considerable, but age, perhaps, allowed that Sanguan to run faster.

A gust of wind blew a few strands of hair across my face.

A wave of pain launched through me. I expected the vampire would show up again.

———————————

An old bell rattled when I opened the door to the antique shop the following night. Vases and fine china sat on dusty shelves and tables. Oriental rugs hung from the walls. Everything had been arranged haphazardly, or not at all.

A voice came from the far corner of the shop. "Hello!"

"Hello?" I called, making my way through the mess.

A chubby old man with glasses came around the corner and stopped in his tracks. "Can I help you?"

"I'm Erin Rose. Udolf sent me about some books."

He frowned. "I'm so sorry, Erin. I received Udolf's message by courier today, but had no way to reply. The books have been destroyed."

"Destroyed?" My tone was harsher than intended.

"In… In a fire… th-three years ago," the man stammered. "I almost lost my whole shop. I'm sorry."

"Do you remember the books? What was in them or their titles?"

"I never read them. I hadn't heard from Udolf in fifty years, but he told my father and me that reading them could be dangerous. As for titles, two had ranges of years, *660-712* and *713-791*. One was called *Kings and Queens*."

I looked around the shop. "That's it? There's nothing else?"

"That's it. I'm very sorry."

I pivoted, marched to the entrance, and flung open the

door, which slammed closed behind me. I scanned left and right for the vampire from the night before, but didn't see him.

In my car, I pulled up directions to Liverpool, over five hours away.

———————————

I began the drive livid and hungry, but gradually accepted that the way Udolf lived, it made sense that news of the books' destruction hadn't reached him. He wasn't modern, constantly plugged in to the events of the world. By the end of the drive, my thirst had grown, but I had calmed a bit. I hadn't come close to seeing those books. *Kings and Queens* was an especially intriguing title, but I had missed it by a full three years. If it had been three days, it would have felt worse.

Liverpool was larger and more populous than Plymouth. As I approached the coastal city, the buildings seemed taller, darker, and those I drove past, dirtier. The setting reminded me more of London than my previous stop.

I went straight to a hotel downtown, not bothering to try the bookstore that had surely already closed. It was three-thirty, and I didn't feel like a pub or club, so I'd wait and see who stayed out after four. On the walk to the Liverpool Marina, I kept watch for the Sanguan from Plymouth.

He never showed, and I ended up sitting at the edge of the wooden dock between a small sailboat and a motorboat. A constant breeze that blew over my parched, chapped lips also kept the water choppy. Licking my lips didn't help. I emailed Zhilan, asking about developments with the synthetic blood we had stolen, hopeful she was having better luck than I was. I opened my RSS app for the news and heard footsteps behind me.

I turned slowly to see a lean man with a white beard approaching. Were there surveillance cameras in Liverpool? If so, could they see out onto the dock? I put away my phone and launched myself at the man.

"Wha—" he started. My fangs pierced his leathery neck, and he got out an "Oh."

My lips grew moist. The clamoring within subsided. My fire burned.

When I finished, I raced us over to his sailboat where I sat him on the deck. He opened his eyes as I left, but he couldn't have gotten a good look at me.

———————

The used bookstore was bright and larger than expected. Four long shelves created five rows of old books. A few people browsed while the owner showed me to a small, cramped office at the end of the rightmost row. Mr. Allen hadn't seemed nervous, though his wife behind the cash register had been when I first entered. He placed three books on the cluttered white desk. A partially crumpled paper covered the bottom of a framed picture of him, his wife, and two sons. I sat in the rolling chair, and he shut the door on his way out.

My excitement became tempered as soon as I inspected the books. The first worn cover read *713-791*. The second

792-846. And the third *847-914.* Those years didn't coincide with the twins' origins, which would have been around 500 A.D.

Past the front matter of *713-791,* the first page contained a handwritten name centered at the top, Timothée, and a black vertical line from it to Urbain. Horizontal lines connected Urbain to Gilebert on the left and Looys on the right. The following page began with Gilebert centered at the top. I didn't recognize any of the names, but it appeared to be a vampire lineage. The next page started with Looys. I flipped through the rest of the book with increasing speed.

792-846 was the same, and not surprisingly, so was *847-914.* None of the names on the early pages of the books were familiar. Under other circumstances, I might have read the rest more carefully, but I felt I had wasted my time coming to Liverpool. Just as I was about to close the books and leave, someone knocked on the door.

Mr. Allen popped his head around the jamb. "I almost forgot this one. I keep it separate." He handed me a small brown book with a golden *VI* on the binding. "Perhaps it will be helpful?"

"I don't know. Maybe. We'll see." The familiar title gave hope. "Thank you."

Mr. Allen nodded and closed the door again.

Like *I,* the sixth volume had a binding of roughly an inch and thick, heavy pages. It was also dated the same year—1408. In English, again below what was probably Old French, and Italian, the first title section read, "The Rescue of Frederick II, Holy Roman Emperor." I turned the page to a drawing in the expected black-line style. Clergymen surrounded a man in a white robe and a tall white hat—clearly the Pope. Amidst a crowd of nobility, another man, presumably Frederick, knelt before the Pope, who was placing a crown upon his head.

The next page was split into two drawings. At the top, a map depicted Rome and Southern Italy with an 'X' covering the strait of Messina along the route to the island of Sicily. In the bottom drawing, a crazed vampire held Frederick by the neck. Eight other angry vampires surrounded Frederick's defeated company of men and two vampires with crosses on their tunics.

Then, Frederick slumped down against the wall across from a wooden door with iron bars near eye level. The room's furnishings were a disorganized mess. Numerous bite marks dotted Frederick's neck and wrists.

In the following drawing, fifteen vampires—two of them female—raided a compound. The raiders jumped over walls and clashed swords with those inside, who were depicted as wild, wearing black, with fangs out and sinister eyes. The attackers, wearing white and most with crosses on their arms, were presumably Spectavi.

Next, twenty Sanguans surrounded six Spectavi who had escaped with Frederick. The two nearest the Emperor resembled Edmond and Victoria. On my cell, I googled "Frederick II, Holy Roman Emperor" and found that he had been coronated in 1220—Victoria would have been a young vampire.

Turning the page, I found a drawing of Edmond and

Victoria defending Frederick in a corner. They wielded two-handed longswords, and hacked-up bodies of Sanguans lay at their feet.

Next, Edmond helped Frederick into a carriage. In the final drawing, he and Victoria were on horseback accompanying men and other Spectavi, who surrounded the emperor.

"The Purge" followed. The Pope, surrounded by clergymen, sat at a table, signing a document. Long pointed stakes and huge mallets were piled on another table. Opposite the Pope, a group of Spectavi, including Edmond, had their hands in the air and appeared to be arguing.

Turning the page revealed three drawings. In the first, with the sun shining overhead, men with mallets and stakes sneaked into a basement where a coffin lay in the far corner. In the second drawing, the enraged, risen vampire attacked the men. The third drawing depicted three small similar scenes in different basements. I turned the page. In the top drawing, with the moon overhead, a vampire carried a dead man toward a house. In the bottom drawing, the man lay on the front porch while the vampire attacked the family inside.

Zhilan had never told me of that particular purge, but stories I had read as a human helped explain the drawings. When humans tried to stake an immortal through their coffin or move a coffin out into the sun, they sometimes succeeded, and their target bled to death or burned to ashes. More often, the vampire awoke and swiftly dealt with those nearby. At nightfall, the vampire would go after the families of their attackers. Zhilan spoke with no remorse when describing how the massive retaliation acted as a powerful deterrent to humans attacking our kind during the day.

On the last page of the section, the Pope tore up the document he had signed.

The next title page read, "Reclaiming Iceland." The twins sat on thrones in a large hall, surrounded by humans in chains. The chapter depicted a military campaign, including maps, battles, and scores of Sanguans vanquished at the hands of Spectavi. The twins fled to Norway at the end.

"The Black Council" came next. Gaunt human bodies with gray, marked skin lined a city street. On the following page, Sanguans, Spectavi, and what I judged to be humans sat around a table. After a few missing pages, three blocks of handwritten text began mid-sentence. The English read, "… two know their names, and only in the presence of both will the three reveal their clues. Until then, the relic remains hidden."

I took a picture of the text, then reexamined each drawing, but I didn't find any hint of wings or flames associated with Caterine and Ariane.

The book had been interesting—extremely, actually— but not what I had been looking for. Those clues and that relic intrigued me, and once everything with Ahmose and Nicolas was behind me, perhaps I would turn my attention to figuring out what the passage meant.

I left the four books stacked neatly on the desk and thanked Mr. Allen on the way out of the store. It was a long way to Dover, and I would have to sleep a day once there, but then I would be off to Calais. England didn't appear to have my answers, and despite my worries that France wouldn't either, I couldn't help being excited to explore the area where the first of my kind had come to be.

9

The white and blue ferry to Calais, France covered a little over twenty miles in ninety minutes. The ship could seat two thousand comfortably inside, but was far from full. I wasn't allowed on the forward deck. Spectavi guards kept that area, and most of the rest, Sanguan-free.

Alone, with my backpack and sword at my feet, I leaned over the railing on the stern deck, watching the yellow cliffs of Dover grow smaller and smaller. The iconic cliffs would have been white during the day, but I had to settle for how the town lights illuminated them.

The sound of water sloshing against the ship relaxed me, and the smell of salt was refreshingly different. I would have enjoyed a cool breeze, but unfortunately, like all winds, the one steadily buffeting my face did so warmly.

I reread Zhilan's email from just before sunrise her time:

Erin,

Nigel has successfully altered the synthetic. We tested it, and our subject responded as we programmed him.

Houjin is planning how we will proceed on a wider scale as an example for the world to see.

How is your search going?

Best, Zhilan

It would have been nice to have been more intimately involved in Zhilan's plans. But I couldn't be everywhere, and my task was also important. I thought it was, anyway.

Two small children cracked open the heavy metal door and stumbled onto the deck, vying to be first. The boy won. They stopped when they noticed me staring at them, and their mother, following a second later, nearly toppled over them. She put an arm on each child's shoulder. "Back inside."

They went in, and when I turned around, the cliffs had disappeared, and nothing remained beneath the twinkling stars and scattered clouds except low, black waves. At least I had gone on *one* boat ride during the day with Todd. On my cell, I found the picture of us out on the blue water of the Potomac that sunny day. And I could find plenty of other pictures or video of daytime water or the bright sun. The ancients had nothing except drawings and paintings…

The door behind me opened again. A Sanguan wearing a black coat and carrying a small backpack stepped onto the deck. I put away my phone and drew Tomori from its scabbard, keeping it low, as the vampire I had chased on the rooftops in Plymouth approached me.

"Hello, Erin."

"Who are you?"

"Nathan Rigby. Most call me Nate these days." He had a youthful face, but his light skin suggested he was far older than I was.

I raised my sword and wrapped my other hand around the handle. "What do you want?"

"To help you."

"With what?"

He smiled with the confidence being beautiful and immortal bestowed. "With whatever you're doing. I overheard you at the pub. Something about a search? Sounds exciting."

"The search is over. I found what I was looking for," I said, so wishing it were true.

He took another step. "That's not what Mr. Allen said at the bookstore."

"Did you hurt him?"

"Mr. Allen? No. Once I mentioned the name 'Udolf'—which I got from the antique dealer—he happily answered all of my questions. The antique dealer is also fine, if you care."

"Who sent you?"

From the level overlooking us, a Spectavi guard called down, "Stop where you are!" He aimed his rifle at me. Neither Nate nor I moved. A Spectavi came out the door on our deck. Another with a rifle appeared next to the one above.

"Put the sword away," the first guard called.

Nate's eyes met mine. I liked my chances against the

swordless Spectavi all by myself. Nate was quick, and if he could fight at all, we'd make short work of the three of them. I tightened my grip on my katana.

"Put it away!" the guard yelled again.

Nate gave a playful smile. "We will have fun." He raised his hands. "But not here. Not now." He turned to the Spectavi.

He was right, at least about fighting. I imagined, with pleasure, Tomori slicing through immortal flesh, blood, and bone, but the ship wasn't the place for it. I grabbed my scabbard, and sheathed my sword.

Nate walked backward with his hands up until he ran into the railing behind me. One of the Spectavi aiming down at us left, then the one on our level went back inside the ship.

The guard who remained above called, "Just give me a reason to shoot."

He had no idea who he was dealing with. The commotion and subsequent attention a fight would draw would have been a nuisance. Those complications, and not his pathetic rifle, were the only things stopping me.

"Not tonight," Nate said loudly. He lowered his hands, then turned to face the sea and dropped his backpack to the deck.

I joined Nate in facing the water. When I glanced up again, the guard had moved away.

"No one sent me," Nate said, answering my last question before we'd been interrupted. "But this is already such fun."

"It's not fun." It was work, and I had found nothing. Yet the conversation at Spectavi gunpoint had brought some relief. With so many questions, learning Nate's identity was better than nothing. He looked strong—solid, but not huge. I guessed he might have been a hundred years old. "You can't follow me."

"Of course I can. I want to help you find whatever you're looking for. I'm already so intrigued. But if I have to, I'll stay just out of reach of that magnificent blade of yours."

I didn't want him with me, but the prospect of looking over my shoulder, constantly wondering if he lurked nearby, sounded incredibly frustrating. "What if I'm faster than you think? What if you run one way and I go the other, but then, at our next move, you guess wrong, and my sword does hit its mark?"

"It's a risk." He smirked. "But what isn't?"

"This isn't a game."

"Sure it is."

"Psht." I looked out to the water.

"So what *are* you looking for?"

I looked up and saw that the Spectavi was once again standing above us.

"Where are you headed?" Nate asked.

I glared at him.

He nodded. "All right."

We didn't talk much the rest of the way. Nate appeared to be quite pleased the entire time.

On the train at the station in Calais, I passed a few half-occupied rows, then stopped and threw my pack and sword onto a backward-facing seat in a group of four. I tossed my coat on top of the rest of my stuff and sat across from the pile, against the window.

Nate took the seat facing me and placed his backpack next to mine. "So, what's in Paris?"

I grabbed my phone, turned off the sound, and casually used my thumb to take a picture that included Nate. "Hmm?" I attached the picture to an email addressed to Zhilan and Hayden.

"Paris. Why are you headed there?"

I wrote, *Ran into Nathan Rigby. Sanguan. Goes by Nate. Know anything about him?* I hit Send and looked up from my phone. The train eased forward. In my mind, on the ferry, I had played out a few different scenarios.

In the first, my train arrived in Paris, where I disembarked and darted into the crowded station. I ran and jumped around and over people and train cars. Eventually, Nate would lose sight of me, and I'd board my next train. Unfortunately, Nate would probably keep up with me. Also likely, the chase would cause the same kind of commotion I had opted to avoid on the ship. It didn't sound like the way to go.

Option two was stabbing him with my knife. I could have tried it before we got to our seats and might have still been able to reach into my backpack, pull it out, and surprise him.

Option three was going the same route with my sword.

Nate had his left leg crossed over his right, eagerly awaiting my answer about Paris. I wouldn't hesitate to kill him if an ulterior motive surfaced, or Zhilan or Hayden suggested it, but maybe he *was* simply out looking for something to do.

"I'm taking another train to Chartres," I said, as the night beyond the window began to slide by faster and faster.

"Ah, the cathedral. You want to see your maker's creation in person?"

"You know who I am," I said.

"I do indeed. Edmond's last fledgling."

I had been called that before. "So what's your story?"

"Not anything so important or so world-changing."

"We've got nothing but time." I enjoyed pointing out something so often thrown in my face.

"Indeed." He uncrossed his legs. "The Victorian gold rush in Australia in the 1850s was similar to the same rush west in America. Canvas towns of tents sprouted up when people raced somewhere new and there was nowhere else to stay. Those towns were especially wild, and for a long time, Spectavi were scarce. Sanguans found humans like me to be easy pickings. I was twenty-five at the time and did all right. I found some gold and made some money…" He grinned. "… which I usually lost at cards, roulette, or dice. Late one night at a saloon in Bendigo, after an appropriate amount of whisky, I was way up at the faro table. The most stunning vampire I had ever seen walked in." Nate's eyes unfocused without moving from me. "Long brown hair, a striking electric-blue dress, her perfect bosom…" He blinked. "Sorry."

I shrugged. "It paints a picture."

"She sat down at the roulette table across the saloon. I watched her purchase chips and lost track of what was going on in front of me. Eventually, the banker got my attention, and I resumed playing, but I kept turning around to look at the vampire. The crowd grew around her, but less and less people were placing bets. One by one, men got up, and eventually, she was left betting and sitting alone. She stood and looked around the room. Her silver eyes met mine for a moment before she sat back down again.

"I left the faro table and made my way over to her. While the white ball spun around the roulette wheel's wooden track, I focused on the Sanguan's exquisite, bare shoulders. The ball bounced and rattled to a stop in the pocket in front of the green double zero. She hadn't bet it.

"When I reached her, she turned around and asked, 'Are you here to play with me?'

"She had such a cheery, precise voice. Staring at that pretty face, distracted by her blue and silver earrings, I foolishly answered, 'You don't need me to play roulette.'

"Thankfully, she gave me another chance, 'It's more fun to play the Devil's Game with a friend. Be my friend tonight?'

"My heart raced. I had plenty of money from faro—a month of work's worth. How could I say yes? But how could I say no? I took the chair to her right, in front of the green cloth betting layout."

I knew virtually nothing of the Australian gold rush. I couldn't wait to hear what happened, and decided that when I had time, I needed to read more history. A world full of immortals demanded it.

Nate continued, "She introduced herself as Josephine, and I told her my name. Half my money got me a hundred chips from the dealer. When he spun the ball, I placed a chip on my favorite number—five. Josephine laughed while spreading ten chips around the board. She took my hand and moved it back over my stack of chips, 'Try to keep up.'

"I somehow managed to scatter another nine chips on different numbers while remembering her firm touch, praying I would get to feel it again. The ball clanked around and landed on twenty-nine—neither of us had bet it. The dealer put his marker down on the number. Josephine simply said, 'More,' while the dealer collected our lost chips. We bet fifteen the next spin, and twenty after that. With everyone watching, cheering at our wins and gasping at our huge losses, she won more than I did. Spin after spin, the dealer dropped his marker, did his math, and stacked our chips in front of him or pushed new ones from those piles toward us. Jo and I didn't say much, aside from her pointing out when I hadn't matched her bet. She smiled when she won and smiled *at me* when I won. I remember those smiles so completely. Her perfect little fangs…"

Nate paused, his face awash with contentedness, before snapping out of it. "Our wagers got so big that it was very sudden when the ball settled in front of the zero, and I was out of chips. 'A pity,' Jo said. 'I liked playing with you, Nathan.' I got out the rest of my money and bought fresh chips. She rewarded me with a smile.

"Betting on the outside and with groups of numbers on the inside lowered my potential winnings and also lowered my risk. The switch improved my luck temporarily and helped the second stack of chips last a little longer. Then nineteen hit, which I hadn't bet. The next spin, it hit again. When nineteen hit the third time in a row, I was out of chips once more, and that time, broke. Jo said nothing. She stared at me, waiting for my move. I reached into my pocket and, to her delight and the delight of the crowd behind us, pulled out a large gold nugget.

"The dealer took a good look at the gold and began counting chips. 'No,' Jo said, 'bet it all.' I couldn't. I shouldn't have been betting it in the first place. After losing my cash, it was close to all I had in the world. The crowd made no sound as the radiant creature gently took my wrist and moved it out over the betting area. She kept a hold of me while my hand hovered above the space that meant any of the red numbers would win. Whether it was her touch or what, I don't know, but I decided to be bolder and kept going until setting the nugget down on the single number five. The crowd cheered.

"Jo quickly moved half her stack of chips onto the board, and told the dealer they were all for the six, because they didn't fit on the space.

"Around and around the little white ball spun. The crowd cheered at first, then grew quiet as the ball slowed. It fell from the track and bounced. My heart plummeted. It was far from the five. Close to the six, the ball rattled to a stop in front of the four.

"Jo gave me a smile anyway. 'What next?'

"'I have nothing else.' I hated saying it. All she wanted to do was keep betting, and she wanted to do it with *me*. Yet I couldn't.

"'Sure you do,' she replied.

"'My tent?' I was only half kidding.

"'Not your tent.' She licked her bright white teeth from one fang to the other. 'Your blood.'

"The dealer said, 'We don't want his blood.'

"He jerked back, Jo turned to him so fast. 'The bet's between us,' she said. 'You will spin when I tell you.'

"Terrified, but thrilled to possess something she valued, I asked, 'How much blood?'

"'All of it.'

"It hit me like a lightning bolt. Even as my infatuation with her deepened beyond any I had ever known, I had a new priority, and an idea of how to push her to it. I said, 'I don't think you have enough money.'

"She chuckled, slid a sapphire ring off her finger, and placed it in front of her chips. I shook my head. The crowd murmured. She pulled a diamond bangle off her wrist and added it to the pile. Again, I shook my head. She looked confused, until she grinned and said, 'Immortality. A fair bet against your soul. If you win, I will still have your blood, but you may have mine in return.'"

Nate had been crazy. And bold. Even with a full understanding of the gifts that came with being a vampire, I could never have left such a thing to chance.

"Jo put her ring and bangle back on, and set the bet. 'I'll take the odd numbers, you take the evens.'

"'I want the odds,' I said.

"'Fine. I'm evens, and if it's one of the zeros, we spin again until it's not.' Her smile was mischievous. 'One way or another, my fangs will pierce your flesh this night.' The crowd gasped. Some turned away. Others left the saloon. I could feel my heart pounding and, in the silence, swore all around could hear it just the same.

"'Spin it,' Jo called to the dealer.

"He took the ball, gave me a long look, shook his head, and did as commanded. Around the ball went, faster than all night. Jo and I stared equally hard, and I had time to wonder what I had done and think about how insane my bet had been. But I swear I didn't regret it.

"The ball kept going, and while we both kept watching, Jo said, 'You will like my bite.'

"As if I hadn't already been thinking that... the most gorgeous creature I had ever seen would sip my life away. The ball slowed. I thought of her fangs slicing into me and what I would feel before the end. I prayed she would take her time. The ball fell toward the eighteen, then bounced past the twelve to the inside of the wheel. The ball shot back out to the track. Unless her drink wasn't the end, and I got to sip *her* sweet blood. The ball fell inward and rattled between numbers before heading slowly for the thirty-four and twenty-two. I imagined what her blood would taste like and later understood the foolishness of trying to guess at such a thing. The ball hit the divider and bounced over the twenty-two to settle in the five slot.

"Jo grinned. The crowd shrieked, clapped, and hollered, while I sat, stunned. Jo lifted me out of my chair. She raced us out to the street and sank her fangs into my neck—for only a second. When she stopped, I kissed her. She kept her word and made me a vampire before sunrise." Nate was left grinning.

"Wow," I said.

"Yeah."

"What happened to Josephine?"

His reaction told me that part of the story was sadder. "We spent years together until she went off on her own. I searched, but never found her."

"I'm sorry."

"Eh, it happens. You'll see for yourself one day."

Odds were, I would, and it scared me, so I didn't think about it often. Most vampires grew apart from their makers and early friends, and many became isolated as they grew older. I couldn't imagine letting go of Zhilan, Grant, or Victoria. And Victoria was a rare example of one who had stayed with another—Edmond—for hundreds of years. So nothing was certain.

"Why did she call it the 'Devil's Game'?" I asked.

"Because the numbers on the wheel add up to the Number of the Beast—666."

"Really?"

"Yeah." Nate pulled his wallet out of his pocket. "And take a look at this. I just had to go back for it." He slid out a thin, plastic-covered, red wooden square with a white five painted on it.

I stopped myself from saying "Wow" again. "That's... that's really cool."

An email from Hayden showed up, saying he didn't know Nate, but had asked around and found him to be reasonably well liked among other Sanguans. He had a lust for adventure and taking ill-advised risks. I had already discovered those characteristics on my own.

I settled in and told Nate that my search was for an ancient vampire named Ahmose, who had information I needed. I didn't tell him what the information was exactly, but Nate seemed to appreciate knowing a little more.

After changing trains in Paris, we arrived in Chartres at three-thirty a.m. A Spectavi guard with mirrored goggles stood on the platform when we stepped off the train. He kept his rifle ready, but not aimed, while giving Nate and me a long look. Like the other Spectavi around, he had a sword at his right hip.

We passed lots of guards while exiting the station among other humans, but none of the Spectavi did anything obvious beyond observing. Nate and I were headed to the cathedral right away. I didn't anticipate discovering anything about Ahmose, but wondered if a reference to Nicolas existed inside Edmond's late twelfth century creation. Plus, I couldn't have gone all the way to France and skipped seeing the cathedral or visiting the city of the first of my kind.

On the train, I had mapped the route on my phone, but Nate said he knew the way, so I followed him. While it had been decades since he had visited, the cathedral would be hard to miss.

Not a minute after leaving the station, past closed shops and small restaurants on both sides of Avenue Jehan de Beauce, to the left, there it was—enormous. The façade Edmond had built above his underground replica of the cathedral at Eure headquarters wasn't full size. Under the starry sky in Chartres, I saw the entire gray stone building for the first time.

At the end of a street of two- and three-story, tan stone medieval and Renaissance houses, an adjacent row of homes obstructed our view of the cathedral. Two blocks later, the west entrance of the massive Gothic structure stood in full view once more. After another two blocks, we stopped at the edge of a long, vacant courtyard.

Two tall spires cut into the sky—the shorter plain Romanesque and the taller ornate Gothic. Between them ran the ledge where the twins had made a scene back in November. The three arched entranceways that dominated the façade at Eure were dwarfed in Chartres by large stained glass windows above them—three narrow rectangular ones with a massive rose depicting the Last Judgment on top.

Across the courtyard, a Spectavi stood at each side of the wide entrance. France owned the cathedral, not the Spectavi. Edmond had overseen its construction and had advocated that it remain open to all. While it was guarded around the clock and Sanguans rarely visited, I had found nothing indicating it would be off limits to my kind.

"More Spectavi around than I remember," Nate said. "I bet because those twins were here."

My knife was packed, and I realized it would have been

less threatening to drop off my sword somewhere, but I didn't feel like waiting. Wearing my coat and with my belongings on my back, I headed for the entrance. Nate followed with his backpack once again slung over his shoulder.

The two Spectavi staring at us while we approached didn't wear goggles and had no visible weapons, except the katanas at their sides. As we neared them, the one on the right called out, "You cannot go in with that sword."

I kept walking. "Why not?"

The guard's hand went to his sword handle. "No weapons inside." The pair moved to block our path.

I stopped. "Edmond's dead. What's it matter?"

Nate let out a little snicker.

The Spectavi on the left revealed massive fangs.

The one on the right said, "No sword, and we'll need to search your bags if you intend to bring them in."

I considered telling them that Victoria had given me my sword or sending her a quick message asking if she could order the guards to allow me to take it inside. The prospect amused me, but ultimately seemed unwise. "I'm not leaving it with you."

"Then you aren't going in."

"I'll hold your things," Nate offered.

I took off my sword and pack. "Give me the wooden five."

"What?" Nate asked.

"I have to know you'll be here when I return."

He pulled his wallet from his front pocket and slid out

the slim plastic case. "If anything happens to this…"

I grabbed it from him. "It won't."

He took my things.

The Spectavi on the right motioned to the side. "That door."

"Why?" I had always gone through the center entrance at Eure.

"Because *that* is the door we will let *you* go in."

It wasn't worth arguing over. While Nate went to the middle of the courtyard to wait, I pushed open the small wooden door and stepped inside. I put his five in my coat pocket.

The door closed behind me, and just as I had at the bottom of the stairs in the replica at Eure for the first time, I stared. The cavernous cathedral was not brightly lit—one of many differences compared to the one in Virginia that jumped out at me. Down the long center nave, rows of plain wooden chairs were arranged for Mass in both cathedrals, but Edmond's replica ended in a simple, low altar. In Chartres, the low altar was halfway up the nave, at the crossing before the choir. Past it, at the end of the choir area, a high altar and a sculpture portrayed the Assumption of the Virgin Mary into Heaven. In Chartres, no massive crucifix hung from the spectacular vaulted ceiling; Edmond had added that dominating symbol in Virginia exclusively.

Scaffolding and wooden beams blocked arched entranceways on both sides of me. Farther ahead, to my left, below a tall, colorful stained glass window, a Spectavi stood like a statue against the wall. Another stood under a window to my right. They carried no weapons I could see. Similar intricate windows ran the length of the church.

As I headed up the aisle between the chairs in Chartres, the sounds of my boots against the stone floor echoed. It was like moving through a dream mixture of the same walk at Eure and images of the real thing I had pulled up on my laptop in my little room there. Row after row, I recalled the Spectavi—young and ancient—sitting as they had each Sunday for Mass. Like then, I would have gone faster if my friend Jennifer were tugging on my sleeve. I stopped before reaching the low altar, at the spot where I had sat in the replica, and ran my fingers over the back of the chair. Across the aisle to my right was Edmond's customary chair—I was walking through a nightmare, not merely a dream.

Far to my left, on the north wall, past more wooden chairs arranged to view the low altar, a guard stood under a large, stained glass rose window. He scowled when we made eye contact. Across the cathedral, another guard stood under another circular window.

Toward the high altar, a partition created the enclave of the choir area, with life-sized white marble relief sculptures depicting Mary's and Jesus' lives. I inspected each one for any mention of Nicolas or the twins, but found none. The marble altar exceeded my expectations from the pictures online.

Like at Eure, the church had been built for God's glory, but unlike then, the Spectavi inside did not seem at all righteous. But what if the Spectavi weren't under control of the synthetic blood? Would the guards have been any different?

Surrounded by angels, Mary ascended to Heaven in the stone sculpture behind the altar. Heaven… I might have glimpsed it in the darkness, in the pure white light, before returning to the world to be a vampire. And the angels… I was a demon. So were the Spectavi. The cathedral was holy, but I was not—yet neither was Edmond, and he had built it.

I turned from the sculpture and took a deep breath. It was too much. I could have spent until sunrise debating with myself, ruminating on so many things unrelated to my search.

I ignored the nearby guard while making my way to the outside of the choir enclave, then I went around inspecting biblical scene after scene, statue after statue. Three deep chapels radiated off the curved eastern end of the cathedral, one of which contained the Sancta Camisa—the tunic worn by Mary at the time of Christ's birth. On the long southern side, below the stained glass windows, a priest's fangs in a relief carving gave him away as a vampire. To the left, above eye level, the aftermath of a battle had been carved. A helmetless vampire knight held his sword high, with vanquished enemies at his feet. I stood up on my toes—it could have been Edmond, victorious. None of the battles or religious scenes included the twins, even them being defeated.

Near the western doors where I had entered, I realized the wooden beams blocked access to the north and south spires. Presumably, the scaffolding meant they were being renovated. I ran my hand over a two-by-four, glanced behind me to see guards taking note, and decided against ripping down the wood.

Instead, I headed to the cathedral's north entrance where, to my surprise, the door to the crypt opened easily. I descended a worn stone staircase with a gray, narrowly arched ceiling. Pictures I had seen gave the place a familiar feel. The air was still, but not cool, as an old mortal instinct led me to expect. I didn't know if Eure's crypt was the same, but no bodies rested in Chartres'.

Under a wider arched ceiling, past a black statue of the Madonna and a well, I stood in the underground chapel. A center aisle separated two columns of four chairs each. A lone Spectavi guard stood beside the altar, his hands behind his back. It must have been a boring post, but with forever ahead of him, I supposed he could afford the dull nights. The place was eerie, yet peaceful. If I were alone, I might have sat for a few minutes, most likely pondering all the same things I had debated upstairs.

Instead, I looked at the bare walls of the chapel. All the way around, I scanned high and low and found nothing. I started to leave, but an irregularity caught my eye. At the very bottom of the wall, partially blocked by a chair leg, the etching was barely visible.

I darted over and crouched low to see the small, crudely drawn cross. Below it read, *Dieu ait pitié de mon frère.* I was pretty sure *frère* meant "brother." Finally, I had found something. I checked my phone—no internet service for a translation.

I looked at the pale guard. "What does it mean?"

He blinked, and after a moment, said, "God have mercy on my brother."

"Whose brother?"

"I don't know."

It had to be Edmond's etching, and the brother *had* to be Nicolas. I took two pictures—one with a flash and one without. I got up and turned to the guard. "Thank you."

He didn't move or answer. On my way out, I scanned the walls high and low, but found no other etchings. Upstairs near the west entrance, I took a few long last looks at the massive cathedral. Of all the mistakes I made at Eure, I didn't fault myself for being overwhelmed with the replica there. What occurred inside was a different story, but Edmond's building itself was magnificent, and his original in Chartres, even more so.

I whispered, "God..." then bit my lip and pushed open the large center door behind me.

Nate sat on a bench far from the entrance, reading on his phone. I headed over to him.

He stood. "Find anything?"

"Not really." He was asking about Ahmose, but my answer also applied to Nicolas. The etching had done nothing except lend credence to Edmond and his sisters' argument in his basement. Nicolas had made "mistakes," Edmond had said. No longer in the secluded crypt or under the spell of the glorious cathedral, I accepted the disappointing fact that I knew no more than I had before. I handed Nate his five and grabbed my things from the bench.

We found lodging for Sanguans scarce in town. After an

hour and no answer at the first three small inns we tried, we finally located a single room above a pub.

A short Sanguan showed us up a narrow, creaky staircase. He opened the door, and a single coffin lay in the small, dingy room. He pointed inside. "Ici."

"We need another," I said.

He didn't seem to understand my English.

With his hands in his pockets, Nate smiled.

I didn't. "No way."

Nate frowned.

I crossed my arms.

"Fine," he said, then turned to the other vampire. "Avez-vous un autre cercueil?"

"Ah. Oui, oui." He disappeared and came back with a second coffin.

10

The following night, the first bartender we spoke to had never heard of Ahmose. He also claimed the same about Caterine and Ariane, which was preposterous.

At the second place we tried, my mention of the twins was met with silence. The response persisted when Nate asked about Ahmose. The bartender didn't force us to leave, but left us no reason to stay.

At the third pub, the bartender said, "Don't know any Ahmose, and I wasn't here when those twins were."

"It sounds like this place was a ghost town," Nate suggested.

The Sanguan shrugged.

"Do you know where their old house was?" I asked.

"Nope, sorry." He went back to cleaning beer mugs. Nate and I left the pub and walked through town.

"This is useless." I was so annoyed. "Edmond... the Spectavi must have such a watchful eye over everything here." While I didn't expect the twins' old home to still be standing, I thought we might have found or felt something there, as crazy as that sounded.

We stopped in front of the Eure River.

"Where to?" Nate asked.

I didn't know if he meant in Chartres or not. "Well, Udolf mentioned someone we might look up, but the books Udolf led me to weren't particularly helpful." Wasting more time sounded dreadful.

"Who?"

"Erec le Roux."

Nate did an about face.

I turned in the same direction. "Where are you going?"

"To the train station. Erec lives in Neuchâtel. In Switzerland."

On the train, Nate explained that Erec was in charge of Neuchâtel, sort of. Erec and a company of other Sanguans had been driven out of France over a hundred years earlier. They found a home in Neuchâtel, and before long, with Erec's men and vampires upholding the law, the area became one of the safest in Europe. A human government remained, but ultimately, the power resided with Erec, and the Swiss were perfectly happy with the arrangement. The Spectavi hated it, but the only concession they received from Switzerland was that the country wouldn't publicize Erec's rule. Plenty knew, but the Spectavi's control over the media in that part of the world ensured Erec was rarely celebrated.

"Erec le Roux," I said. "It sounds like a medieval knight's name."

"You are correct," Nate confirmed. "Back then, the name

'le Roux' was usually given to red-headed children. Erec earned it for all the blood he spilled from his enemies on the battlefield. It still fits, considering his notorious thirst for blood as a vampire—rare for one so old."

"Do you know him?"

"I met him once, briefly. Did Udolf say *why* to seek him out?"

"No, but he already sounds more interesting than all those books."

Sunset in Chartres had been after nine and sunrise in Neuchâtel came at a quarter past six, making nighttime aggravatingly short. We waited until the following night to take the twenty-minute cab ride around the lake that shared its name with the region. Erec's predominantly white mansion stood on a small island a quarter mile into the lake, accessible by a narrow causeway.

Parked on the circular drive were a Ferrari, a Maserati, three Mercedes, a Porsche, and a Bentley. Carrying all of our things, Nate and I walked onto the brightly lit front porch, where two columns supported a high roof. We exchanged glances, then he knocked on the door.

Two seconds later, a slender woman wearing a white gown opened the door. A handsome, tan man in a suit stood behind her on the marble floor. A framed painting of a medieval battle hung on the wall.

"Please, come in," the woman said.

We did, and she closed the door. One hallway led behind

the man, and another went to the right.

"Are you here for business?" The woman glanced at my sword, and finished, perfectly pleasantly, "Or the tournament?"

"We're here to speak to Erec," I said.

"He's not available at the moment, but if you'd like to wait, he should be soon."

"What's this tournament?" Nate asked.

The woman appeared surprised. "Erec's monthly tournament. A million-dollar prize." She gestured to my things. "Wooden weapons, though."

"Let's—" I started.

"Do you have room for one more?" Nate interrupted.

"We do. That would make eight."

"Perfect," Nate said.

"Please, follow me." The woman headed down the hall to the right.

I fell into step behind Nate and tapped him on the shoulder. When he turned, I gave him a questioning look. He just smiled and faced forward again.

The sound of wood meeting wood echoed ahead. It had only been a week and a half, but I already missed sparring with Zhilan. The hall opened into a spacious room with a slightly elevated surface where two male Sanguans fought— one with a long staff, wearing black pants and a matching, sleeveless shirt, and the other in a simple white robe, wielding a wooden sword. At each of the four corners of the mat, thick, round columns ran to the high ceiling.

"Has it already begun?" Nate asked.

The woman descended the two steps of a staircase that

ran along the entire length of the room. "No, but soon. Who shall I say is filling the last spot?"

"Erin Rose," Nate announced.

"What?" I blurted.

"Don't you want to?" he asked.

"No." It *did* sound fun, thrilling, actually. Zhilan had told me of such tournaments, but I had never seen one, let alone fought in one.

His eyebrows rose. "Why not?"

The woman looked at me expectantly.

"It's not why we're here. *You* fight if you want to." I really hoped he wouldn't take the advice. Sitting out and watching him would have been unbearable.

"Come *on*," Nate pushed. "What'll it be, an hour or two?"

"Yes," the woman confirmed.

Nate crossed his arms. "You looked pretty eager on the ferry and in Chartres. Have some fun."

Crack! Thwack! The vampire with the staff smacked his opponent's arm.

The two stopped sparring. I didn't think they were better than I was. "Fine."

Nate clapped his hands. "Excellent."

The woman went to a desk near the mat and spoke to a pale, gray-haired man sitting in front of a notebook.

I didn't need the money, but fighting sounded so fun. Actually, a couple hours doing *anything* to take my mind off my so-far fruitless search sounded appealing. Plus, it would be good practice, and we had to do *something* until Erec was available.

Up eight steps to our left, on a platform adorned with red drapes, sat two vacant wooden thrones with high backs. The right wall had two large windows with views out to the dark water that surrounded the house. Ahead, past the mat, two long, recessed rooms with wide-open fronts contained an assortment of old tables and chairs. Paintings and a long mirror covered the walls in each. In the room on the left, four male Sanguans and a female sat around a table talking, and two other males sat in chairs in the corners. One read and one listened to music. All were dressed to fight in athletic apparel and robes of various colors.

I didn't feel like joining the group. They watched as Nate and I made our way to the other room, where a white wall separated us from them. I brought my things into a small bathroom in the corner and changed into my black athletic pants and tank top.

When I emerged, Nate pulled cash out of his wallet. "Do you think you'll win?"

I dropped my things in the corner. "Did you want me to fight just so you'd have something to bet on?"

He counted his money. "No. But since you are, I'll bet. How good are you?"

From racks of wooden staffs, swords, knives, and nunchucks, I grabbed a wooden katana and took a few cuts. The bokken felt very similar to the one I used when practicing with Zhilan.

His betting wouldn't affect me. The gambling was unexpected, and not at all the purpose of my being in Switzerland, but I had already rationalized my fighting, so how could I take issue with Nate's fun? "I didn't fly from Virginia with my sword and carry it with me from city to city because I'm bad."

He nodded. "All right then."

I sat down next to Nate to await my turn.

The man at the table with the journal stood. Two Sanguans with straight swords on their hips appeared at the room's entrance. The man pointed to the side of the mat near Nate and me and said, "Selim Demir." Then he pointed to the side near the thrones. "Jan Rauber." Presumably, the newly arrived guards would intervene if things got out of hand.

Selim, who was fairly dark-skinned, stepped onto the mat first. Jan, the one in white who had been sparring earlier, joined him. Jan carried a curved bokken, the same length as mine. Selim's was shorter and straight.

Two oversized flip-boards displaying zeros hung from the man's desk. He gave instructions. "First to three points wins. A solid hit with a weapon is a point. Touching the ground off the mat is a point for your opponent." The man looked from side to side, then yelled, "Fight!"

The vampires charged each other and clashed wooden swords. It became clear how confining the combat to the relatively small space would speed things up. Each of them darted from place to place, but it seemed unlikely either could run indefinitely.

Crack! Their blades met.

Crack! They met again.

Woosh! Selim ducked under a cut from Jan.

Thwack! Selim smacked Jan in the side.

"Point," the scorekeeper called, flipping over a 1.

"Ya!" a vampire in the other room yelled. Clapping came from a few.

The combatants stepped back from each other.

"Fight!" the scorekeeper called.

The battle resumed. Selim was faster. After a quick cut of his sword, he thrust and grazed Jan's arm. The scorekeeper shook his head as the fighting continued with no point awarded. Then, I realized what was about to happen.

Thwack! Selim's bokken sent Jan's head sideways. Blood splattered to the mat.

"Point!"

The gash on Jan's face stopped bleeding, but didn't go away. He growled and flashed his fangs, but Selim didn't appear moved.

"Ya!" another holler came from the spectators, along with loud clapping.

"Fight!"

Jan's rage cost him. He swung harder and harder, until instead of blocking, Selim dodged a blow, and then had no trouble scoring the final hit.

"Point! Match!" the scorekeeper called.

"Aghh!" Jan screamed and growled all at once. He threw down his bokken and headed out of the room.

Selim returned to his seat. I liked my chances against him.

"Gorak Miloszinski and Erin Rose," the scorekeeper called.

I stood and picked up my wooden sword. A huge Sanguan in navy sweatpants and a dirty white undershirt emerged from beyond the wall and walked onto the mat. He had dark stubble, and in his large hand, his bokken seemed like a twig compared to mine.

Nate gave me a concerned look.

I placed my hand on his shoulder and smiled. "Go bet on me."

He grinned and hurried off with his wad of cash. I could hear him negotiating his wagers while I approached the mat. As my bare feet touched the soft surface, my last reservations about taking the time to compete dissipated. I couldn't wait to fight and resolved that if it was going to be practice for real battles where a single blow could end my life, anything short of winning the tournament would be a failure.

Gorak ripped off his shirt with his free hand, exposing a chiseled, pale chest. We stood fifteen feet apart, swords down at our sides. I kept my shirt on.

"Edmond's last pet, how nice of you to pay us a visit."

That nickname I had also heard and did not like. "Ready!" the scorekeeper called.

I raised my sword and wrapped my other hand around it. Gorak didn't raise his weapon.

"Fight!"

Rushing me more quickly than his size suggested he would, he swung his blade down with one hand. I reacted late, but not too late, and moved to my right beyond his reach. Before he finished his swing, I lunged and—*smack*—hit his arm.

"Point!" the scorekeeper called. A lone pair of hands clapped twice firmly, once softly, and then no more.

"Grrr." Gorak showed me his long fangs while we took our spots at the center of the mat.

I scolded myself for assuming he would be slow. Size didn't matter.

"Fight!"

I raced toward him, while he came at me. He hadn't expected my aggressive move and—*thwack*—I chopped across his thigh before his block got there.

"Point!"

"Gha!" Gorak grew enraged. He finally took hold of his sword with both hands as we returned to ready.

"Fight!"

Two steps in, we cut high. *Crack!* Our bokken met.

I cut low. *Crack!* Gorak repelled my blow and stepped back.

Crack! He retreated again.

Crack! Crack! I drove him farther back.

Crack! He stepped off the mat before realizing how far he had gone.

"Point! Match!"

Gorak swung, but I ducked under it, backing away.

"Grha!" He threw his bokken at me. I easily avoided it.

Gorak fumed. The guards came down a step, and my defeated opponent darted from the arena.

Nate collected his money while I made my way to my chair. I rested my bokken at my side, and Nate returned.

"How much did you win?" I asked.

"Twenty thousand."

"Twenty thousand!" I assumed he meant Euros.

"Eh, it's nothing. I got good odds."

Based on his reaction and considering his age, he probably already had a fortune. "So..." I motioned to the mat. "... what did you think?"

"I think we should have taken our chances against the Spectavi on the ferry."

My smile lasted a long while.

In the next match, a female named Alina Senn used two short swords to win easily. She was tall, pale, and had her long blond hair in a ponytail. Wearing red leggings and a red sports bra as a top, she reminded me of one of the twins. Alina fought precisely and carried herself calmly.

After that, Rohit Gaude, the Indian vampire who fought with a wooden staff, dispatched his opponent three to one. Rohit seemed intense, but composed.

Nate had bet against them both, so he was down for the night.

"Erin Rose and Rohit Gaude," the scorekeeper said, not as loudly as his earlier announcements. With only the four victorious fighters remaining, tension filled the quiet room.

I grabbed my bokken and stepped onto the mat. Rohit's sleeveless top revealed strong arms. He stood with his staff vertical, its end on the ground.

"Ready!"

I estimated his weapon to be nine feet long.

"Fight!"

Rohit stepped forward and snapped his staff straight at

me. I leaned far to my left to avoid it. He tried again. I hit down on the staff and rushed him, landing a solid blow on his shoulder before he could react.

"Point!"

Rohit remained calm.

"Ready!"

He had done nothing to warrant anything but calm from me, either.

"Fight!"

Rohit tried the same move again, and again, it failed. He grabbed his staff with both hands. Before long, it became obvious he used the long weapon because he fought slowly in close. Once I forced him into that kind of fighting, I scored the last two points quickly. I had a hunch he was pretty young.

I sat down. "How much?"

"A little over a hundred thousand."

I didn't see a bag. "Where's all the cash?"

"We've moved on to credit. I'll send you after them if they don't pay up."

"Wonderful." Clearly, we were both having fun.

After the other semifinal, the scorekeeper announced the championship.

"Erin Rose and Alina Senn."

Rohit and Alina's last opponent stuck around to watch.

I stood.

Nate looked up at me. "A million dollars, Erin. Go get it."

The money didn't matter, but with victory so close, I had

to win. I had arrived underestimated and mocked. Most Sanguans appreciated the role I had played in ending Edmond, but that role had been standing by while his sisters did the deed. When I had defeated Kastor, Alexander's fall was the big story. Zhilan received the credit for besting Silas. If I won the tournament, word would spread that I was more than a celebrity vampire.

On the mat, I saw the resemblance to the twins again, but let the idea go. Tall, thin, and blond didn't equal demonic twin. Alina's blue eyes didn't burn red like Edmond's sisters did.

"Ready!"

With her two swords, Alina appeared confident and collected, not psychotic.

"Fight!"

She stepped to her right, so I did the same. One foot crossing in front of the other, we circled, waiting to see who would make the first move. We drew nearer each other, circling some more.

I darted at her, and she was ready. *Crack.* She blocked with one sword and swung with her other. I jumped back to avoid the blow and cut down. *Crack.* She blocked and swung high. I ducked, leaving my back vulnerable.

She swung down and, taking my only chance, I cut up.

Smack! I hit her armpit, lifting her body off the mat.

"Point!" A purple bruise formed on her light skin, then faded.

She said, "Good hit."

"Ready!"

I nodded.

"Fight!"

Alina charged. *Crack-crack. Crack-crack.* Her swords' strikes came quicker than before, and I struggled to keep up. I pushed myself to be faster and succeeded until Alina started to swing, stopped, and—*thwack!*—her other sword smacked my shoulder.

"Point!" I stumbled and saw Nate wince.

"Ready!"

I stood straight and raised my arm to test my shoulder. It was fine.

"Fight!"

I charged Alina. Unexpectedly, she retreated to near the corner of the mat. I cut high. *Crack.* She crossed her swords to block it. I cut low, and she flipped backward, toward the stone column. Her feet hit it, and horizontally, she flew at me. *Crack.* I blocked one sword—*smack!*—but not the second that hit my hip and sent me stumbling left.

I got back into position. "Good hit."

She nodded.

"Ready!"

I hadn't realized the columns were in play, but that had been impressive.

"Fight!"

We circled. I didn't know if it would last, but Alina seemed content to play it safe with the lead. One mistake from me, and the contest would be over. We kept our distance. She was fast, but I didn't think faster than I was. Her moves had been precise, but so were mine. We drew closer. Her two swords were the problem. Zhilan had fought with two swords occasionally in our practice, but not nearly as often as with one.

Alina came at me, and I had a new idea. *Crack.* I blocked her attack, but did it with greater force than necessary. *Crack!* I blocked again, even more firmly. I avoided two strikes and, when cutting at her, focused on being precise while swinging harder than I had all night.

CRACK! Our bokken met, and hers flew from her hand. *Crack*—she managed a block as her lost sword fell to the ground, but—*smack!*—failed to stop a blow to her hip.

"Point!"

Fear or perhaps shock filled her face, and the expression lingered while she slowly collected her weapon.

"Ready!"

I never forgot my body's resilience, or the speed at which I could run and fight, but the tremendous strength I could summon often slipped to the back of my mind. I had remembered.

"Fight!"

Alina charged, and I avoided her. She charged again, and I moved to the side again. The third time, I stayed just close enough to engage her. *Crack-crack. Crack-crack.* I swung harder. *Crack!* She almost dropped her sword as her arm flew out wide. *Crack!* She stumbled back, blocking a blow with her other blade. *Crack! CRACK!* Alina stepped to the edge of the mat, glanced down, and—*crack-smack!*—I hit her shoulder, driving her to a knee.

"Point! Match!"

A massive bruise formed on her skin. I stood, she knelt,

and we caught our breaths. She got up and nodded. I returned the gesture.

Clap-clap-clap. A barrel-chested Sanguan wearing a fine suit, white shirt, and no tie emerged from down the hall. "Well fought, Ms. Rose."

The two remaining fighters left. Alina walked to the source of the clapping, put her arm around him, and went straight for his neck. He did the same, and they held each other and drank for a few seconds. Alina's bruise faded away.

When they finished, Alina said, "I'm glad you missed it."

"Get changed. We have to leave soon," the other vampire said. She left the arena, and he addressed me. "I am Erec le Roux. Welcome to my home."

"Erin Rose." I pointed at my companion. "Nathan Rigby."

"'Nate,' isn't it?" Erec asked. "Did you make any money tonight?"

He came to my side. "She won, so I won."

Erec nodded. "Erin, if I had known you would be joining the tournament, I would have returned earlier to watch."

I lobbed my bokken onto the mat. "It's not why we came."

"No? Why then?"

"I have a question." I glanced at the guards and lowered my voice. "Udolf Gloster thought you might be able to help me."

"Udolf, hmm?" Erec motioned for the guards to leave, then pointed at the chairs where the others had been sitting earlier. "Please." We took seats at the round table. "How is Udolf?"

"Fine," I said. "Alone in his cottage in the woods."

Erec rolled his eyes. "Such a waste. But that does sound like Udolf. So, what question brought you to Neuchâtel?"

"Ahmose. Have you heard of him?"

Erec leaned back in his chair. "I have heard of the historian."

"Do you know where he is?"

"I know where he was when he last surfaced... ten years ago. I know what drove him to hiding."

"Where was he?"

Erec gazed out at the mat. "You beat Alina."

"In a close match," I offered. "She's one of the best I've ever fought."

That didn't seem to please him. "My Alina has been training for fifty years. You stole Edmond's blood not a year ago. I do not know how you won, but will you let me defend her honor?"

The tournament had been fantastic, and fighting Erec sounded even better. "I didn't come here to fight." I tried to get myself back on track.

"If you win, I will tell you about Ahmose." He stood, took off his suit coat, and folded it on the seat of his chair.

Fighting him also felt wrong. "Please, I just—"

"Come now," he said. "Don't you want to know?"

About Ahmose? Or if I could defeat the old knight? There was only one way to know both. While he untied and took off his shoes, I walked to the mat and picked up my bokken.

"Thank you." Erec found a matching weapon leaning

against a chair. He turned to the long hallway and called, "Louis!"

The scorekeeper's hurried steps echoed before he appeared at the arena's edge.

Erec asked, "Three points?"

"Sure," I agreed.

The scorekeeper took his seat. Erec moved onto the mat with his sword down at his side, but not lazily like Gorak had held his.

I brought up my blade.

"Ready!" Louis called.

Erec's entire face intensified. Out of the corner of my eye, I saw Nate sitting on the edge of his seat.

"Fight!"

Erec brought his second hand to his bokken and came at me fast. *Crack!* I blocked. *Crack!* He blocked my cut. *Crack!* I blocked, but my blade flew out wide. *Swoosh.* I leapt back to avoid a cut. He swung drastically harder than Alina, Rohit, or Gorak, and it took all my strength to match his.

Erec stopped. "Word is, Zhilan trains you. You fight like her."

He stepped toward me, and I ducked under another cut. I swung low. *Crack!* His block came just in time. I swung at his neck. *Crack!*

"And *that* reminds me of old Victoria. You *have* been well trained." He came at me.

Crack-crack-crack. Erec got close, so I raced to my right. He followed. *Crack-crack-crack.* I went right again. *Crack-crack.* I ducked—*swoosh*—and spotted an opening. I swung up, but he avoided it. Guessing his next move exactly while he swung, I ducked low and—*thwack!*—hit his calf.

Louis flipped over a 1 without saying anything.

Erec shook his head.

I stood straight. "I do have a few tricks of my own."

Without waiting for a "Ready" instruction, Erec came at me. I blocked blow after blow. He fought faster and harder, but didn't boil over to the point where his moves became sloppy. As his relentless attacks came one immediately after another, I struggled to keep up. When I retreated and darted from side to side on the mat, Erec followed almost instantly to resume his assault. My speed didn't seem to be an advantage. Retreat after retreat, he caught up to launch his next attack.

He huffed and puffed, and I raced to the left side of the mat. *Crack-crack!* He forced me to the edge and let loose a guttural growl.

I darted right. *Crack-crack!* I darted left, and when Erec followed, for the first time in a long time, I rushed him. *Crack.* I passed him—*thwack!*—and hit him square in the back.

"Yes!" Nate yelled.

"Ghraa!" Erec growled.

Louis flipped over a 2.

"Enough!" Erec hurled his bokken at a column, ran to his thrones, and punched down through the elevated floor between them. His hand emerged with a gleaming metal longsword, like the huge two-handed blade Victoria often used.

"Whoa!" Nate stood up. "Erec!"

I raced to my things in the corner and drew Tomori. After holding wooden toys all night, the leather-wrapped handle felt incredible.

Nate raised both hands in front of him. "Erin, no."

Erec and I came at each other. If the old knight wanted a real fight, he'd get it. While he bled at my feet, he'd reveal all he knew of Ahmose.

Tyn! Our blades met. *Tyn-tyn!* His sword's length was going to be a problem. No longer confined to the mat, I darted to the window side of the room.

Tyn-tyn! Tyn!-TYN! I repelled a mighty blow and raced to the foot of the throne platform. *Tyn-tyn-tyn!* I jumped up past the chairs, and when Erec followed, I lunged at him. *Fswht!* My blade sliced into his side. Red covered his shirt and pant leg, but Erec didn't flinch.

He swung harder—*tyn!*—I blocked and backed up. *Tyn.* I retreated another step, and my back touched the wall in the corner. I glanced right—a way out. Erec swung ferociously. *Tyn.* My block was weak. I raced to get past him. His hand shot out and grabbed me.

"Grahh!" He threw me to the ground in the corner, got both hands on his sword, and swung—*tyn*—my left hand flew off my katana. *Fswht!* He severed my right arm below the elbow.

My hand and my blade hit the ground. In horror, I watched blood pour out of me.

Erec turned and screamed, "Louis!"

I tried to move my fingers and saw them not respond, attached to my hand on the ground.

Bleeding from my arm slowed. Louis stood, but didn't move. I had to run. I started to get to my feet, but Erec drove his knee into my stomach and forced me back to the floor. He dropped his longsword and ripped off his shirt.

"Louis!" Erec grabbed my severed limb and held it to the cut end of my arm. "Nathan! Bring him!"

I punched Erec's cheek with my remaining hand, but he ignored me. Aching for the blood I had lost, I tried to stand. Erec drove me down, hard. He wrapped his shirt around my arm, which suddenly felt longer. He pulled the bandage tighter, and as I commanded, my pinky twitched. Nate appeared and knelt with Louis next to Erec.

The old knight grabbed the terrified man and forced his neck to my mouth. "Drink!"

I leaned up, and my fangs pierced Louis's flesh. *Vvwwooosh!*

My eyes closed as my void filled. The fire blazed, and when I sucked, my arm burned hottest of all. I flexed my fingers, then opened my eyes and watched myself do it again. Thank God. I tore my fangs from the man.

"Drink!" Erec urged. "For the sake of your arm, drink!" He forced the struggling man's neck to my mouth.

Hot blood fell into my throat, but I didn't suck.

Erec pushed Louis at me. "DRINK!"

Blood streamed over my tongue, filling my mouth and dripping down my chin. *Vwoosh!* The inferno roared back to life. I dug in my fangs and sucked. A burst of flames shot from my shoulder out to my fingertips, and to save my arm, I drank more.

And then, the blood cooled. I withdrew my fangs.

Erec leaned back, lifting his weight off me. He laid poor Louis's lifeless body on the ground. I flexed my fingers and watched them respond exactly as instructed. I rolled my wrist around, then pushed on the ground, wondering if my limb would snap at a weakened point where it had been cut. It didn't. My arm felt strong. I unwrapped Erec's shirt, and a dull purple ring remained under crusted blood, but otherwise, my arm seemed fine.

"That will fade," Erec said.

"When?"

"Not long." He got up and offered me his hand.

I stood without it.

"I'm sorry," he said. "I should not have done that. Come to my study, and I will tell you about Ahmose." He left his sword and stained shirt on the floor and headed out of the arena.

I almost apologized for killing Louis, but aside from the fact that Erec had pushed me to do it, the words sounded so insufficient.

I picked up my sword, ran to my things to resheath my blade, then washed dried blood off myself in the bathroom.

Nate waited outside. "What do you think?"

"We need to hear what he knows." I shook water off my hands. "I don't know, but it seems foolish to leave at this point."

Nate nodded.

Walking down the hall, we passed paintings and tapestries showing a variety of medieval scenes. The corridor ended at a study with small statues and busts on pedestals and tall wooden bookshelves on two sides.

Erec entered wearing another white dress shirt. "Please, have a seat."

Nate and I sat in front of the desk in chairs upholstered in plum.

Erec fastened the second to top button as he took his seat across from us. "I'm relieved you are all right, Erin."

I didn't respond.

"So why does Ahmose interest you?"

"I want to find him." I decided he would get nothing more from me. "Why, is my business."

"Fine." Erec didn't argue, perhaps having left all his fight in the arena. "Ahmose was not always so withdrawn from the world. In the seventh century, a wave of Justinian's Plague stole his family from him. Since the century before, that plague had killed tens of millions in Europe and nearby, an even more staggering toll back then, considering the world's population. I don't know why, but Edmond took a liking to the Egyptian, and that affection endured for centuries after he made him a vampire."

Nate interrupted, "You knew him back then?"

"No. But I met him not long after my transformation in 1180. We captured him in battle and, since he was Edmond's, held him for ransom in my lord's castle, instead of burning him with the others. Ahmose was the oldest vampire I had ever seen prisoner, so I visited him repeatedly in the dungeon. I asked why he didn't struggle like the rest. I actually feared our chains and bars would not hold him.

"Ahmose told me that he was content. If God's will was

for him to be a prisoner and meet his end, so be it. I was young and couldn't fathom such a frame of mind. We started talking, and eventually, Ahmose got to the heart of it. As a young immortal, he couldn't understand why God had sent the plague that ravaged the world and his hometown. Our kind was not affected, but humans had been powerless to fight it, and Ahmose wondered if it had been the will of Satan, not God.

"Then, as centuries passed, without a recurrence of plague on that scale, Ahmose grew confident that the event had cleansed the world as God intended, or else God had stopped Satan from inflicting another like it. Either way, he reasoned, the world had moved from darkness into light, and the Lord had prevailed against his adversary.

"After a few nights, we traded Ahmose for three of our own. Almost two hundred years later, the Black Death in the fourteenth century wiped out half of Europe, perhaps a hundred million people. Sanguans and Spectavi met to discuss what the cause of the disease could have been. I attended the council, as did Ahmose. His understanding of the world had been shattered anew. Some argued that God punished the unjust with the disease. Ahmose couldn't accept that death on such a scale should be necessary so often, and he left the meeting very abruptly. I hardly saw him after that."

Nate leaned forward. "How was going into hiding supposed to help anything?"

"I don't think he wanted to help," Erec said. "Or he accepted that he could not. He was angry with God and chose to remove himself from the world. At one point, when I didn't hear of Ahmose for hundreds of years, I thought his depression had led him to take his own life—not that I thought of him often. As it turned out, he was not dead. He was watching the world from afar."

"You mentioned you knew where he was in 2000," I reminded.

"Rome," Erec said. "He may have been other places, as well, but I had him followed to an apartment in Rome. By the time I arrived, he had gone. I returned a year later, and the dwelling remained unchanged and vacant. Who knows? Maybe he left clues behind."

Alina appeared at the entrance of the study, wearing a long red gown. Her diamond necklace and earrings glistened in the low light. She held Erec's suit coat.

Erec got to his feet. Nate and I did the same.

Erec asked, "Will you go to Rome?"

I nodded.

"Let me send you on my jet. It's the least I can do." Erec went to Alina and put on his coat. "Julien will take you to the airport."

I picked up my things. "Fine."

Erec added, "Give him your information, and he will wire your winnings."

Alina took Erec's arm, then said, "Come by if you're ever in Switzerland, Erin. I'd like to spar again."

They walked out as the man from the foyer earlier entered. "Ms. Rose, Mr. Rigby, there's a car out front that will take you to the airport."

Nate turned to me. "Are you sure?"

"I doubt we'll find anything in Rome," I said. "So we might as well get it over with."

11

During the three-hour plane ride, I filled Nate in about Nicolas, the strange drawing of the twins, and why I was trying to find Ahmose. We landed in Rome a few hours before sunrise and took a taxi to the address Erec had given us. Disappointment struck even more spectacularly than expected. Nate and I stood in front of an empty hole in the earth, surrounded by rubble and old construction equipment—backhoes, trucks, and a bulldozer. I double-checked the address and map on my phone.

"I'm sorry," Nate said.

"I should have known." I almost had. I figured we'd get to the apartment, break in, and discover nothing useful. That the entire building had been razed hit me like a superfluous slap in the face. "Let's go."

"Where?" Nate asked. "A club, a pub?"

Blood sounded good, better than the ever-disappointing search. But I had killed Louis… "I'm fine. Do you need to drink?"

Nate stepped toward me and placed his hand on my arm. "From them? No."

I pushed his hand away and started on the cobblestone sidewalk. "Let's just find a place for the day." The forearm I pushed had been so strong, like the rest of him looked, and what he had in mind did sound drastically better than the search.

Nate caught up to me. "You fought well."

I hated that I had lost. All the victories, the entire tournament, they meant nothing. My hand had been hacked off, and if it had been done by a Spectavi, or even a different Sanguan, I would not have gotten it back.

Nate continued, "And what you're looking for… it's hard. Ahmose wants to be hidden. You're trying to track down one of the most ancient vampires. You couldn't have expected it to be easy."

"I know. I didn't. But I had hoped we'd have found something, *anything* that would narrow the search. We're talking to the right vampires, I think—ones who've met Ahmose. Erec almost did recently. Yet we've gotten nowhere. How many old Sanguans do we have to meet before we know if he's even in Europe?"

In my second story room at an inn, I sat on the rough maroon couch, reading the news on my phone. An old coffin lay on the floor in front of me. There was no television. Nate had no trouble securing his own room, as we were the only customers for the night, and probably for many nights.

I checked my email and found one from Zhilan.

The plan is in motion. The week after next, simultaneously, ten Spectavi from an office in San Francisco will march themselves onto the Golden Gate Bridge and set themselves ablaze. They will die. There will be witnesses, and we will post the video online. An anonymous release will explain how it was done, and the humans will not be able to ignore how the Spectavi are using their synthetic.

Her unquestionably good news made me upset to be so far away with no success of my own to report. Should I respond that my search was going horribly? That I had almost lost my hand? Through the slightly raised window, I could hear a few of Rome's young inhabitants laughing and joking with one another. I felt so alone. Unlike ever before in my life, I had an entire list of those I cared for and who cared for me. Zhilan, Grant, Hayden, and Houjin—it was different with all of them, but they all meant a great deal to me.

Hysterical laughter came from outside. I stretched out on the couch with my head on a small pillow. I missed Blaine's jokes—the bad ones as much as the good. I missed the way June looked at me each time we met, and the way Zack watched me drank from her. My insides ached. My throat became parched, and my tongue brought no relief to my dry lips. I pulled up a picture of Luke on my phone, then switched to my music and hit play. I closed my eyes while my cell did the best it could with his hard rock with no headphones connected. I was so far from them all and not one bit closer to finding Ahmose.

Knocking came at the door.

I sat up and spotted my sword leaned against my backpack. "Who's there?"

"It's me," Nate said.

I went to the door and checked the peephole. Nate's tight t-shirt stretched over his hundred-fifty-year-old vampire body. I opened the door.

"May I come in?" he asked.

I stood aside, then closed the door behind him.

He turned to me. "What are you afraid of?"

Losing sight of the goal. The search was the priority, and things had gone so badly in Neuchâtel. I dreaded continuing to make terrible choices, of being the same fool who had made so many mistakes before. Nate came close. I darted past him to the other side of the room.

"Not tonight," I said softly.

I blinked, and he stood before me. "Why not?"

"I killed that man." I stared past Nate, remembering it.

"You're a vampire," Nate offered.

"I don't have to kill people."

He tilted his head into my view and grasped my shoulder. "Sometimes, you do."

I met his brown eyes. "I shouldn't have fought Erec. I was a fool."

"Would you fight him again?"

The lion within me stood up.

Nate asked, "Right now, if he had something else you wanted, would you?"

I sighed. "Yes."

"Why?"

I spoke plainly. "Because I'd win. I'd be smarter." I recalled the points I had scored. "I wouldn't get caught in that corner."

Nate squeezed my shoulder. "You don't sound like a fool to me. You sound brave, and I love it."

The lion prepared to pounce. I listened to the powerful heart beating in the chest across from me. More than anything, I feared being meek.

I wrapped my arms around Nate, pulled his hard body to me, and brought my mouth to his neck. His tough skin proved no match for my sharp fangs.

Phzz. His searing blood hit my throat—*no!*—two pricks came at the left side of my neck. I withdrew my fangs and as Nate sucked, the void within spread and spread. Both our bodies grew warmer. I pushed and drove Nate across the room, back first, into the door. Nate held me and stopped drinking. My neck healed, as his already had. I bit back into him and sucked hard.

Vwoosh! The void filled.

Nate bit into me. I waited while he drank. I grew hotter and loathed losing my blood, but knew what was to come.

Phwoof! Fire flared when I bit. He stopped drinking while his juicy blood oozed into me, out to the corners of my body. Unlike when I drained humans, it required no extra effort to draw more as I went. Nate had no less than when we had begun.

I ripped my fangs out of his neck. "When should we stop?"

Nate's moist lips kissed high on my cheek, then lower. He kissed over my cross. "First light." He bit my neck and drank.

I didn't wait for him to stop. I sucked and pulled the

mixture of our blood into me. My insides boiled. He spun us around and held me against the door while we both drank. I opened my eyes, wondering when we'd resume taking turns, but he didn't stop, so I didn't either.

I shut my eyes, and in the absence of memories from Nate, and without fear of draining him to the point of death, I became lost in my own thoughts. Why had I waited so long to bite him? It didn't matter. I had done it! A flame flared, and I replayed the battles from earlier. Against Alina and Erec, I had fought faster than ever. I dug my fangs deeper, and Nate responded in kind. I had to fight even better! I couldn't afford not to. I sucked hard, the fire rose, and a wave of heat surged.

Nate drank slower, and I followed his lead. Another wave gently radiated. I would learn from the fight with Erec, and I'd improve. Nate pulled out his fangs. I kept sipping while he lifted me and brought me to the couch. He laid me down, and I felt the back cushions being removed and thrown to the floor. From on top of me, Nate pushed on my shoulders. I stopped drinking and watched blood trickle from his neck while he shifted himself down and slowly bit through my tank top and bra.

My mouth opened, my eyes closed, and I gave him a few seconds to make up for the lead I had gained before grabbing his arm with both hands, pulling it to me, and biting into his bicep. I sucked hard. Flames flared. I *would* defeat Erec when next we fought.

Raspy vocals and lightly punching bass from my cell provided the soundtrack for the blaze that danced within me until sunrise.

12

Blood!—BLOOD! I flung open the lid of my coffin. My throat felt bone dry, and my eyes stung whether opened or closed, but the deep ache hurt worst of all. I stumbled stepping out of the coffin. Holding my stomach didn't help, and the throbbing pain expanded beyond there, to my arms, legs, and head anyway.

Someone knocked and the low sound pounded through my head. I yanked open the door.

"You look terrible," Nate said.

Hardly flattering after events of the previous night. "You have no idea what this feels like."

"On the contrary, I know *exactly* what it feels like."

That made sense, but my own aching was so excruciating, so… all encompassing, that I struggled to accept it.

"Let's go," he said.

"Where?"

"A club. *We* need blood."

He wouldn't feel whole and satisfied until I did, and peace for me rested with him. I felt like such an animal, much further apart from humanity than normal.

"I'll be out in a minute." I closed the door.

Ahmose would have to wait until we dealt with our thirst. From my backpack, I pulled out the first black skirt I found and decided it would do. The bra I had on would serve the purpose, but I switched to a light gray tank top that hadn't been bitten through, then sat on the couch and zipped up my knee-high boots to complete the outfit. When I stood, while noticing that the purple ring on my forearm had gone away, a wave of hunger like tiny knives stabbing my insides sent me to the wall for support. I skipped makeup and jewelry.

———————————

Despite steady rain we hadn't prepared for, we ran the nine blocks to the Sanguan club because it was the quickest way to get there. Nate appeared to be handling things better than I was, but did seem distracted. He assured me he felt as wretched as I did.

From a block away, we could see strobe lights flashing at different speeds on each of the top two floors. Inside, we found that the first level consisted of little but a simple bar.

I picked out a middle-aged man in the mirrored wall behind a row of liquor bottles and raced to him.

"Ciao," he said, rotating on his backed barstool.

He was bald and had a pudgy, round face. It made no difference. His neck throbbed to the beats of the Italian music, at least to my starving eyes.

I reached to tear the shirt at his neck. "Ciao."

He grabbed my hand and placed it on his upper chest. I showed him my fangs. I wouldn't be told no! Frantically, he undid his top two shirt buttons, which I then realized he had meant *me* to do. It didn't matter. With both hands, I ripped open his shirt, then leaned into him and bit his plump neck.

Boom! His succulent blood flowed. Gulp after gulp, it filled me, coursing through me like a raging river of fire, washing away my miserable pain.

I withdrew my fangs and took a calming breath. "Thank you."

Vittorio gulped. "Prego."

I felt my face contort as emptiness launched from my core. Vittorio looked scared. My hunger hadn't been vanquished. He had to give me more!

A firm hand grabbed my shoulder. Nate was right. Another drink from the man could have been the end of him. I nodded, and Nate let me go. I followed him to the second floor.

Three steps from the staircase, under louder, faster music, Nate found a tan girl and began dancing with her. He held her wrist, and a few seconds later, he bit—and I felt a little better.

I opened my mouth to... I didn't know what and grimaced. Warmth coursed through me, far more subtly than when I drank, but undeniably spreading. Nate stopped, and as my thirst returned, nausea came with it. My pain tied intimately to another felt so unnatural. The creature I had become disgusted me.

A young man in a tight shirt watched me suffer. Driven by suddenly preferable thirst, I moved through the crowd to him as he headed my way. He put his hand on my back and danced. I shook my head, pushed his arm away, and sank my fangs into his neck.

We stood still while bodies danced around us. Nausea departed, the glorious flames rose, and when memories came with his blood, the Italian words didn't prevent all understanding—his emotions made perfect sense. I savored a long, last sip. Disgusted? What a waste of a thought. I was powerful. Beautiful. A vampire!

When I stopped, hoots and hollers came from the crowd, for Rocco, or me, or both. I licked my lips for traces of his blood on the way over to the wall. I leaned against it and watched Nate bow slightly to his flattered partner.

He joined me. "Feeling better?"

"For now." I crossed my arms and didn't mention that I wouldn't be drinking from Nate again anytime soon. I couldn't stand being so dependent on another and couldn't afford to put the search for Ahmose on hold for long. I winced.

Nate noticed. "Tell me this isn't better than sitting on a train? Or hearing another story from some ancient out in the woods."

It had taken longer for the aching to return, and it didn't reach quite as deep, but I was already searching for another target on the dance floor, imagining the impending drink. Unwilling to give Nate the satisfaction of knowing that, I said, "Udolf's cottage was lovely."

I pushed myself off the wall and made my way to a tall couple. She danced while I drank from sturdy Paolo. Then he danced while I sipped slowly from Rochelle's delicate neck.

"Who is better?" Paolo asked with a thick accent.

I deliberated for longer than necessary to drag out the moment for them. "Paolo's blood burned hotter." I kissed his neck over the mark I had left, and he shuddered. I told his girlfriend, "Rochelle's tasted sweeter." I returned to the wall and watched the crowd.

In contrast to the rapidly flashing strobe lights, Nate danced slowly across from the girl who surely yearned for his bite. She hoped at any moment he'd grab her and have her, and then take her somewhere and sip until sunrise. I had read enough thoughts to know that was what most craved. Finally, Nate bit, she melted in his arms, and I warmed slightly. I wouldn't have hated to be the one he held. He finished with her. Our bites could have gone on, song after song.

A pang of hunger became a series of pangs that didn't stop. I headed back into the crowd.

"Dance?" a hunky Italian called over the beating music. Word must have been spreading that the Sanguan who kept coming and going was an American.

I shook my head. "No. Drink?"

"Dance," the man said firmly.

My pain wasn't as overwhelming as it had been, so I started dancing, confident I'd taste his blood before long. The song began to fade—time for my drink. A new song started—I'd wait. He gently took my hand and, when I didn't react aggressively, pulled me toward him. We held each other and moved to the music. When I thought the song had ended, I bit into his neck, but I was wrong. The electronic beats picked up, so I brought my fangs out of him, and we resumed dancing. I sipped on and off, very briefly, until the song finally did end.

"Grazie," Antonio whispered into my ear.

"Thank you," I echoed while letting him slip out of my grasp.

"So you *do* dance," Nate called, coming over to me.

I glared at him.

He put his hand on my hip. "Tell me dancing wouldn't be preferable to standing against the wall, waiting, counting the seconds between cravings, wondering if you've finally had enough?"

"Not tonight." I walked past him.

He spoke to my back. "Tell me you haven't had a great time."

Still close, I spun around. "It's been *too* great." The pain I had woken to had been excruciating, the unnatural tie to Nate sickening, but the intense rush of feeding again and again was freshest. My initial hunger wouldn't have killed me, and all ending it took was more people—more delicious blood and more fascinating lives. "It's not what I'm supposed to be doing."

"We're vampires, Erin. It's *exactly* what we're supposed to be doing."

My damned aching returned, and I knew Nate's blood would cure it—temporarily. I pictured us holding each other as the music pulsed: my arms around his neck, then sliding down so I had room to bite, the flames rising and falling to our sips and the beats. That dance would mean waking twinned with another, to an unbearable, savage thirst. Except we *could* bear that pain, and we *could* tame that thirst, over and over…

It was *supposed* to sound wrong, but didn't. A circle of eavesdroppers had formed around us.

Nate grasped the top of my arms. "You're stronger than me; we both know it." He leaned close. "Push me away if you want, or bite back."

He brought his mouth toward the left side of my neck while I watched the crowd behind him. His fangs pierced my flesh, and I winced as the delectable mortals danced. Blood oozed out of me. Ahmose wasn't going anywhere for another ten years. I rested my fangs on Nate's neck, spotted Antonio, and hoped the Italian would be around the next night. I bit down and tasted our thick, immortal blood. My void began to fill.

I woke to a thirst I swore plunged deeper than the night before, terrified of the pain persisting if anything had happened to Nate and he couldn't feed. A minute later, he knocked at my door with a particular lounge in mind. There, we sat in a booth for hours, receiving visitors as they came to us. Nate and I bought them drinks, talked, and laughed with them, until our hunger returned. Then, we had *our* drinks and warmed each other with each sip that warmed ourselves.

I began the evening disappointed with my lack of focus, but soon found myself focused wholly on the taste of every new person or couple. My penetrating, hell-born pain came again and again, and hot human blood satisfied it without fail. Drinking in such rapid succession, I was fascinated by their lives and emotions for being both unique and similar. No two were identical, most not by a long shot, yet so many dealt with slight variations of the same hardships and heartache—relationships gone wrong, goals unachieved, sickness, death—and rejoiced in the same triumphs—long sought after first kisses, dreams fulfilled, children born healthy and full of promise.

Flush with the memories and the blood, Nate and I drank from each other's immortal body anyway—at the lounge, on our way back to the inn, and finally, on my couch. When purple light filled my window, he kissed me one last time, then shut the heavy curtain on the way to his room.

When the sun set, I rose from my coffin, and Nate came to my door. After drinks at a pub, we made our way to massive St. Peter's Basilica. On the crystal clear night, the central dome dominated the skyline and was impressively illuminated along with the column-lined façade. The church was closed, but Nate had been inside and said Michelangelo's Pietà alone warranted a better-timed trip. Nate sipped from my wrist, then I took a turn from his while gazing at the architecture and wondering about the Lord, his son, the earthly pope, and how a creature like me could set foot in a building like that. A group of people passed by, pointing at us and conversing in Italian. Nate informed me they were arguing over my tattoo.

At the first hint of thirst, we raced to the Roman Forum. The plaza, filled with ancient ruins of temples and tall columns in brick and white marble, was splendid in its own way. As we strolled, a couple noticed us, had a quick word, and flashed inviting smiles. Nate made introductions, and we led them to an area under a canopy of tall trees, away from most of the ruins. Nate and I took turns drinking from the couple before they went happily on their way. Afterward, we lay on the ground, and I rested my head on Nate's chest between taking sips from him.

The Coliseum came next, the Pantheon after that, and then the Spanish Steps. For hour after hour, we crisscrossed the city as fast as our immortal bodies could carry us, but taking our time wherever we stopped. Outside, without blaring music, we could talk, and without a dancing crowd, we were content to sit or lay at countless fountains, piazzas, and churches until compelled to move on by our recurrent thirst. I loved that night.

The following evening, in an attempt to silence our pain immediately, Nate and I drank from each other before leaving his room. Unfortunately, our thirst lingered, grumbling for mortal blood. During the thirty-minute limo ride to a fancy club outside the city, those grumbles grew into moans, wails, and growls.

From across the room, a short, tan young man with a shaved head and a cord necklace made eye contact with me, then rushed away with his bottle of beer, bumping through two groups of people before I lost him in the crowd.

Nate and I split up, and Chase was my first human of the

night. Defying the loud music, he whispered the sweetest things into my ear in French before I sipped, then English, before I sipped again.

Nate found me, held my back to him, and sank his fangs into my neck. I let him drink for a few seconds, then brought his wrist to my mouth. As I bit, I spied the same tan man standing against a wall, watching another vampire with a woman. The man's jeans were out of place, and he had a different beer than before. I left Nate and made my way toward him.

He didn't notice me, and when very near, I called to him, "Hi."

His eyes grew wide. I smiled. He pushed his way past people to his right and into the crowd.

"Hello," a man said from behind me.

I located the voice and, after drinking from Mario and learning that he had grown up in Virginia, a few miles from where I lived, had a good time chatting with him until Nate came by. Back in his vampire arms, loving his boiling blood, I saw the man with the cord necklace once again.

I approached more carefully than I had the last time. He shouldn't be so scared, I thought, at least not of me.

As he took a drink of his beer, I darted to his side. "Hi."

He stopped drinking.

"I'm Erin." I gently took hold of his back.

"I... I..."

"Relax." I smiled.

"Does it... hurt?"

"It's incredible."

"What should I do?"

"Just relax." I leaned down, held him close, and bit. Matt's recent arrival in Rome had been nothing short of fulfillment of an almost lifelong dream. Matt had come from England and, before that, spent a few weeks in Hawaii after a long trip at sea.

I slowed my sipping and enjoyed seeing Matt perfectly at peace in my arms. His voyage had begun when he stowed away on a private yacht. He had escaped from the island where he had been born—an island in the central Pacific. He wasn't supposed to leave. None of the hundred inhabitants were allowed to, according to the crazy old vampire, who only left every twenty years.

I ripped my fangs out of him. "Seorsum."

Matt stumbled and tried to compose himself.

The pale white vampire with no name, the lone immortal on the island with no connection to the outside world, hardly drank at all, and had never drunk from Matt. Matt wanted to know what it felt like. The vampire had to be Ahmose.

Matt fled into the crowd. I didn't follow. His blood had already told me enough. I sat down in the nearest empty booth, pulled out my phone, and searched for "Seorsum." No useful results appeared, while image after image of the island raced through my mind. Southeast of Hawaii, near the equator—nothing more specific, but the tiny island was there. I had a hunch who could make an island disappear and messaged Victoria: *Seorsum Island, central Pacific. Can't find it online, but I know it's there. Any ideas?*

Nate came over to me.

"Sit," I said. He did, and leaned close to bite. I pushed him away. "Not now. I might have found Ahmose."

"Really?"

"Yeah." My phone chimed. "One second."

Victoria had responded: *No, but I will investigate. Where are you?*

I told her we were in Rome and brought Nate up to speed on where Matt had lived.

―――――――――――

The following night's trip to a local club was all business. As much as I wanted to focus on Seorsum, our thirst simply had to be dealt with first. The debt Nate and I owed for our nights of pleasure was non-negotiable. I drank from seven or eight people in a little over an hour and found the hunger that came after that bearable, so I returned to my room while Nate stayed at the club.

Thousands of miles from a major land mass, Seorsum didn't have an airport, so even if we discovered its exact location, it was unclear how we could reach the island. On my laptop, I researched ships and seaplanes to charter and even the possibility of skydiving, which sounded a little crazy.

Victoria messaged:

I have found your lost island. Even Reinald didn't know Edmond had it hidden for his old fledgling. He still doesn't. Good work. Get yourself to the airport before sunrise, and I'll send a plane to take you the rest of the way.

I responded that we would be there, then headed to the club to tell Nate and to drink a lot more blood.

13

Our trip began with twenty-five hours aboard a private plane Victoria had arranged, with two Spectavi and two men for pilots. As we readied for takeoff in Rome, bound for Tokyo, I lay in a coffin with my headphones on, listening to Luke's music. For the first time in days, I had time alone, at peace.

Did I really deserve Victoria's praise? Those nights of drinking... all the blood. Neck after neck, wrist after wrist. How many had my fangs pierced?

But so what? I hadn't taken any lives at those clubs. I was a vampire, and vampires drank. The blood, the emotions, and the lives had been wonderful—sublime. And frankly, it was about time I had some good luck.

But I *had* killed Louis, and that nagged at me. That it happened because I had lost the fight with Erec made me feel even worse.

While the humans flew the small aircraft, all the vampires slept for the start of the first twelve-hour leg of our journey. When we awoke, Nate and I climbed out of our coffins and took seats in the partitioned-off rear cabin. The two Spectavi in the forward cabin were heavily armed.

"I feel like a prisoner," Nate said.

"We're not," I assured him. "Victoria would be upset if any harm came to us. Besides, we've got our weapons. If it came to it, I like our chances."

He reached into his backpack on the floor, pulled out his huge knife, and inspected its edge. "Let me see yours?"

I handed my knife to him.

He flipped it open and compared mine to his straight blade, which was two inches longer and considerably wider. He folded mine closed, then hit the release to unfold it again. "That's so cool. I may need to get one of my own."

We landed in Tokyo at three-thirty a.m. local time. Over the intercom, the pilots instructed Nate and me to remain on the plane while they refueled. But I was thirsty, and my body and head hurt from it. I slid open the door to the front of the plane. The Spectavi sitting across from the exit stood up with his rifle hanging over his shoulder.

"I'm going out," I said. Nate moved to stand behind me.

The guard gripped his gun. "Where?"

I took another step. "Were you ever *not* a Spectavi?"

He aimed at me. "What do you mean?"

"Did you ever thirst for real, human blood? Did your entire body ever scream for a taste, so loudly that it hurt to be awake at all?"

"Yes."

"How does it compare to drinking cans of synthetic?"

"It doesn't. I drink at the same time each night, and there's no thirst."

I resumed walking to the exit. "That's a shame."

He kept his gun on us, but never fired. We went into the airport and found a cute couple happy to feed us both.

An hour later, we were back aboard, headed for Honolulu. Before long, we had to retreat to our coffins to once again avoid the rising sun.

————————

We awoke during our descent to Hawaii.

Nate climbed out of his coffin. "What do you think of Ahmose?"

I took my seat next to him. "What do you mean? Where he's hiding?"

Nate rolled his head, stretching his neck. "Where, yeah. But mostly that he is at all. It's kind of crazy."

I had tried to imagine what it would be like. "I'm not sure. When you get to be that old—"

Nate waved away the notion. "Edmond was old. Erec's old. Victoria's old. Others are as old as Ahmose, and they aren't hiding."

"Yeah. It is weird." A rationalization came to mind. "But there is something to be said for it, the peacefulness of his life. He's just living, watching the world change. He's not judging, not taking sides. He's not making decisions that will affect his life or anyone else's."

"*You'd* want to live like that?"

"Of course not. Not now, probably not ever, but I can

imagine the peace Ahmose feels, night after night, not burdened by the weight of any choices."

"It's crazy," Nate said.

———————————

After our stop in Honolulu, we had a four-hour flight southeast to A17, a secret Spectavi island used for research. Victoria would not reveal its specific purpose. Three hundred and fifty miles south of the small island was Seorsum, which meant "apart" in Latin. I assumed Ahmose had contributed to its naming and also assumed that if that were true, he did not name A17. None but a select group of very high-ranking Spectavi knew the research facility existed, and tiny Seorsum was an even deeper secret.

With our travels nearing an end, as I had many times already, I replayed Matt's memories of the island in both sun and moonlight. I would never see the water in its perfect blue, but that didn't matter. I would see Ahmose and, whatever it took, would convince him to tell me Nicolas's story.

———————————

We stepped off our plane on A17 into a clear night with a warm breeze. On a connected section of runway, an extremely pale Spectavi waited in front of a black military helicopter with fuel pods attached. The rear sliding door was open, and two pilots sat up front. A third Spectavi guard sat in the back. Nate followed me toward them.

"I will bring you to Seorsum," the pale vampire said.

"Any trouble, here or there, and you will never return home." He climbed into the back of the chopper. Not surprisingly, we weren't going to be allowed anywhere near the research facility.

Nate and I boarded the helicopter, and as the blades starting spinning, the armed Spectavi slid the door closed, then returned to his seat beside the pale one across from us.

"Two hours," the guard said.

I nodded as we lifted into the air. All I saw of A17 out the window was the landing strip, some jungle, and then the beach before moonlit ocean surrounded us completely.

I checked my phone—a little after two. And I had missed a message from Caleb because of the noise and rattling of the helicopter.

Fernand Bisset and his daughter were murdered in France by Sanguans. My brother was at work at the time, at least according to the logs I checked.

Fernand had been the man on the phone with David that Caleb had mentioned when we last spoke. With no cell service, I expected to have to wait to respond until we returned from Seorsum.

———————————

A few lights dotted the crescent-shaped bay of Seorsum as we approached. I located the main street that ran to the Baker family's house, where Matt's blood had told me the old vampire dwelled.

The chopper descended until it hovered a few feet above ground. The pale Spectavi yelled over the blade noise, "Call when we are to retrieve you. The vampire knows how."

The other Spectavi slid open the door.

"Where will you spend the day?" I asked, my mind on the impending sunrise.

"The far side of the island. We'll be left alone," the guard explained.

I nodded, grabbed my things, and jumped down to the sand. Nate followed. The helicopter rose.

Nate grinned. "We made it."

I matched his expression. Not only had we found Ahmose, but we had made it somewhere hidden and secret. The Spectavi flew away, and waves crashing against the shore became louder than the helicopter. A child stood at the far end of a wooden deck that led to the main street.

"Now we'll see if it was worth flying all the way around the world." I headed to the deck and, ignoring the steps, jumped up to the end opposite where the boy stood. His eyes grew wide. He wore mesh shorts and an old t-shirt and, aside from being very tan, appeared perfectly normal. I remembered his image, but not his name, from Matt's memories. He turned and sprinted the other way.

Two voices came from around the corner to the right. The boy appeared at the end of the deck. His older brother—Stuart, nineteen years old—ran in front of him and stopped.

"Who are you? What do you want?" Stuart asked in only slightly accented English.

"I'm Erin. This is Nathan. We're here to see the old vampire." I figured if Matt didn't know his name, Ahmose might not have wanted it to be known.

"Why aren't you in uniform like the others?"

I glanced over the trees where the helicopter had gone out of sight. "We're not with them."

"Why do you have a sword?" Stuart asked.

I smiled. "I bring it everywhere. We're here to talk, not fight. Can you take us to the vampire?"

"No." He shook his head. "You aren't supposed to be here. Call them back. Go away."

"It's the Bakers' house, up the hill. We'll go without you if you won't take us."

"We live peaceful lives here," Stuart said. "He will make you pay if you've brought any trouble."

"We just want to talk," I reiterated.

Stuart looked up the hill for a moment. "Follow me." With his brother, he headed up the dirt road.

In between tall palm trees and lush, green vegetation, we passed small, mainly single-story houses on both sides of the street. A light came on inside a house to our right. A woman peered out, and then another window lit. We kept going.

I checked and, sure enough, no cell service.

"What's that?" Stuart's brother asked.

"What's what?" I responded.

He pointed at my phone. "That."

I put it away. "Nothing." Had he ever seen a cell phone? Had he ever heard of one?

When the child turned around, I got my phone back out and shut it off. We continued up the hill, and eventually, the Bakers' relatively large home came into view. The two-story house was nestled directly in front of a large, black volcanic mound that rose above it.

The front door opened, and a bald, pale vampire in a thick red robe emerged. He shut the door and stood, stone-faced, with his arms behind his back.

Stuart and his brother stopped a few steps before Nate and I did.

The vampire looked past us and smiled kindly. "Thank you both. Get some sleep." The two scampered back down the hill. Warmth fled from the vampire's face. "What brings two Sanguans to Seorsum?"

"I'm Erin Rose. This is Nathan Rigby. I have a few questions for you."

"It's a long way to come to ask a few questions."

"No one else had any answers. Victoria thought you might." I was prepared to reveal all that had happened in the world in order to convince him, but would attempt to proceed cautiously.

"Victoria…" he said. "She found me?"

"No, I did."

"How?"

"Luck. I came across a young man in Rome—"

"Matthew," the vampire interrupted. "Matthew… he often asked to hear my stories about the Eternal City. Was he hurt?"

"He was fine when I found him and fine when I left him."

The vampire nodded. "I am Ahmose. I am a guest in the Bakers' home, and I will see that you pay for any harm that comes to them or anyone on this island. Do you understand?"

"Yes," Nate and I said in unison.

"Follow me." Ahmose opened the door.

Nate and I followed him inside, where Ahmose brought a finger to his lips, signaling for us to keep quiet. He led us through a home with furnishings that might have been half a century old. The living room conspicuously lacked a television in what seemed the perfect spot for one. The opened door of an office revealed an old desktop computer with a bulky monitor and papers stacked on it and the keyboard.

Between the living room and the kitchen, at the rear of the house, Ahmose opened a plain white door to reveal a metal one, which a large key on a rope around his wrist unlocked. Ahmose led us down a black staircase.

As soon as the door closed, he said, "This basement is carved into the rock."

That accounted for the low, uneven ceiling. Yellow bulbs hung along the black walls. The single room was by no means spacious, but the three of us would fit without trouble, and I imagined it being plenty for Ahmose alone, during the long hours he doubtless spent down there.

A large wooden desk against a long wall had papers and books all over it. To its left, a small round hollow had been carved into the rock. Books, new and old, filled shelves on all four sides and were stacked in front of them on the floor. A few rolled scrolls topped some piles.

Nate stepped off the last stair. "You need an e-reader."

I glared at him.

"So they are widely used now?" Ahmose's face lit up a little. "Eh. That development was easy to guess. But please, nothing more or you'll ruin my game."

"Sorry," Nate said.

Ahmose brought a wooden folding chair from the wall and set it up in the middle of the room, then moved a closed cardboard box next to it. "Welcome. Please, have a seat."

I took the chair, and Nate sat on the box.

At the desk, Ahmose spun his chair around and sat. "Do you need to drink? Erin, you look thirsty. I could wake someone."

My skin might have taken on a subtle drab tint, though I couldn't tell if so. He could have noticed my dry lips. However he knew, he was correct, but I denied it. "I'm fine."

"Perhaps tomorrow, then." Ahmose folded his hands on his lap. "Please, what brought you so far to see me?" He pointed at me. "Actually, I suppose it wouldn't hurt to know why you changed your name from Vera."

Apparently, he recognized me from my first few years at Eure. "I didn't change it. Edmond did. It's... related to why we're here."

"I see."

I got straight to the point. "Did you know Nicolas Duchart?"

"Why do you ask?"

I considered how to explain without revealing what had transpired, but came up with nothing. "It's important."

Ahmose rubbed his chin. "Has something happened to Edmond?"

"Yes."

Ahmose squinted at me. "Then, I should know of it. Please, tell me what you must."

"I don't remember being Vera. As Erin, I found my way to Edmond's side. I trusted him and thought I loved him. Then, I discovered he was lying to the world about Sanguans and their crimes. To see what else he had lied about, I freed his sisters from their steel coffins. Edmond confirmed he had wiped away my memory of life as Vera, then his sisters killed him."

"How did he die?" Ahmose asked.

"They ripped off his head and threw his body into his coffin." Ahmose didn't react, so I continued, "Then they fled. Victoria nearly drained me, and I drank Edmond's blood from a crack in his coffin to survive. But a few minutes before that, before the twins attacked Edmond, they argued with him about their brother Nicolas and his part in what happened to them. No one I've asked has heard of Nicolas. Or at least they haven't been willing to tell me. Do you know what role he played?"

Ahmose waited a moment before responding, "Why does it matter what Nicolas did?"

It sounded like he knew. I *had* to get him to tell me. "Caterine and Ariane are out there, and they've caused some damage, but I feel like there's more going on. I found a book with blackened out drawings depicting their transformation. There was mention of a search and a drawing of the twins with wings, wrapped in flame, but I have no idea what it means. Those two are evil, and I'm the one who let them loose. I *have* to find out what they're planning."

"Evil?" Ahmose scoffed. "They are vampires, the same as the three of us."

Nate spoke up, "They're insane."

"No, they are not," Ahmose said. "They're angry, and they know how to act to make people and other immortals fear them. They always have. When you've seen all I've seen, you realize that you cannot be certain what constitutes good and evil. I have my morals, and I try to teach those here to live right, but I no longer presume to have any idea if those morals align with God's."

The twins were evil in my book, but it wasn't important that Ahmose agreed. "Tell me about Nicolas," I urged. "Please."

Ahmose's raised an index finger. "Did Edmond pick your tattoo or did Vera or Erin?"

"I did."

"Who knows what the Lord is up to?" Ahmose clasped his hands. "I trust you know who my maker was."

"I do."

"You and I share his ancient blood, Erin." Suddenly, Ahmose focused on Nate. "Why are *you* here?"

"Erin." Nate didn't turn to me. "I had to know what she was looking for. I couldn't not follow her to find out. I couldn't not follow her here."

Ahmose nodded. "I suppose I should tell you the story of how Edmond's sisters came to be as they are, and what they searched for—fought for, really. The history should not be lost, and whether any of us is good or evil, whether letting them free or imprisoning them in the first place was right or wrong, I understand why you desire to know the whole truth, Erin."

"Thank you," I said.

"I will tell you tomorrow." Ahmose rose. "It is late, and the tale will take time." He went to the carved-out hollow in the wall and lifted a box to its left, revealing another tubular opening with a level bottom and round top. "Guests are rare, but over two hundred years, you are not the first."

Nate got up and moved another stack of books out of the way. I moved a box from in front of a third opening, then returned to run my hand over the smooth rock that would be my resting place for the day.

14

My eyes opened to black all around me. Past my feet, yellow light filled Ahmose's basement. My arms were folded over my chest, and for the first time in a long time, my sword was not within reach when I awoke. I slid out of the hollow to find Nate leafing through an old book and Ahmose writing at his desk.

The ancient vampire put down his pen. "Shall we go for a walk?"

———————

The three of us strolled on the beach. I did my best to ignore my growing thirst while enjoying the grains of sand between my toes and marveling at the scintillating canopy created by the most stars I had ever seen.

"Seorsum is home to over a hundred people these days," Ahmose said. "They produce what they can, and other supplies are shipped to us. My presence ensures there's virtually no crime. No one needs to fear war or other vampires. It's not a perfect life, but it is a simple one."

"And in return, you have blood to drink while you wait out the years?" Nate asked.

A loud wave crashed, and water ran up near us.

"I hardly drink anymore," Ahmose said. "But yes, when I do, they give me that and company. I ask that they do not try to leave, to protect the secret of my location. Some have, like Matthew, but I don't go after them. Few, if any, are looking for me, so the risk is low. Edmond, in spite of his frustration with me, graciously helped keep this island off the map. The Spectavi patrol the waters around it and keep most others away."

"How long have you been here?" I asked.

"On Seorsum since 1800. I've been other places since the fourteenth century."

"Don't you miss the rest of the world?" Nate asked. "Modern technology, if nothing else?"

"No. I lived for a long time before anything considered modern. I am consistently fascinated by new developments each trip away from this island reveals—especially recently—but so far, I've always been eager to return to the simple life." He smiled. "I will admit that my game of guessing at what may happen—in politics, science, and everything—is vital to keeping me occupied as the years pass."

"I'm sorry to have ruined some of it for you this time," I said.

"Please." Ahmose shook his head. "Edmond is to blame, it seems, and this news will give me more to ponder for the next ten years."

I recalled Erec's story. "Was it the plague that led you to live like this? The Black Death?"

"It was that," Ahmose said, "and a great deal more. Why

are there earthquakes and plane crashes? Why…?" He paused. "Even out here, where it is peaceful enough to ponder the mystery and even with forever ahead of us, I will spare you a list you can make for yourself. Why is there so much death and pain that seems to have no reason?"

"Maybe so we appreciate life and the good times," I offered, while not totally committed to the answer.

"Sure," Ahmose said. "But it isn't enough."

"Says you," Nate added.

"Quite true, quite true," Ahmose agreed.

I thought of the black void I had found myself in after Victoria sucked me to the point of death. The pure white light that flickered, then solidified as I approached had been so good—perfectly good—yet evil was everywhere. It vexed me as it did Ahmose.

Another loud wave hit the shore. Had that white light been Heaven? That night on the sanctuary that was Seorsum was not the first time I realized that by choosing to live, I had chosen against knowing the true nature of the light. *Had* it been some perfectly good place? Or had it been death, and clinging to my earthly existence, I had simply envisioned the end that particular way? Ultimately, every single time, I ended up thankful with all my heart for having chosen life, yet continued to wonder.

Ahmose stopped. "Erin, you must be ravenous. I will admit that while I still enjoy blood immensely, I can hardly remember the sensation of a terrible thirst. But I do remember there being a time when I had such a nightly thirst."

"I'm fine," I said, despite craving blood nearly as much as I craved for him to tell me of Nicolas. In the company of Nate, who didn't need to feed as often as me and could have gotten directly to Nicolas's tale, I didn't like feeling so young—like a child pining for a meal. More accurate, and worse, having left humanity behind, I was a baby *demon*.

"You don't look fine," Ahmose said. "One of the Bakers will surely not mind, and then I will tell you about Nicolas."

"Okay," I relented.

———————————

Nate, Ahmose, and Mrs. Baker's husband sat around the kitchen table while I sipped on the tanned woman's wrist, experiencing her forty-five years on the island. Her ancestors had arrived in 1800 with Ahmose. Mrs. Baker had been married at nineteen. She knew of impossibly thin TVs, cell phones, and the internet, but struggled to imagine a world filled to the brim with such high-tech things. Her only exposure to them came from the books and updates Ahmose brought back with him in 2000 and 1980—and those updates were plenty. She loved her life of gardening and helping with the maintenance of the homes and common buildings on the island. She loved her son and daughter, and she loved cooking with her husband—often the fresh fish he caught. On weekends, the family spent hours on the beach, listening to waves rolling ashore.

Her blood hit my tongue, lush and deliciously warm, yet within it, calmness reigned. Few dramatic twists filled her past and weighed on her present. Her humble aspirations painted the picture of a bright, fulfilled future. She had known ups and downs, but they had been only modest deviations from her usual. Mrs. Baker wondered why Nate and I had come to Seorsum. She was fearful a crisis had brought us and wished we would leave, so everything would return to normal.

"Thank you," I said when I finished drinking.

"You're welcome." Mrs. Baker nodded and exited the kitchen with her husband.

"Shall we?" Ahmose motioned to the basement door, then led the way.

We took the same seats as the previous night.

Ahmose checked an old pocket watch he had on his desk. "Edmond told me of Nicolas even before making me a vampire. We discussed him often."

I could hardly stand the preamble, afraid Ahmose would be interrupted at any moment and not get to the meat of the story.

He continued, "My maker swore me to secrecy, which I will honor by not telling you of our discussions about the meaning of it all. But with Edmond gone, I will tell you the tale I have never told anyone. In return, I ask that you not reveal the location of this island, or that I am here, to anyone."

"We won't," I assured him.

"You have my word," Nate confirmed.

"Good. Edmond pieced together his version of the story from events he lived, as well as a number of other sources. Determined to know the whole truth, I spoke to Caterine and Ariane hundreds of years after they became vampires. Their account matched Edmond's, for the most part." Ahmose gave a sly smile. "What I will tell you is the sum of those sources, as best I have been able to organize them over the last fourteen centuries."

15

June 2, 507 – Chartres, France

A fire burned in the middle of Edmond's single-room house. Edmond, on leave from his post as a personal guard to the Frankish King, Clovis I, sat alone with his wife, who lay on a long, dark wooden table and had stopped breathing minutes before. The tall, brown-haired beauty had gone into labor, but their first child had not been delivered. Blood covered the table, the dirt floor, Edmond, and his wife.

The fire died while he held his wife's hand and wept.

June 13, 507

"This concludes the Mass. Go in peace," Nicolas said from the altar of the small church in the center of Chartres. He wore a long black robe with a brown pouch on his belt.

"Thanks be to God," the townsfolk responded in unison. A few approached Nicolas for a quick word, and the rest filed out. His fair-skinned, eighteen-year-old identical twin sisters exited from the front row. Thirty-two-year-old Edmond, two years Nicolas's senior, waited outside with them, as did their father, Guillaume, and the twins' betrotheds.

Nicolas, who lived in the church, emerged last, and under a sunny sky, the group left town and walked up the long dirt path to the home where the two girls and their father lived. Nicolas did his best to comfort Edmond along the way.

Two sturdy horses were tied to a post in front of the small thatched-roof house. The walls were made of interwoven branches and mud, with a single window to the left of the door. Nicolas went inside.

Before following him, Guillaume addressed his daughters' husbands-to-be. "Good luck to you both."

"Thank you, sir," Michel responded.

"Thank you," Fabian echoed.

Both young men were dressed to ride in earthy-colored trousers, tunics, and cloaks, and needed only to collect their swords and supplies before being on their way.

The tall twins each wore plain, long-sleeved dresses that had faded from white to eggshell some time ago. Ariane's long blond hair was a few inches shorter than her sister's same-colored locks.

Edmond stopped at the entrance and could not manage the warm face he intended for his sisters. "Don't keep them long. The fighting in Nantes will not wait." He looked to the ground, then went inside and shut the door.

Michel gazed into Caterine's hazel eyes and stroked her cheek. "It will not be a month," he said softly.

Ariane kissed Fabian before he could offer his own assurance of their safe return.

Michel kissed Caterine and added, "Then we will be married."

Caterine's face lit up.

"Fabian," Michel said. "We must go."

Fabian and Ariane ended their kiss, and the two men untied and mounted their horses. Michel led the way back down the dirt path.

Ariane pouted while Caterine beamed. Once the men were out of sight, the girls grinned at each other and joined their family inside the house.

July 21, 507

A horse galloped up the path. Caterine and Ariane rushed outside. They had never seen the lone rider before. Caterine brought in the letter the messenger carried for their father.

August 13, 507

Early that warm night, in the middle of the single-room house, a fire surrounded by stones burned under a black pot. Two months had passed with no word from Michel or Fabian. Guillaume Duchart labored to breathe in his bed in the rear right corner of the room. The twins stood over him with tears sliding down their checks. On the other side of the bed, Nicolas held a large cross necklace over his journal. His eyes were closed as he mouthed prayers. Edmond stood beside his brother.

The dying man's light skin had turned dark, and his

fingertips had blackened. Nodes had swollen under his armpits and on his neck. His last words had come hours earlier.

He took his final breath.

Nicolas read fear on his sisters' faces. "Our father lived a full life."

Ariane coughed. Then, Caterine did the same.

———————

The next morning, Edmond waited outside the open door. His sisters, after having woken up with fevers, aching joints, and dizziness, lay a few feet from each other in narrow beds opposite from where their father had rested. A large wooden cross hung on the wall above them.

Nicolas stood between the beds. "Rest today. Pray to the Lord, and this will pass." He joined his brother out front.

Edmond reached in and shut the door. "They will die in two days as our father did, or maybe three or four because they are younger. I know not what ails them, but it is the same as what took him."

Nicolas smiled and put his hand on Edmond's shoulder. "You are not sick, nor am I. It has been a hard year for you, brother, but our fair sisters are strong. Death will not take them."

———————

In her bed, Ariane rolled onto her side and said, "I don't want to die."

"We will not." Caterine turned toward her twin and

coughed. "Michel and I will be wedded, and my little sister will be standing beside me, marrying her Fabian, just as we planned."

"One minute does not make me younger." Ariane coughed twice. "And I'm taller than you."

"You are not," Caterine said sternly. Then, unable to maintain her sharp expression, she broke into a mixture of laughing and coughing.

Ariane's own fit overcame her. "I know," she managed.

Over the course of the day, the sisters' fevers grew worse. Edmond stayed past midnight. Nicolas prayed almost constantly, sometimes with them and other times on his own, before spending the night in his late father's bed.

The following morning, Nicolas sat at the rectangular wooden table, writing in his journal. Edmond entered to see his sisters staring wide-eyed up at the ceiling. They were covered from neck to toe by thick blankets. Their hair had thinned, lips grown pale, and faces become light gray. Edmond lifted the corner of Caterine's covers and discovered her shoulder and arm similarly tinted and marked with boils. Farther down, he found blackened fingertips. He replaced the blanket and checked on Ariane, finding her in the same condition.

"You should go, lest this illness takes hold of you," Caterine said.

Softly, Edmond assured her, "I will not leave you. I swear it."

Ariane gulped. "Nicolas says this will pass. Will it?"

After a moment, Edmond said, "Our brother's faith is

strong, as yours should be, no matter what."

The twins slept off and on for the rest of the day, while their brothers watched their health deteriorate. With Nicolas again in his father's old bed, Edmond managed a few hours of sleep in a chair at the table.

At sunrise the following morning, the sound of approaching horses excited everyone in the sullen house. Nicolas and Edmond greeted Michel and Fabian out front. The twins could hear them talking to their brothers, but could not make out exactly what was said.

"Please go to them," Nicolas urged. "It could help."

"Gray skin?" Michel asked Edmond. "Is it some new plague?"

"May be," Edmond answered. "My father grew ill first, and then they did, the day he passed. Nicolas and I remain healthy."

"Hm." Michel said, "We dare not go inside."

"I have to see her." Fabian stepped toward the door.

Michel grabbed his arm. "You cannot."

"Please." Nicolas focused on Fabian. "Please, just for a moment."

Fabian tried to pull away, but Michel tightened his grip.

Edmond suggested, "Perhaps you will return tomorrow and see if they have improved?"

Michel shook his head. "No. If it's plague... we must leave this place at once."

After another attempt to go to them, Fabian broke from Michel's grip and mounted his horse. Michel did the same.

To the twins' horror, they heard hooves galloping away.

Ariane tried to get out of bed, but ended up slumped half off of it with her hand on the floor keeping her from falling all the way. Edmond came in and rushed to her.

"When will they return?" Ariane asked while he helped her back into bed.

Her sister answered, "They will not."

Edmond took a seat at the table and wept.

August 27, 507

At the table, Edmond sat across from his brother. Edmond took a bite of bread. "What are you writing?"

Nicolas looked up from his small brown book. "It is a miracle our sisters live so long after their affliction. I am keeping a record, so when they recover, their story can be told for generations to come."

Edmond chucked his bread onto the table and stood. "It is no miracle that they are made to suffer."

The twins had been unable to keep down food for three days.

September 5, 507

Nicolas wrote in his journal:

Their skin seems a shade grayer each day. Their lips, paler. Their hair, thinner. New boils and blisters form, and old ones fade. Some leave scars. The girls hardly sip any water, have not eaten, and grow weaker.

September 29, 507

Nicolas wrote:

Caterine called out for Michel in the night. It was the first I have heard either speak in two weeks. They have not eaten for over a month and remain dull gray, yet have not grown thinner. Their faith is sustaining them.

October 9, 507

"I cannot stand seeing them like this. How long will it go on?" Edmond asked his brother. "No word of spreading plague has come. Why would God make them suffer so?"

"I know not," Nicolas said. "Have faith."

November 30, 507

Nicolas wrote:

I have asked the Lord what more I should do for my sisters. "Pray" is the answer I feel in my heart. I kneel between them and pray. I stand over them and pray. I go to my church and pray. Nothing changes. The promise of each rising sun grows dimmer. I fear my brother has lost hope.

December 8, 507

Amidst lightly falling snow, Edmond split a log with his axe.

Nicolas returned from his Mass. "No one will visit them."

Edmond readied another log. "As they should not." He

swung and split the wood. "Whatever curse has hold over our sisters should not leave this house." Edmond put down the axe. "Come with me." He led the way inside.

The twins' heads had been propped up on pillows. They opened their eyes slowly.

"Tell Nicolas what you told me," Edmond urged.

Caterine rasped, "End it."

"No!" Nicolas rushed to their beds. "You do not mean it."

"We are not strong enough to do it ourselves," Ariane whispered. "Please."

"I will not!" Nicolas turned and pointed at his brother. "You will not!"

December 17, 507

Edmond stood over the twins' beds before sunrise. He whispered, "My sweet sisters." Their eyes opened as he knelt between them. "If I do as you ask, I will not be able to live with myself. If I stay, I will not be able to stop myself from doing as you ask. I will pray for you day and night." He rose to his feet. "I will always love you."

Edmond left the house, mounted his horse, and rode away.

April 20, 508

Nicolas wrote:

Four months since Edmond left. Spring has come. He has written from the Rhine, Cologne, and farther east, reporting no plague like what has befallen Caterine and Ariane. I have responded each time with: our sisters have not changed. They hardly move or speak any longer. Still, they do not eat, and yet they grow no thinner. I remain healthy. Why them? God has not revealed an answer to that question. Not even a hint.

June 15, 508

Nicolas wrote:

A girl in town a few years younger than my sisters grew feverish and ill. Her family followed. After a grim three days, the girl and her family improved and are nearly completely recovered. I know the Lord has a plan, but why heal them, and heal them so quickly, yet leave my sisters lingering in their sad state?

August 3, 508

Nicolas wrote:

I returned from Mass angry. Townsfolk tell me how they pray for my sisters, but none will visit them. I grow tired of relaying the same well wishes. Tell them to my sisters yourselves!

August 13, 508

"What day is it?" Ariane whispered.

Nicolas told them, and then closed the door on his way out.

"It has been a year," Caterine rasped to her sister.

"Why is this happening? Why are we not dead?"

"I do not know," Caterine answered.

November 19, 508

Nicolas wrote:

Bishop Fabrice skipped Chartres on the way from Paris. I wrote to ask why, and he responded that he did not have time. I think he lies. He fears my sisters' illness as everyone else does.

February 26, 509

Nicolas wrote:

I suffer along with my sisters. The Lord answers none of my prayers. Every day Caterine and Ariane awaken to lie helpless in their beds, I fail them anew.

March 13, 509

Nicolas wrote:

I wrote Bishop Fabrice, asking that he send an experienced priest to determine if my sisters are possessed by demons and, if necessary, to perform an exorcism.

April 4, 509

Nicolas wrote:

The Bishop does not believe they are possessed and will send no priest.

August 13, 509

"Do you still pray?" Caterine asked, staring at the ceiling, while Nicolas was at church saying Mass.

"No," Ariane answered.

"Nor do I." Caterine summoned all her strength to turn her head so she could look at her sister. "Do you remember our prayer from when we were little, playing by the old oak tree?"

Ariane managed to turn her head. "Yes."

"Will you say that prayer with me tonight, in your head?"

"Yes. When?"

Caterine turned back to the ceiling. "All night. From sundown to sunrise."

September 4, 509

Nicolas wrote:

A sinister voice in my mind told me to sacrifice a goat and to ask for his help. I forced Lucifer away.

January 7, 510

Nicolas wrote:

Hope! Bishop Fabrice returns from Constantinople with a fragment of the wooden cross upon which Jesus Christ was nailed and crucified. A woman, ill and bedridden, was shown the cross and rose from her bed, healed! I will write to the Bishop in Paris and ask him to bring the relic to Chartres.

January 9, 510

Nicolas wrote:

I dreamed Bishop Fabrice came amid great celebration to Chartres and brought with him the True Cross. Standing in my doorway, the sun shining bright behind him, he handed it to me, wrapped in a fine golden cloth. I took the Cross to my sisters and knelt between them. Their eyes opened, they turned to see, and they smiled. Their skin became fair, their hair became full, and strength returned to their bodies. Healed, they rose from their beds and praised the Lord!

January 27, 510

Nicolas wrote:

No word from Bishop Fabrice. The serpentine voice tells me the bishop will not answer, but I know he will. My sisters will be healed at the sight of the True Cross.

February 16, 510

Nicolas wrote:

The snake was nearly correct. Bishop Fabrice did respond, but says he will not take the Cross from Paris because of the risk in traveling with it. He suggested I bring my sisters to the Cross. I tried to move them, but it was agony for either to be lifted.

February 17, 510

Nicolas wrote:

I tried again to move Caterine and Ariane, but the pain was still too much for them. I asked God why he would reveal their salvation yet keep it out of reach. The serpent answered that the bishop is being greedy, hoarding the Cross's power for himself.

February 27, 510

Nicolas wrote:

After Mass, a young man who had returned from Paris the evening before spoke joyfully and passionately to all who would listen. He had seen the Cross fragment. He related how being in its presence filled him with such joy that he feared he would burst at any moment. My sisters would not even need to see the Cross. Merely being near it would heal them. I know it would!

March 2, 510

Nicolas wrote:

It is so close. I can see their salvation. I can feel it! Yet it remains kept from me, and them.

March 5, 510

Nicolas wrote:

I dreamed Caterine and Ariane died in the middle of the

day while I was praying for them and while others prayed before the True Cross in Paris.

March 10, 510

Nicolas wrote:

I brought a goat behind the house and cut its throat. The voice in my head praised me while I held it and watched the animal bleed. Afterward, the voice scolded me for not drawing a pentagram on the ground first.

April 3, 510

Nicolas wrote:

I placed a shard of wood on my table. I stood and stared at it for hours while Caterine and Ariane lay unmoving and unspeaking. I joined them in silence and imagined the plain wood as the holy Cross that would save them.

April 29, 510

Nicolas wrote:

I wrote to Fabrice again, pleading with him to send a priest to perform an exorcism, in case the rite could help my poor sisters. The serpent tells me the True Cross will heal them, and I know it could.

June 1, 510

Nicolas wrote:

They appear so ill. So weak. I fear their end is near.

June 2, 510

Ariane whispered, "Sister?"

"Yes?"

"I promise to always be with you."

"As do I." Caterine took a breath. "In life or in death, I promise we shall never be parted."

June 3, 510

Nicolas wrote:

I could not bear to be with Caterine and Ariane today. I sat outside until long after sundown, looking to the northeast, to Paris, to my sisters' only chance for survival.

June 4, 510

Nicolas wrote:

The Bishop has finally dispatched the priest I requested. Does fresh hope come with him?

June 8, 510

"Adnot, thank you for coming," Nicolas said, closing the door behind the old priest.

Adnot grunted while looking around the home. Long years of his intense, specialized work in the name of the Lord had worn his face and hands and thinned his long gray hair. He wore a brown robe and had left his leather satchel outside with his horse.

"Do you need anything?" Nicolas asked. The fire below the metal pot smoldered.

"No. It is late." Adnot went to the twins. While the girls stared up blankly, Adnot felt their foreheads and pulled back the blankets of each to see their dark, boil-marked arms. Adnot crouched, checked under the beds, and grunted. "Three years, you say?"

"In August," Nicolas replied.

Adnot got up. "And they no longer move?"

"No."

"Have they spoken in foreign tongues, in languages they should not know?"

Nicolas shook his head. "No."

"Do they speak at all?"

"No."

Adnot pointed to the wall, at the cross between them. "How long has that been there?"

"Their whole lives," Nicolas answered.

Adnot walked out the front door, reached into his satchel, and returned to the twins with his hands hidden inside his loose sleeves. He stood between the sisters and watched the sheets over them rise and fall nearly imperceptibly as they breathed.

Adnot prayed, "Our Father in Heaven, hallowed be your name. Your kingdom come, your will be done, on earth as it is in Heaven."

Crack! The dying fire flared. Both priests gave it a long look.

Adnot brought his hands from his sleeves and placed identical silver crosses on the blankets over each sister's stomach. "Give us this day our daily bread and forgive us our debts, as we also have forgiven our debtors." He moved the crosses to their foreheads. "And lead us not into temptation, but deliver us from evil. Amen."

Adnot glanced between them, then picked up the crosses. "The Lord be with you both."

He led Nicolas outside and shut the door. "They are not possessed," Adnot said.

"What?"

He gave Nicolas one of the crosses to hold in each hand.

"The house is cold… very cold." Adnot took the crosses back and put them in his bag. "But none here are possessed."

He suspects, the serpent said.

"What, then?" Nicolas pleaded. "Why do my sisters suffer so?"

Adnot frowned. "I know not. But I cannot help you." He turned to his horse.

Kill him.

"What?" Nicolas said aloud.

Adnot looked back. "Hmm?"

Fool! He knows we speak. You must kill him!

"Nothing," Nicolas replied.

You know what you have to do for your sisters. It is their only hope. The Bishop will not let you near the Cross when Adnot reports what he has learned about you.

Adnot placed his hand on Nicolas's shoulder. "I will pray for your sisters."

Kill him!

While Adnot prepared to mount his horse, Nicolas drew a small knife from his waist pouch.

For your sisters' sake, do it!

Before the old priest got all the way onto the animal, Nicolas launched himself at the man and stabbed into his robed back.

Adnot screamed and tried to push himself up from the dew-covered grass, but Nicolas forced him down and stabbed again.

"Ah." Adnot's face hit the ground. "Agh!"

Nicolas stabbed and stabbed, until Adnot's struggling, and then his breathing, ended.

June 10, 510

Nicolas wrote:

Thibauld, whose wife recently passed, will stay with my sisters while I travel to Paris to plead my case to Bishop Fabrice. Thibauld will sleep in a tent outside for fear of entering the house, but he is strong and will keep them safe. The serpent assures me I will return with the True Cross.

227

June 12, 510

Riding Adnot's horse, Nicolas arrived in Paris an hour after sunset and went to find the Bishop at the church.

"Your Excellency," Nicolas said. He stood between the two guards who had escorted him into Bishop Fabrice's office.

"Nicolas, what a surprise. Please, have a seat," the bishop said, without taking his quill from the parchment in front of him.

Nicolas sat across from the Bishop, and the guards left. "Thank you," Nicolas said. A thick candle burned on one corner of the desk, the only light in the dim, windowless room.

"I imagined you'd be at home, waiting for the priest I dispatched at your request."

"I was. Thank you for sending him." Nicolas shifted in his seat. "Adnot sent word he would be delayed, perhaps by as much as a month."

"Oh, I had not heard." Fabrice put down his quill. "What brings you to Paris, then?"

Nicolas scooted forward in his chair. "I hoped I might convince you to lend me the healing relic of our Lord's suffering."

"Nicolas—" the bishop began.

"Did it heal that woman?"

"It did."

"Then it can heal my poor sisters. I know it can! They were fair and true servants of Jesus, and they will be again."

The bishop frowned. "I told you, I will not let it out of Paris. Bring your sisters here if they wish to see the Cross."

"They cannot be moved; they are too weak." Nicolas leaned forward. "Please, I beg you."

"If they are so ill, perhaps they are beyond the Cross's healing power. Perhaps Adnot can help them when he examines them."

Nicolas slumped back in his chair. *I told you,* the serpent said. Nicolas tried to push the voice away, but failed. *Ask to see it.*

"May I see the Cross?" Nicolas asked.

The bishop hesitated.

"Please," Nicolas urged. "If I could see it, perhaps describing it to my sisters will lift their spirits. They may not last until Adnot arrives."

Bishop Fabrice nodded. "Certainly."

By candlelight, the bishop led Nicolas into the large congregation area. To the right of the altar, in an alcove protected by a metal gate, a brown sheet covered a lump on a small table. The bishop put down his candle, produced a key from under his robe, and unlocked the gate. He slid it open and removed the sheet, revealing a small golden box.

Nicolas stepped forward and reached for it.

The bishop grabbed his arm and gently pushed it down. "Allow me." He lifted the lid of the box.

They both leaned over to see the single strip of three-inch-long, half-inch-wide, dark brown wood. Grains and grooves ran the entire length from one sharply cut edge to a jagged end.

"Isn't it beautiful?" the wide-eyed bishop said.

"It is," Nicolas agreed. *So were Caterine and Ariane,* the serpent added.

The bishop tilted his head. "I do hope your sisters can see it one day."

It will heal them, the snake pushed.

"I share that hope, with all my heart, your Excellency."

Bring it to them, and they will be healed!

"You're certain I cannot bring it to them? For but a day?" Nicolas begged. "I cannot possibly return to them with nothing."

The bishop stared at the wooden shard. "We will pray for them at Mass for the rest of the month. You may share this news with them when you return."

Nicolas reached into his pouch. "Your prayers will go unanswered, as mine have."

The bishop finally tore his gaze from the cross. "Nicolas, listen to yourself."

Nicolas leaned toward the Bishop. "I am." He pulled out his small knife, slid it across the Bishop's throat, and covered the old man's mouth so he couldn't yell for the nearby guard. While Nicolas held him, blood poured from the Bishop's neck until his eyes closed, the blood slowed, and his body went limp.

Nicolas laid him on the ground, wrapped the cross in the cloth that had covered it, then shoved the shard into his pocket. Nicolas moved to stand beside the door and called to the guard, "His Excellency has fainted. Come quick!"

When the guard ran in, Nicolas lunged and stabbed him

in the gut, while forcing him to the ground. Blood spurted, then streamed as Nicolas withdrew his knife. The guard struggled, and Nicolas stabbed his neck. Then he stabbed again into the man's stomach, and again, and again.

When the guard finally lay still, Nicolas reached into his pocket and pulled out the fragment of the True Cross. He held the relic at arm's length. "What have I done?"

What you had to, the familiar voice assured him. *For your sisters!*

Nicolas looked at the cross upon the altar and the stone statue of the Blessed Virgin Mary against the wall, then back to the scene in front of him. He put away the Cross fragment and ran from the church, while figuring out how he would kill the two guards who had led him into the Bishop's office. The serpent had instructed Nicolas not to leave any record of his visit.

Nicolas rode hard back to Chartres. *You had to do it,* the snake told him over and over. *I told you that you would return with the True Cross. I told you!* Nicolas thanked the serpent.

Mid-morning, Thibauld exited his tent in front of the Ducharts' home.

Nicolas dismounted. "How are they?"

"I know not." Thibauld began taking down the tent. "None came near."

Nicolas tethered his horse and hurried inside. Nothing had changed. He crouched between his sisters' beds, took the wooden shard from his pocket, and unwrapped it. "I've brought it! See the cross upon which your Lord and Savior bled his holy blood. See the True Cross and be healed!"

They opened their eyes in unison and rolled their heads to see what Nicolas held. He looked from one to the other, until they returned to facing the ceiling, and closed their eyes. Nicolas lowered the Cross fragment.

He didn't hear your prayers before. He will not hear them now. But I will.

Nicolas stood and ripped down the large hanging cross from between the beds. Seething, he threw it against the far wall.

Thibauld swung open the door. "Father! Is everything all right?"

Kill him! He might have seen the True Cross or heard you. He cannot know what you've done!

Nicolas stared at the broken cross on the ground.

Do as I say, and I will reveal how your sisters will be healed.

"Father?" Thibauld asked.

Do it! One more life for your sisters!

Nicolas walked to the entrance. "I must give you something more."

Thibauld raised his hands in front of him. "Not necessary."

"I insist. A token of my appreciation. My sisters are so dear to me, and you kept them safe." Nicolas motioned out the doorway toward the side of the house. "Please."

Thibauld led, and when he reached the side, said, "I don't see anything."

"It's around back," Nicolas explained.

"Oh." Thibauld kept going and Nicolas pulled his knife from his pouch.

As Thibauld rounded the corner, Nicolas stabbed into the man's upper back, then shoved him to the ground, burying his face in the dirt, and stabbed again. The attack continued long after Thibauld had died.

Nicolas went back inside and sat down at the table to record what he had done and why.

———————

An hour after sundown, with a fire crackling and the Cross fragment hanging from a rope around his neck, Nicolas wrote:

My sisters will be healed! The serpent commands me to slit my wrists, so I will. He promises that when my sisters taste my blood, their skin will regain its fair color. Their boils and blisters will fade. As they drink, their strength will return. After tonight, no sickness or injury will ever touch them.

Time will not age them. They will thirst, but will possess the power to quench that thirst. When my sisters have drunk the last drops of my blood, they will be beings of flame and fly away from this house. At a thought, they will be able to travel anywhere in the world.

The serpent swears it will be so.

Nicolas closed his journal and put it in his waist pouch. With a piece of chalk, he went to the twins. Their eyes remained closed while he drew an inverted pentagram on the wall behind their beds, then circled the figure and threw the chalk into the corner. "I will end your suffering this night. I will trade what remains of my mortal life, so you two may be immortal. I will see you healed before I die."

Nicolas knelt and brought his hands together with his knife between them.

He focused on Caterine, and then Ariane, seeing them as young girls playing in the grass under the sun's warm rays. He remembered their baptism.

He abandoned them, the serpent said.

Nicolas recalled the day he decided to enter the priesthood and how excited his sisters had been for him. He remembered a prayer they all used to say together and began reciting it in his head.

He abandoned YOU!

Nicolas stopped praying. "In sight of this True Cross, but without the God who remains blind to our family's suffering, you will be healed. Drink when the blood hits your lips. Drink it all!"

With a flick, he cut his wrists. The knife clattered to the floor, and he began to bleed. Swiftly, he brought his arms out to hang inches above each of his sisters' mouths. The first drops hit their pale, parched lips.

Fzzz. The boiling blood burned them.

"Drink," Nicolas whispered.

The twins' lips twitched as blood flowed onto them. Where the liquid ran, color slowly returned.

"Drink, my sisters!"

Their cracked, black tongues slipped out in unison and gradually moistened and reddened as they tasted the healing nectar. Their dark faces began lightening. Their chests rose and fell with deeper breaths than they had taken in years.

The girls leaned up to Nicolas's wrists and covered his wounds with their mouths.

His blood streamed. "Yes…"

The twins breathed faster as their hearts picked up pace.

CRACK-vwoosh! The fire in the middle of the house flared high.

Under their covers, the tips of each girl's fingers brightened. They made fists, while boils, marks, and gray faded from their bodies. Their skin became soft again, and then firm.

They wrapped their arms around Nicolas's and sucked harder.

Vwoooosh. Flames roared to the ceiling.

Nicolas whispered, "Yes…" Red seeped into the hazel of the girls' eyes, then Nicolas's eyes shut, and his head drooped forward.

With strength in their legs that had been useless for so long, the pair sat upright and drank on. Their fingers dug into their brother's arms when they gripped tighter than they had ever gripped anything. Their hair grew full again.

They ripped their mouths away.

Crack-crack!—went the raging fire.

When each saw her twin sister, they saw what they had become: their skin, once more fair and healthy; their hair, long and radiant as ever; their eyes, blazing red. Unexpectedly long teeth nicked their tongues. They opened their mouths to reveal razor-sharp fangs. Ariane let go of Nicolas and leapt out of bed. Caterine dropped his other wrist, and he fell forward when she got up.

The fire settled. The sisters smiled at each other, then watched Nicolas bleed onto the floor.

"Thank you, Nicolas," Caterine said.

"Yes, thank you, Nicolas," Ariane repeated.

"Ghaa!" they roared, as the first awful aching thirst hit them. Ariane ran to the far side of the room faster than she had ever moved. Caterine followed her lead. Ariane tore a loaf of bread and threw half to her sister.

After a few quick bites, Caterine asked, "Can you taste it?"

"No," Ariane answered while they kept trying.

When they had finished, Caterine announced, "I starve as if I had not eaten a single bite."

Their lips and throats became dry. They gulped down water, and as soon as they finished, they became parched again, and their hunger deepened.

"What new curse befalls us?" Caterine asked.

Near the beds, they examined the chalk pentagram on the wall above their brother's body.

Ariane smirked. "Our prayers were answered."

"And yet, we remain afflicted. What kind of God would make us suffer so horribly? For so long?"

"The God we prayed to. The God we lived for."

Caterine shook her head. "Damn him."

Ariane ran her tongue over her fangs. "Damn his men and his women…"

"Damn them all!" Caterine yelled.

"Yes!"

Caterine and Ariane sped down the dirt path into town,

intent on inflicting pain like that they had endured.

Upon their arrival, all praised the Lord for miraculously curing the twins. As the ravenous pair attacked and overpowered the townsfolk with inexplicable strength and speed, praise and all thoughts of God gave way to terror. While the vampires chewed their prey's flesh, those who died last had time to curse Satan.

Caterine and Ariane discovered that blood could make them feel better and by the last of their victims, had begun drinking exclusively and not eating. The twins fled west, and at twilight, at the same instant, both knew to seek shelter from the coming sun.

That day, a brave survivor in Chartres ventured to the home that all had avoided for so long. He found Nicolas lying in a pool of bubbling, boiling hot blood. The man didn't touch the liquid while he carefully cut the rope necklace off the priest's limp body. He didn't know what he had taken until learning of the True Cross's theft from Paris.

When stories of twin girls haunting the countryside reached Edmond, he rode for home. On a calm, clear night, he found his sisters missing and his brother lying in still-bubbling blood. Nicolas's journal remained in his belt pouch. Edmond read the chronicle of Nicolas's descent into madness, his murders, and the evil he had brought into the world.

Edmond stood over his brother's body and reread the final entry.

When my sisters have drunk the last drops of my blood, they will be beings of flame and fly away from this house. At a thought, they will be able to travel anywhere in the world.

The last drops of Nicolas's blood remained, never drank. Edmond kept the journal and set the house ablaze with his brother's body inside. Fearful of what he'd find, but overjoyed they had risen from their beds, Edmond rode off in search of Caterine and Ariane.

16

"And the search?" I asked. "Was it for the True Cross?"

"Ah, yes," Ahmose said. "A few nights later, Edmond caught up with his sisters and found them no longer ill and, somehow, incredibly strong and fast. They hated Edmond for abandoning them after swearing he would not and laughed at his persistent faith in God's goodness. They cursed him and fled while Edmond followed with all the speed his horse could muster. A week later, for fun, Caterine fed a man they had tortured from her wrist. To their amazement, Gosse became the third vampire. He shared their wild ways and went off on his own.

"It was a while before the twins learned to fight properly, but from the outset, Edmond couldn't match their superhuman speed. When news spread of Gosse, Edmond did manage to track *him* down. Knowing he had no other choice if he wanted to keep up with his sisters, Edmond persuaded Gosse to turn him into a vampire."

Exactly how close to the source Edmond's blood—my blood—was became clear.

Ahmose continued, "Edmond was a more skilled warrior

than Gosse, so he managed to do away with his maker. After that, Edmond prayed to be forgiven for breaking his oath not to leave his sisters, then swore to God he would help them. He hoped to talk some sense into the twins, and if they would not be reasoned with, to capture them and find a way to heal them. He would never kill them, he told me.

"As word spread of the twins, most rumors of their identities were false, but not all. Edmond also swore to clear his family name from its association with the evil Nicolas had brought into the world, however long it took. To accomplish all he promised, he needed other vampires loyal to him because his sisters were two, and had made others. Those first years, rapidly creating fledglings didn't result in as weak offspring as today.

"Edmond shared the information in Nicolas's journal with his companions, which was a mistake. One of them found the twins, and in exchange for a taste of their first vampire blood, he told them of their brother's last journal entry and how the twins could have possessed greater powers, if only they had drunk Nicolas completely dry.

"After that, the twins searched for the True Cross with hopes of replicating Nicolas's ritual and attaining the additional powers that had been promised to them. Edmond and his vampires, who would become the Spectavi, sought the Cross to prevent the twins from having it. Edmond also held out hope that the holy relic could return his sisters to their human form."

"What happened to the Cross fragment?" Nate asked, while I wondered if a "being of flame" could be harmed by a sword—or any weapon.

"The twins found it," Ahmose answered. "But they only held it for a single night before Edmond reclaimed it. Two years later, his sisters stole it back, but as you can see, they remain vampires with the same powers we all share. Once again, Edmond reclaimed the Cross.

"Then, one day, the relic disappeared. Fifty years later, a man came to Edmond, claiming the Cross was hidden and safe. Edmond demanded he turn it over, but the man would not. Edmond drank from him and discovered that the man had received an anonymous letter instructing him to seek out Edmond and tell him that vampires could not be allowed to possess the True Cross. Such a holy thing would not be destroyed, but would be kept secret and in human hands.

"Edmond searched for a long time, but never found it. He did agree that information about the Cross was highly sensitive, so he destroyed Nicolas's journal and, to avoid repeating his earlier error, only disclosed its contents to a few of his most loyal friends. I never heard him speak of it to anyone after the turn of the century—last century, the year 1000. I did suspect he kept searching from time to time."

I asked, "Weren't there other pieces of the True Cross? Aren't there still?"

"Yes," Ahmose confirmed. "Edmond collected many, as did the twins. It quickly became evident that the others did not hold the same power as the one Nicolas stole."

"So they're still looking for it after all these years…" Nate said.

"I wouldn't know." Ahmose shrugged. "I've been here."

"To be honest, we really have no idea what they're up to," I said. "What happened to Michel and Fabian?"

"The twins ensured they suffered mightily before their deaths."

Nate and I spent the rest of the night asking Ahmose to retell parts of the story and about his long life. A lot of what he shared matched Erec's account.

Ahmose was born in Alexandria, Egypt, in 610, when the Byzantines controlled the city. Later, the Persians took over, and he lived through a decade of their rule until it ended when he was nineteen. His trade was carpentry, and he had a wife and two sons.

The Plague of Justinian, which had originally struck in 541, thirty-one years after the twins' transformation, continued to crop up in waves each generation until the middle of the eighth century. Edmond was in Alexandria in 640, and had already met Ahmose when the plague claimed the lives of Ahmose's wife and children.

Ahmose was crushed. When Edmond came to console him, in a heated argument, he screamed at Edmond about how God could let such a thing happen. Ahmose nearly took his own life, but Edmond talked him out of it and then showed up every night for a few minutes, or sometimes hours, of arguing some new point on the same subject.

Eventually, the debates cooled into discussions when Ahmose found what Edmond had to say reasonable, if not convincing. Edmond enjoyed Ahmose's company greatly, and in 641, when the Arabs captured Alexandria, Edmond offered Ahmose the chance to become a Spectavi and go with him to France. Ahmose accepted.

The two continued their discussions, and as the centuries passed and no new plague came on the scale of Justinian's, Ahmose's faith returned and strengthened. His role in the war against the Sanguans with Edmond was mostly strategy, but he claimed to have become decent with a sword.

When the Black Death rocked Europe in the fourteenth century and so many millions died, Ahmose couldn't fathom why God would allow such an atrocity. To Edmond's great disappointment, his friend lost all interest in fighting, arguing, or discussing anything with him. Ahmose went into seclusion and eventually traveled to Seorsum.

Just before sunrise, Ahmose used the island's only phone, which he kept in his bottom desk drawer, to call A17 and arrange our helicopter ride for the following night.

———————————

The three of us stood on the beach while the Spectavi helicopter approached. Stuart and his brother, along with a few others, watched from the deck.

"I'm tempted to ask what you'll do," Ahmose said. "But of course, I cannot."

"Then, I'll ask you," I said. "How long will you stick to the twenty-year routine—on Seorsum or otherwise?"

Ahmose smiled. "Tonight, I like it here, and I like what I'm doing. I expect I will like it tomorrow, and the night after, as well. Beyond that, nothing is certain."

He extended his hand, and I shook it. "Thank you," I said.

"You're welcome." He shook Nate's hand.

Questions about the world, its history, and other vampires rushed to mind, but time had run out. When the helicopter hovered fifteen feet above us, I glanced back at Ahmose, then jumped up and inside.

———————

Nate and I once again sat in our own compartment on the plane, with the Spectavi and humans up front. We taxied to the runway for our eastward flight home.

"Are you going to tell Victoria?" Nate asked, leaving out details in case our cabin had been bugged.

"Of course." I put my phone down—still no service. I didn't want the Spectavi leadership knowing the story of the True Cross, but Victoria was different.

Nate put his hand on my leg. "What now? Will you stick around and look for it? It could be anywhere."

Luke came to mind first, then June, Zack, and Blaine. I had to write Caleb back and see if anything had come of Fernand Bisset's murder. The world seemed far larger and more diverse than it ever had, and the new perspective fascinated me, but also felt intensely foreign. My own coffin sounded wonderful, as did my house, my neighborhood, and all the familiar things that filled my nights. "I think I need to be home for a while."

Nate's face fell. "I understand."

I'd miss him, but I had found what I had gone to Europe for. Nate had played a huge role and would always be special to me.

"But I'll be back," I said, thinking it might be soon if

Victoria suggested I get right to searching for the True Cross. "Or you'll be in America. Or I'll run into you somewhere else."

"And it will be like we never parted." Nate leaned over to me. "You will be exactly as beautiful as you are tonight." He kissed me. His tongue ran over my fangs, and I jerked away.

The fire flickered when I swallowed. I kissed his forehead. "And so will you."

My phone buzzed with two new messages as soon as it had service. The first, from two days earlier, read:

Erin, are you still in Europe? I'm going to France with my brother. I asked him about Fernand Bisset, and he said it would make sense when we got there. I'm worried.

The second message was from a day later:

Erin, please contact me. I'm in Tours, France. On the flight, David wouldn't answer my questions about Fernand Bisset, but he did say that "God had spoken to him," and that we wouldn't have to be scared of vampires any longer. David said, "A lost relic that's been in our family will bring a divine rain to wash the vampires from the earth."

I think David's gone crazy. But what if he hasn't? He and my father had lots of secrets.

I wrote instead of calling in case David was around.

I'll be in France in two nights. Can we meet?

I looked at Nate. "I'm not going home after all."

"What is it?"

I pointed to David's name on my phone. "He might be on the trail of... the same thing Nicolas killed for."

During the flight, Nate questioned whether telling Victoria made sense for exactly the reasons the Cross had been kept from Edmond. What would she do if *she* found it? David having it seemed worst of all, so ultimately, we agreed to take our chances in trusting the ancient warrior who had always appeared devoted to the Lord. I tried calling Victoria, but got no answer. I emailed her, saying that we had found Ahmose and that it was important for her to get in touch with me.

Gradually, the idea of immortality had been sinking in. It *was* reasonable to live as though I had forever in front of me. And then, all of a sudden, that attitude might not have been such a safe bet if David really did know how to find the True Cross.

While a truck refueled our plane across the tarmac at JFK Airport in New York, I shared what I had read in Liverpool with Nate. "According to the book, '... two know their names, and only in the presence of both, will the three reveal their clues.'"

"Two families, I bet," he said.

I agreed, but didn't want to influence his reasoning. "Why?"

"A person might die. Have a heart attack. Get in an accident. Anything. A family would be more reliable and better suited to passing information on over time."

"Exactly. And I think the Sartoris were one of the two. Massimo never went out after sunset, even though it drove away his wife. It sounds like Massimo was committed to keeping his secret hidden from vampires at *any* cost."

Nate nodded.

I added, "Plus, David and Massimo hardly ever traveled together until that night in the limo."

"What about Caleb?"

I recalled my drink from him. "He didn't know. He was fed the same lies about his father and brother his whole life, and eventually gave up trying to dig deeper."

"So the Bissets were the other family? It could work. Fernand hadn't agreed with whatever David planned, so David killed him—or had his four Sanguan bodyguards kill him."

"Maybe. It does add up."

"And Fernand's daughter knew the secret, too?" Nate asked.

"Either that, or she was just in the wrong place at the wrong time."

"Right."

The refueling hose was disconnected from our plane.

I said, "Presumably, David's headed back to Europe in search of three 'clues' to the Cross's location."

"Without the Bissets, he'll have to take the clues by force."

"Yup. Another reason to have those Sanguan bodyguards around."

The truck drove away.

"Come on," Nate said.

While we headed back and boarded the plane, I thought through the discussion with Nate. Once I was comfortable with our reasoning, I focused on the most ominous part of Caleb's message—the "divine rain" that David intended to bring. That it could be the end of immortals, and of *me*, was almost incomprehensible, yet with the story of the twins fresh in my mind, the possibility felt eerily imminent.

———————

We landed at Le Bourget Airport, north of Paris, after one o'clock in the morning. Victoria had written that she was in South Africa, following rumors of the twins' whereabouts. Like Hayden, Victoria expected to join us the following night. Nate and I rented a car and drove to Tours.

I hadn't heard from Caleb, so I wrote him:

I'm here. Where are you? Can we meet?

Nate and I found a hotel downtown, then a lounge for a much-needed drink. Nate went trolling while I found a young man and took him to a back booth. After I finished drinking, the man left me alone and I checked my phone.

Nate returned and sat down next to me. "Anything from Caleb?"

"No."

"I don't get it. The True Cross was supposed to make the twins more powerful. David wants to wash away our kind. Maybe he's found a different relic."

"Maybe," I responded doubtfully.

"And why would Sanguans be helping David?"

"I don't know."

"In any case, it sounds like David cracked. His father's death was too much for him."

Two young women smiled at us as they strolled past. Ignoring them, I recalled Massimo Sartori's uneasiness in the video before the car accident, and then my drink from Caleb. "It was tough for Massimo after he woke up from his coma. He spent his life protecting a secret in the name of God, and then the accident happened so suddenly. He lamented to his oldest son that he didn't understand it. That must have been brutal for David to hear."

As clearly as I had seen it in Caleb's blood, I pictured Massimo staring up at David, whispering the charge, "It's up to you now. Don't forget. It's up to you."

My phone buzzed with a text from Caleb:

David murdered the entire Foquet family. Can't explain now. Will during the day.

"Do you know the Foquets?" I asked.

"No."

Nate brought out his cell, and we searched online and found a few people named Foquet in Tours. The most well-known was a wealthy banker who didn't live far away. When Nate and I drove by the row house, police and Spectavi vehicles with flashing rooftop lights surrounded the place.

17

I read Caleb's explanation first thing the next night:

We've been traveling by night, resting during the day. It's easier to write without his bodyguards around. David knew one of the Foquets had a clue to the location of the relic, but he wasn't sure which. We went to their apartment, and the family claimed to know nothing. David ordered one of the Sanguans to drink from their teenage son to read his thoughts. The boy didn't know anything, but was drained anyway. When the vampire neared their daughter, the father blurted out, "'Come to the meadow, to the forest.'" He swore he didn't know what it meant, or what secret the clue hid.

David had him drunk from, and the Sanguan confirmed the information. Then I watched while David's vampires drained Mr. Foquet, his wife, and their daughter.

David told me he needs two more clues. Someone in Paris is next.

The police are blaming local Sanguans for the murders. I know I should call them or the Spectavi, but I don't want to see my brother rotting in a French jail for the rest of his life. What if God does speak to him? There have been others in the past, allegedly. What if he's not crazy?

Please catch up with us, drink from David, and know the truth. If you tell me he's gone mad, we'll turn him in. Come to Paris. I'll let you know exactly where once I know where we're going.

Nate and I ran to our car and raced to Paris, two and a half hours away.

———————————

"Hell on Earth," I whispered, sitting on a long stone bench outside Notre Dame Cathedral. A thinning crowd ambled through the square. We waited for word from Caleb, and the building hadn't held my attention for long. I preferred Chartres' sharp, unmatched spires and its small city setting.

"What?" Nate asked.

"When enough live and enough have died, hope will bring the red rain, and Hell will be on Earth." I turned to Nate. "It's from the end of *Figli del Diavolo*. I read it a month ago in a library in D.C."

"What does it mean?"

"I don't know, but perhaps it's an appealing outcome for the Sanguans helping David."

My phone buzzed. *Leconte. 354 rue du Cardinal. Eighth floor.*

I mapped the address, showed it to Nate, then strapped my sword to my back and ran. Nate carried his long knife sheathed on his hip.

Twenty-five Parisian blocks later, we came to a stop. No police or Spectavi surrounded the modern apartment building with eight floors of mirrored windows. Deciding against the wide revolving entrance, I cautiously pulled open a smaller side door and peeked inside. At the center of the predominantly steel-colored lobby was a vacant reception desk with two elevators to its left. I went in, and Nate followed.

We checked behind the desk and found a man lying in a puddle of blood on the floor. His wounds appeared to be recent and from a knife.

"Looks like the place," Nate said.

I drew my sword, went to the elevators, and hit the up arrow. Nothing happened, and I tried again with the same result.

To the left, Nate ripped open the locked door to the stairs. "After you."

Silence filled the concrete stairwell. I led the way, carrying my sword and trying not to make too much noise. We climbed and climbed, until near the eighth floor, a dull scream came from above us. I continued to the top of the stairwell.

A scream beyond a door to the roof sounded like, "No!"

I drove my shoulder into the door, then darted left while Nate went right. Ten feet from a narrow swimming pool, I stood ready with my blade. Greenish light came from underwater at the end of the pool and from regularly spaced glowing squares at the base of the two-foot high wall surrounding the roof.

Standing on the wall to my left, halfway down the pool, a Sanguan held a middle-aged woman dressed in nothing but a nightgown. She sobbed while staring in the direction of the

Eiffel tower, instead of at the city street below. David Sartori stood next to them, along with two other Sanguans. Farther down, Caleb sat on the wall, looking terrified and upset, with David's fourth Sanguan holding him by the shoulder. At Caleb's feet lay the motionless bodies of a man and two children, I assumed Mr. Leconte and the rest of his family.

"Stop this!" I shouted.

David turned to us. "Who are you?"

"Let her go!"

The French woman sobbed. "'Come to my home from the north… no, come from the east.' Please let me go. I already told you, I don't know what it means. None of us did. Please!"

The Sanguan holding her let go, and David pushed her off the roof.

"Ayee!" she screamed.

I darted toward David, but had to slow down when the nearest bodyguard came at me with a long knife. I ducked under his swing and slashed back, clean through his midsection, cutting him in two.

"… yeeee…" *Splat.*

I ran to the edge. The woman's body lay sprawled on the pavement. Nate rushed over to me.

David took a few steps back. "She had to die." He appeared confused. "He told me she had to."

"*Who* told you?" I asked.

"God," David said.

Caleb tried to stand, but the Sanguan who held him pushed him back down.

David pointed at his brother. "Did he tell you where to find me?"

"What are you after?" I asked, hoping when I rushed the bodyguards, Nate would have the sense to go after David.

"The cross that God's son suffered and died for us on. Men have been afraid of its power for too long." David's momentum built. "We live in fear of vampires, *powerless* to fight them, but we need not lead such a pathetic existence. There is hope!" He slammed his right fist into his other palm. "Our only hope is to use it. It took my father until his slow, agonizing end to realize that we should act, that he should have acted years ago." He shook his head. "I didn't want to kill anyone, and I don't want to kill anyone else, but I have to. After a few more, I will find the True Cross, and a holy rain will wash the vampires from the earth."

"*That* cross started all this," I said. "Whatever it *was*, it's evil, and it will only bring more evil."

"You're scared, like everyone else. But I have heard God's will. He speaks to me even now. He tells me you will not leave this roof alive."

I stepped toward him. "It's not God you hear."

Two streaks of black shot out from the stairwell. My heart sank.

"Vera, what a pleasant surprise." Caterine stood at her sister's side between David's group and Nate and me. She pulled her katana from her back.

The ghostly pale twins wore stiletto boots under leather pants and sleeveless leather tops with red trim. Tight ponytails kept their long hair out of their faces.

Ariane drew her identical sword. "Who's your friend?"

The Sanguan holding Caleb jumped off the roof with him. Another lifted David and did the same, followed by the last of his bodyguards.

"Lausanne!" Caleb yelled as they fell. "Tomorrow!"

"Finally," I called to the twins. "I've been waiting for this."

They turned to me. I'd rather have David on the trail of the Cross than the ancient demons seeking it, aided by all he knew. While I had battled them frequently in my mind, I set a more realistic goal on that roof than in those dreams. With luck, Nate and I would last a few minutes to give David a head start, and then we would flee.

Ariane showed me her fangs and pointed her blade at me. "You've been waiting? We've been craving… no, salivating for the night Nanny Victoria wasn't around to help you."

"What about you, Ariane?" I spun my sword once. "Big sis still protecting you?"

Ariane tilted her head and squinted for a moment before charging me.

Tyn! I blocked a lightning-quick cut while Caterine rushed after Nate, who had darted away. He blocked her blow with his knife, then retreated again.

Tyn! I blocked a low cut from Ariane. *Tyn!* She swung so hard! *Fsswht.* She sliced into my arm, but not deep. *Tyn!* I blocked high, then swung low. The opening had vanished. *Tyn!* Ariane blocked and resumed her offensive. *Tyn! Tyn-tyn!* I blocked and blocked and, out of the corner of my eye, saw Nate under siege from Caterine. Blood dripped from his side. He raced from place to place, but his knife was short, and her strength was taking a toll on him.

"Nate, get out of here!" *Fsshwt!* "Ah!" Blood spilled from a gash in my side.

Ariane smiled. "Fear not. I will end you before you have to see your friend die."

"Agh!" Nate stumbled from a slash to his leg. "You go, Erin. Run!"

Tyn! I blocked Ariane's mighty strike, then darted right. She came at me, and instead of preparing for her attack, I ran toward the pool. She swung and missed as I leapt across the water to Nate.

Tyn! Caterine met my blade.

"Run, Nate!"

Fsshwt! Ariane sliced high on the back of my left leg. *Thwack!* Caterine kicked me across the face, sending me flying into the pool. Sword in hand, I fell backward, and a growing plume of red-stained water obstructed my view. My rear end hit the bottom, and then my head did.

With a weak left leg, I pushed off with my right and leapt up, landing across the pool from the twins. Caterine held Nate, withdrew her fangs, and passed him to her sister. He tried to break free until Ariane wrapped her arms around him and bit into the other side of his neck. I focused on the sound of his slowing heartbeat.

Dripping wet, I looked eight stories down, and then back to Nate. His heart stopped, and I jumped to the street.

Screee! A car lurched to a stop in front of me.

I sheathed my sword, ignored my pain, and sprinted with a limp.

I ran five blocks before checking behind me—no twins. I began zigzagging away from the penthouse, and ten blocks later checked again—still no tail. Across the street, a man strummed a guitar with an open case in front of him. I rushed over, pushed him against the building, and with his guitar pinned between us, sank my fangs into his neck. *Dammit, Nate! Why didn't you run?* I gulped, sucked hard, and felt myself healing. Tears slid down my cheeks. *Why didn't you run?*

I tore my fangs away and wiped my face with my arm.

Breathing heavily, wet from my embrace and steaming hot, the man slumped low against the wall. I resumed my sprint with no limp.

———————————

Two hours later, on a bench on the hill of Montmartre, I sat with Hayden, looking out at Paris's expansive skyline. Not far below, men, women, and a few vampires chatted outside restaurants. The mortals sipped on wine and other late-night drinks. I had changed into dry clothes in my rental car.

I tapped my sheathed sword, which rested against my leg. "I should have done better."

"You did well enough," Victoria said from behind me. "You are alive and had the sense to run."

I stood. "I left my friend." I had briefly explained the night's events when we picked a place to meet. I hadn't mentioned how worried I was about Caleb.

Hayden got up. "Victoria."

"Hayden." She nodded. "Erin, you couldn't have saved him. You know that, so let it go."

"I shouldn't have brought him with me."

Victoria remained steady. "He didn't flee because he didn't want to leave you. He made his choice."

He had proven to be a true friend, and I had failed him. Maybe we both should have run from the outset. But I would have hated not even trying to keep those fiends off David's trail.

Victoria continued, "Are you ready to tell me what's going on?"

I looked around. "Do you think here's safe?"

"You said the twins would be on their way to Lausanne, Switzerland?"

"Probably."

"Then here is fine." She sat on the end of the bench. I chose the middle.

Hayden glanced at her, then me. He had said he'd meet with her, but clearly didn't trust her as I did. "I'm good standing."

"Fine." I scooted over to the end. "Ahmose told us the story of how Caterine and Ariane came to be the first vampires. The twins got sick and lingered that way for years, just like Edmond said. But he wasn't alone at their side. His younger brother, Nicolas, who was the priest in Chartres, watched over them, as well. Nicolas urged his siblings to keep their faith, but after months of bedridden pain, the twins asked Edmond to end their lives. He wouldn't, but he couldn't watch them suffer, so he left them with Nicolas."

I had their full attention. "Every day that the twins didn't heal, Nicolas suffered his own pain, wondering why God would torment his sisters. He began hearing a voice in his head. Two and a half years after they grew ill, a True Cross fragment…" Victoria tilted her head skyward. Hayden crossed his arms. "… was said to have healed a similarly ill woman, and then been given as a gift to the bishop in Paris."

I filled them in on the rest of the tale, including what Caleb had told me and the events since I had returned to Europe. "So it seems David is after the Cross for his reasons, while the twins want it for their own. I don't like the idea of either succeeding in finding it." I imagined the twins' bodies wrapped in empowering fire, and then tried to picture the flames of Hell all over the world. "Who wrote *Figli del Diavolo*?"

"A Sanguan in Rome," Victoria answered.

"The passage about hope and the red rain, is it true? Could the rain David intends to cause actually bring about that hell?"

"Who knows?" Victoria shrugged. "It may be fiction, the creation of an imaginative immortal. Or it may be something else entirely."

Investigating that sounded time-consuming and unlikely to lead to anything definitive, so I moved on. "Do the two clues we have mean anything to you? 'Come to the meadow, to the forest.' 'Come to my home from the north… no, come from the east.'"

"There are meadows and forests everywhere," Hayden said. "North, east, that doesn't help either."

"I bet it's in Europe," Victoria said.

What had she read in the clues that I hadn't? "Why?"

"European families hiding a relic that was in Europe during the Merovingian dynasty… it's a hunch, nothing more."

"Do either of you have any idea who's in Lausanne?" I asked.

"Lots of people," Hayden said. "But no idea who David's after."

"But we know where, most likely," Victoria said. "There's a ball tomorrow night. The Martineau family puts it on each year."

"A *ball?*" I asked, stunned at the thought.

"A masked ball." Hayden uncrossed his arms. "*La Masquerade.* Humans and vampires, mingling and dancing, kissing and quick bites—I've been. You never know who you're talking to or whose blood you're about to taste. It was fun."

Victoria added, "Whether it's a Martineau or someone else, David must know they'll be at the ball."

"Surely David will find them another way, since Caleb screamed out his plan," I said.

Victoria shook her head. "I don't think we can assume that. With the last two, David knew the specific family he had to go after. In this case, it seems David does not know his target's identity so precisely. Perhaps it's one of a few brothers or their wives, who share a family name. People come to the ball from all over the world, and my guess is that David will be unwilling to pass up the opportunity of having them all in one place."

"Then what do we do?" I looked at Victoria. "Can you cancel the event?"

"Perhaps," she said. "The Swiss government will not be pushed around by the Spectavi, but Madame and Monsieur Martineau might like to know that they or one of their guests are in danger."

"Exactly," I said.

Victoria continued, "But I don't think informing either is the wise course of action. I think the ball is an opportunity for *us*."

"What?"

"There is no complete guest list for the event," she explained. "Half will arrive unannounced and uninvited. David has the advantage because he knows what family he's looking for and apparently that they are likely to attend the ball. If the event does not take place, questioning the hosts may not reveal who we seek."

"So? What? We go ourselves, roll the dice, and hope we find them first?" I couldn't believe what she was suggesting.

"Yes. If the ball is canceled, we're left without the last clue. In *that* case, we're rolling the dice in hopes we find David before the twins do or that we come across the clue another way. It seems a long shot that we would. If we attend the event, we're taking a calculated risk. We know David will be there with his bodyguards. I imagine Caterine and Ariane will also be present."

"Hell on Earth," I reminded her.

"You're scared," she remarked.

"Of course! Just like I'm scared of the twins being any *more* powerful. Aren't *you* scared?"

"No. I do not look forward to either outcome." She

pulled her black chain necklace over her head, kissed the red cross that hung from it, then grasped it tightly. "But at the moment, I am relieved. For eight hundred years, I have battled those two. Others fought them before me. What I fear is the twins on the loose, doing as they please, while I am blind to their true aim. We were very nearly so blind. Only out of curiosity did you befriend Caleb Sartori. On a hunch, you went in search of an ancient who had fallen off the face of the earth. In a bout of bloodlust, you stumbled across that ancient's whereabouts. Whether it is God's will or dumb luck that we know what we do and have this chance, I cannot say. But I count myself fortunate to have the chance."

The old vampire had a point. "Do you think God would do it?" I asked. "Do you think he'd cause Hell on Earth over the actions of one man?"

She rubbed her cross with her thumb. "I do not know. My heart tells me that the Lord would not end the world as we know it because of one man's murders. But my mind tells me not to presume to understand how the Almighty operates. After all, He alone knows why we are immortal in the first place."

"We can't let them get to the Cross first," I said.

"We won't." Victoria looked at her cross. "And if we do, we'll take it back, like Edmond did, twice before."

18

I awoke to an email from Zhilan:

Everything is set for tomorrow in San Francisco. When it is over, we will post video of the event, our explanation, and detailed science of how it was done. Then, we shall see what happens.

I pictured Spectavi obediently marching themselves onto the Golden Gate Bridge, then following a lab-engineered command to set themselves on fire. Unfortunately, with the time difference, it would be daytime for me soon after nightfall in California. Even if I didn't have my own task at hand, I probably wouldn't get an opportunity to see the first news reports.

La Masquerade. I couldn't believe that with Houjin's plan in motion, the True Cross near to being found, and so soon after my friend's death, I was preparing for a *ball*. I recalled the gala in the underground cathedral at Eure, where I had clung to Edmond's arm, scared, naïve, and weak. I pushed the memories away. Hayden would arrive by limo in a few minutes for our twenty-mile ride. Victoria would be joining us later.

S.M. PERLOW

At her instruction, I had covered my arms, shoulders, hands, and face—all of my exposed skin—in pale white makeup. Everyone at the ball would do the same to help hide their identities. Peach lipstick and blush kept me from looking perfectly white. My floor-length black gown had a high collar that hid my cross tattoo. I wore sandals with high heels. My black mask had feline cutouts for my eyes and didn't run as narrow over my nose as some of the others I had seen.

At my bathroom mirror, I hooked a dangling steel earring through my ear. The chestnut brown wig I had chosen was nearly the same length my hair used to be— straight down to the middle of my back. I looked as I might in a few hundred years, with skin naturally so pale—if I lived that long. I put in my other earring.

Victoria had rejected my idea of filling the ball with planted people. As soon as David's Sanguans drank from one of them, they'd learn of the setup and leave. We had to let the event go on and hope one of us would be the first to drink from whoever had the final clue. Failing that, we would follow David and the twins when they left, so our secondary objective was to figure out who among the masked they were.

I trusted Victoria and reluctantly understood why she considered the ball a fortunate opportunity. That I hadn't heard from Caleb worried me immensely. So much was at stake in such unfamiliar territory. My sword rested against my coffin and would have to remain there, but at least my gown was loose enough that my knife and cell phone strapped to my thigh weren't easily noticeable.

The highest point of Hayden's black mask reached the middle of his forehead, its lowest, his nose. The cloth tapered narrower to over his ears, where it wrapped around his head. He wore a black tuxedo with a bowtie, like almost every other male—mortal or immortal—in the huge, already crowded ballroom.

The event began at midnight, and soon after, we descended wide steps on a narrow red carpet at the entrance. Thick ivory columns lined the long walls with thin, vertical strips of gold filling the space between them. Chandeliers sparkled under a vaulted roof. Old portraits of kings, queens, lords, and vampires and paintings of coronations, battles, and world-changing happenings hung throughout.

Near us, over loud, but refreshingly classical music, humans held drinks while they conversed, some at high round tables that dotted the wood floor. Hayden had indicated that English would be the dominant language for uniformity. At the far end of the room, a small group of couples danced gracefully to the elegant music a DJ played from an elevated platform in the corner. The DJ wore a red frock coat, a long, white, curly wig, and sunglasses. Just then, his song's violins, horns, and piano faded to silence, and each couple kissed, bit, or both.

The women's dress ranged from short cocktail attire leaving white painted legs exposed, to long evening and ball gowns with hoop skirts. Some masks were simple like mine, in black or colored to match their costume, while others had intricate designs and dramatic flowers, ribbons, and feathers attached. Men's masks varied from those like Hayden's to solid shields in gold, silver, or white covering the tops of foreheads down to upper lips.

Hayden had matted his typically spiked hair. I imagined many of the women, and even some men, wore wigs. Looking out at everyone, I had guesses as to who was mortal and who was immortal, but unless I caught a glimpse of fangs, I couldn't be certain.

In stark contrast to the pounding music of Sanguan clubs, but fitting with the colorful ballroom, strings and woodwinds began the next song.

"Have you fed tonight?" Hayden asked.

"No."

"Good. Be quick with them, but not so quick you cause a scene and give us away. Call if you find anything."

It made perfect sense to split up to cover more ground, but I hadn't been looking forward to it. "Will do."

Hayden disappeared into the crowd. I scanned left and right, expecting Victoria's large frame to give her away if she had already arrived, and considered again why someone holding such an important piece of information would put themselves in a room with so many vampires. I accepted the same conclusion as before: not knowing what their clues hid and only having a piece of the riddle, the individuals and families couldn't grasp the importance of their secret.

Loud laughter overpowered the music for a moment. The ballroom wasn't my preferred battleground, but it was going to be one of the most important battles of my life. Short, sharp violin strokes came in succession. It was time to get to work. I made my way toward a few high tables in front of the bar to my right.

A male with brown hair and a simple black strip of a mask came near. "Madame, good evening."

"Good evening." I tried hard to sound genuine. His scent and heartbeat hinted human, but surrounded by so many other bodies, I wasn't certain.

He motioned to the bar. "Would you care for a drink?" His fangs appeared rather dull.

"No, thanks." I tapped my tongue against my two sharpest teeth, so he could see.

"Ah, then perhaps a drink?" He extended his wrist.

An unhealed bite mark revealed itself as his arm extended out of his shirtsleeve, and I figured it out. I wouldn't have normally gone for someone wearing fake fangs, but it was not the night to be picky. I took his wrist in my left hand and wrapped my other arm around his back so he wouldn't fall. The first drops of his mortal blood showed me when he had put the plastic imitations in his mouth. In his eight previous years at the ball, he had been tricked by vampires who drank wine, liquor, or champagne to throw off those they approached. He wore the fangs in an attempt at a similar deception.

I found no riddle or clue anything like the other two, so I let him go and continued toward the bar. The sip had been quick, and the sight of my next targets fueled my craving for more. At the end of the short line for beverages, a female in a yellow ball gown tensed at the touch of my fingers on her bare upper back. Her male companion turned to me as she did.

"Perhaps a drink, before your drink?" I asked, sliding my hand across her soft skin.

She gulped. "Yes." She had a slight accent.

I pushed aside her long golden locks and found her neck unmarked. Moving close, pushing into her skirt, I spoiled the white painted flesh. *Mm*, I heard while sipping. She was terrified. Not of me specifically, but of the entire event. Danish and married for a year, she wanted to make her husband happy, so at his urging, she had gone to her first Sanguan club with him six months earlier. Attending the ball was her present for his birthday.

I withdrew my fangs and moved her hair forward to cover the mark I had left. She didn't have the clue.

Her husband had already rolled up his sleeve. I took his forearm and brought his wrist to my mouth. He loved vampire bites—the rush of heat, the waves of joy, and most of all, the time apart from the cares of his life for as long as the drinking continued.

I opened my eyes and watched her catching her breath, watching him intently.

He loved his wife so much for going to clubs with him and for the birthday gift. I loved experiencing the differences in what they felt for each other, then discovering why. I let go of his wrist. I missed June and Zack. The man grinned from ear to ear while leading his wife to the bar.

A male voice behind me yelled, "I won't do it again! I swear!"

The music stopped, and all eyes went to two maskless vampires in trench coats forcing a guest out the main entrance.

"I swear!" he yelled again with the barrel of a pistol pressed into his spine.

Hayden had warned me about there being zero tolerance for overaggressiveness at the ball. If it was a vampire, he had probably drunk without asking or from someone who had declined.

As if pouncing on the moment, two females in slinky, red satin dresses descended the stairs at the entrance. A single strap covered the left shoulder of each twin, and a slit ran from high on their right thighs down to their ankles. Their red eyes shone from under their glossy black masks. Each wore a thick, glittering diamond bracelet and double strings of the same stone for earrings. With their blond hair tightly up, I couldn't tell them apart. They darted into the crowd, then stopped and had their first drinks. Cheers rose, and they raced the rest of the way to the front of the room. High-pitched whistles of a recorder heralded the return of the music, with the string section not far behind. The twins joined the line of women in the lively dance, and two males shot from the crowd to be their partners.

Hopefully, whoever had the last clue wasn't in that part of the room. The two had made quite an entrance, but I had actually been expecting more—a grander spectacle, or perhaps outlandish attire. Regardless, I really wished Victoria would show up.

A male in a shiny silver mask that covered most of his face approached. He flashed small, sharp fangs.

"No, thanks," I said. It didn't take long for him to find his way to the neck of a nearby man, who melted at the vampire's bite.

I surveyed the crowd. Some men and women ended up in the arms of the immortals they had come for, and others found humans offering kisses that ranged from pecks to passionate. An apparently universal thrill for each new encounter pervaded. No one jumped out as being David or one of his bodyguards, not that I could have easily distinguished them—unless they traveled as a pack. I decided to start checking for any sign of such movement in the recent memories of those I drank from.

I headed across the room in the direction of the opposite bar and noticed a low arched entrance to a hallway on the left. Dark wooden paneling ran on the lower half of the walls, with forest green painted on top. Just inside a room on the right, a vampire pressed a woman against the wall, slurping from her neck. Far ahead, a black gate blocked the way. Before the barricade, an old wooden door was ajar. Through the opening, I saw two male vampires and two women sharing drinks from each other on an antique couch. I continued down the hall to the iron gate and wrapped my hands around the bars. More hallway lay ahead to a corner I couldn't see beyond. I pushed a little and had no doubt I could tear down the obstruction if need be. I made my way back out to the ball.

Fingertips ran across my bare right shoulder. "Hello there," a deep voice said.

I turned to a tall, imposing male, whose golden mask left his forehead and chiseled jaw uncovered. "Hello."

"Care to dance?" he asked with a British accent.

Having not seen any fangs, I moved closer. "I'm not here to dance."

The visible parts of his face remained steady. "Why, then?"

I slid the back of my fingers from his masked cheek down to his firm neck. "You know why."

"I do. For a dance, you may."

I could hear his heart pounding louder than the music, yet outwardly he kept his cool. Impressive, but I pushed his hand off me. "I don't have time."

"You're looking for someone," he said.

How did he know? Did he really know?

He added, "It might be me."

I glanced toward the front of the room. "I don't know how to dance to this."

"It's easy." He put out his white painted hand. "Follow my lead and mimic the others who know the steps. You're fast enough."

He was, of course, correct. I took his hand, and we made our way through the crowd. While he appeared stoic, his heart raced faster. The song ended. We stepped onto the dance floor as Caterine and Ariane selected new partners—humans, I thought. The twins paid no attention to me as they took their places at the opposite end of a line of ten females. When a violin and piano sounded, the male line bowed, and I did a subtle curtsey to copy the females next to me.

Violin strokes came faster, forward we all went, and then I held my partner's outstretched hands while we spun. I let him bring my left hand above us and took his back with my right, as he did mine. I couldn't believe I had curtsied. And

I never knew what step would come next, but had no trouble keeping up.

We stopped and, back in line, the female beside me moved around me, while her partner circled mine. Mine nodded at me.

To light notes of a piano, we came toward each other, and I held his solid body closer while we spun some more. He took my hand, and we headed up the floor. Across the circle of couples, the red-eyed twins appeared obsessed with their prey-to-be. I focused on mine, picturing him with no mask. If nothing else, I would enjoy my drink.

We twirled individually as we circled, which felt strange—no, silly—then ended up back in our lines, before a step forward led to a close embrace while the warm melody continued. I couldn't have done it all night, but the dance was something fresh, and after a twirl, when I found myself wishing my partner would crack a smile, I realized the fun of such a thing shared with someone so fresh. We held each other tight when a long violin stroke ended the song.

My partner brought my hand over his pounding heart. "You were wonderful." His soft lips caressed my neck, and while I leaned toward his, I wondered, but no pricks came at my skin.

I kissed him twice before sinking my fangs into his neck. Hot, thick, rich—his blood didn't disappoint. Strong, confident, powerful—the football striker didn't disappoint, until he did completely. I sucked more, but already knew he did not have the clue. I withdrew my fangs.

He opened his eyes. "Perhaps another dance later?"

"Perhaps."

He nodded and retreated toward the rear of the ballroom.

A rolling drumbeat started, the dim lights darkened, and the area began filling much more densely than before. I moved off to the side while an electric guitar sounded, and the growing crowd bobbed. After the first vocals of the night gave way to louder drums and guitar, the bobbing progressed to jumping, and the transition to punk music was complete.

The twins adapted and would certainly have no trouble maintaining their energy for the half hour before club music started. I wondered if any mortals had guessed the twins' true identities or merely flocked to the identical pair who were happy to drink from any who came near.

While the punk rock was more my kind of music, I had other priorities. I walked down another hallway where a couple sat against the wall, eyes closed, resting—perhaps weary from loss of blood. I found two side rooms and reasoned that David might have been hiding in one. Out in the ballroom, all he knew would have been up for grabs if he were to be bitten. I checked the rooms, but found nothing interesting. I decided to check all the hallways, repeatedly if necessary.

On my way back, a male approached me. Vampire, I guessed, then recognized Hayden.

"Erin." He lifted his mask momentarily with both hands and raised his voice over the music. "You find anything?"

"Not yet. You?"

"No clue. And no obvious glimpses of David or his

bodyguards in any memories. A few potential candidates, but they'd be hard to re-locate in the crowd."

"Right," I said. "At least Caterine and Ariane are still here. They must not have found anything yet, either."

"Yup."

"Have you seen Victoria?"

He shook his head. "No. You sure she'll show? That we can trust her?"

"I think so." I crossed my arms.

Hayden tilted his head, and I imagined a hidden eyebrow raising.

"I do, really." She had never lied to me or misled me since my time at Eure... I didn't think she had, anyway.

"Okay," Hayden said, and we headed out of the hallway.

In the ballroom, I drank from the first man who approached. He felt so good to hold that I ran my hand through his long hair and took far more blood than necessary to find out he had no useful information.

Back up front, I watched the crowd give the twins more space than anyone else. The pair used it, jumping, twisting, and contorting their bodies to the rapid beats, sometimes in inhuman ways at inhuman speeds. They held each other for half a song, then one pulled a male's shirt collar down and chomped into his neck. The total calmness that shot over his face gave him away as human. She passed him to her sister. After her drink, he stumbled away, and two immortals raced to dance near the twins. One of the males came close for a sip, but was rebuffed and had to settle for the feel of the most ancient, rock-hard skin, instead of the taste of the most ancient blood.

A hand on my shoulder caused me to turn to the same vampire as before—I was fairly confident—with a silver mask and a thick head of jet-black hair.

"No," I said. Visions of my time in Rome with Nate raced to mind, and I added softly, "But thank you."

He moved on. If we all survived, perhaps I'd come to another ball and be more cavalier about whom I drank from. I headed back toward the entrance.

At a high table, a male wearing a simple mask put a lowball glass full of ice down when I came near. "Hello, beautiful," he said with an accent that I guessed was Japanese.

I crossed my arms. "Is that the best you can do?"

He chuckled. "You're right." He motioned around the room. "All these painted faces will become a muddled memory before long. But your emerald eyes will haunt me after this night. I should like to know if I am to be haunted by a woman or an immortal."

"Better." I reached for his wrist.

He stopped me, loosened his bowtie, and undid his top shirt button. I used both hands to separate his collar, then bit.

Li's blood told me he had spent the night before with a woman far younger than his wife. It started with drinks at a high-end lounge, then quickly escalated in his hotel room. I considered sucking the jerk dry, but after a huge gulp, ripped out my fangs.

He needed both hands on the table for support.

I slapped him across his face. "Be true to your wife or get divorced."

He huffed. I walked past him. He knew full well he had betrayed her expectations for their marriage.

A tall female in a deep blue ball gown approached from near the bar. Long, matching gloves reached high up her arms, and three white feather plumes sprouted from the side of her blue mask, hiding most of her brown hair's high bun.

"Thank you," she said when close enough not to have to yell. A blue ribbon choker adorned with a large diamond in the front wrapped around her smooth white neck.

"For what?"

Her eyes shifted toward my last drink. "I saw that. He must have deserved it." Her sharp fangs told me she was a vampire.

"Yeah," I admitted.

"A drink?"

"Oh, no… thank you, though."

"Please? Everyone here is so spineless, the men and women grazing, ready to be sucked from, the vampires aimlessly doing the sucking. Each year, I search for the few who aren't so weak. I haven't found many tonight." She touched my arm.

I tensed, imagining the taste of her luscious, inhuman blood. She ran her hands over my shoulders and down to my back, then tilted her head to the right.

"What's your name?" I asked.

She pulled me a step closer and straightened her neck. "No names here." The blue in her eyes flared.

What was I scared of? What would it be, a few seconds? I reached for the back of her choker. My fingers found the chain clasp, which I undid. "Just a quick bite." I held the blue ribbon and focused on her pristine neck while wrapping my arms around her waist. I chose my spot.

"As you wish," she whispered.

I felt two pricks in my shoulder. *Black!* She sucked, and the darkest black I had ever known poured through me. My fangs pierced her hard neck. *Red!* Boiling blood filled my void. The pure red gave way to a violent mixture of orange, red, and black flames. She sucked harder—*black!*—nothingness—I sucked hard—*red!*—sweet, perfect red.

She withdrew her fangs, and I followed suit.

"Thank you," she said, taking her choker from my hand.

I nodded as the fang marks in her neck closed. She walked away. That suffocating black was gone, I assured myself. I glanced at my healing shoulder and gulped. Why hadn't I pulled out more of the sweet red? I watched her disappear into the crowd.

I closed my eyes and remembered the red, then the total black. I shuddered. I couldn't dwell on that. But it hadn't taken long. It was no big deal.

On the way to the last hallway leading from the ballroom, I drank from a short man. Intense memories of the vampire drink I had just finished distracted me, so it took longer than it should have to determine he didn't know the last clue and hadn't seen anything useful.

The hallway was like the others—from the arched entrance to the rooms filled with Sanguans feeding on humans to an identical metal gate. I was turning to go back to the ballroom when a sweaty, wiry man with bright blue hair stumbled near, reeking of alcohol. Red splotches stained his loosened white collar.

"Another bite?" I asked, amused at how far my standards had fallen.

"Yeah!" He wrapped his arms around me and kissed my cheek.

I bit while forcing his arms away. No clue. Lots of dancing since the classical music ended. Lots of bites. He had noticed two males disappearing behind the DJ on two separate occasions, then the same thing a third time with a third male. I stopped drinking. Sergei tried to kiss me. I pushed him, and his alcohol-impaired balance left him crashing to the floor.

I ran out of the hallway, then rushed through the crowd to the front of the ballroom, where the twins' dancing hadn't slowed. The DJ bobbed away up on his platform. Behind him, for the first time, I made out the folds of a dark curtain. I had missed a hallway. I kept watch on the twins while casually making my way to the side wall. No one appeared to notice as I slid behind the DJ, then parted the curtains just enough to enter the hall.

I didn't see anyone, but the iron gate in the distance was swung open. I crouched low, reached under my gown, and pulled out my knife. With a flick of my thumb, I unfolded the blade.

The first door was closed. I turned the brass lever, pushed open the door, and peered into a dim room with a coffee table and vacant couch. I made my way down the hall to the second door. Light bled from the cracks around it. I turned the handle.

"Mmmm!"

Hearing the muffled scream, I flung open the door and darted in, ready for battle, but found no one to fight. I rushed to the bed, where Caleb's wrists had been handcuffed together around the bars of the headboard. His ankles were bound the same way at the other end. A bitten man in a tuxedo lay beside him, unmoving. I pulled the gray strip of tape off Caleb's mouth.

"Erin," he panted. "David left. He's going to sacrifice himself. He's gone insane."

"Where'd he go? When?" I ripped each ring of Caleb's handcuffs open, then did the same with those at his feet. Bite marks littered his neck, but thank goodness, he was alive.

He sat up and rubbed his wrists. "An hour ago? Maybe. I don't know. I don't know where to."

"An hour!" I heard no heartbeat in the man next to Caleb. "What did he know?"

"'However you speak, come find the peak.'" Caleb looked at the man on the bed. "David made me watch his bodyguards do it. He's crazy. He left me so I could see the 'new world.' What does it mean? What's going to happen?"

"I don't know. Hell on Earth? We have to go. Are you all right?"

He stood. "I'll be fine."

I texted Hayden and Victoria to meet me in the hallway behind the DJ. If Victoria still hadn't arrived, Hayden and I would proceed without her. Caleb followed me out of the room. The vampire in blue that I had drunk from earlier approached from near the curtain.

I closed my knife. "It's not what it looks like."

"I'm fine," Caleb added.

"Are you?" She continued toward us.

Rolling drum beats grew louder as the curtain parted and another female in a hot pink ball gown and matching mask appeared.

Crrnch! The one in blue rammed me into the wall, denting it, and pinned my arms out wide. I got my knife unfolded, but couldn't use it. She had been so fast. Caleb ran, but the other vampire caught him immediately. I tried to push my arms off the wall, but my captor was too strong. I couldn't believe she was so strong!

"Who are you? What do you want?" I yelled.

"All I've ever wanted," the vampire who held me said. "Pain and suffering. Nothing new."

"Pity *he* won't suffer." The one in pink bit, and Caleb's body relaxed.

Ignoring the drumbeats, the whining guitar, and the crowd screaming along with the song in the ballroom, I heard my friend's heart race as sweat seeped from his pores. She sucked, and beads of water slid down his face.

Wielding a thin blade longer than my knife, a vampire in a tux and silver mask shot through the curtains behind the back of the vampire in pink.

"Caterine!" my captor yelled.

The new vampire stabbed into his target. Caterine let go of Caleb and swung an elbow at her attacker, while moving so the blade cut out of her side. Blood spilled, and the vampire in the tuxedo—who appeared to be the one who had approached me twice earlier—grabbed Caterine and threw her against the same wall where I stood. With a blade pressed against her neck, Caterine didn't move. The blood seeping into her gown stopped. Caleb took a few cautious steps away.

"Ariane," I said to the Sanguan holding me.

"Victoria," Caterine named her assailant in the tux.

Ariane said, "Victoria, if you hurt my sister, your beloved Vera will find herself with no arms, and then, no blood."

Victoria removed her mask. "Harm Erin, and your sister will find herself with no head."

I tried to push free, to no avail. Ariane's eyes flared. Contact lenses could apparently change their color, but not hide the bursts of flame.

"David's already gone," I said. "You're too late."

Ariane broke into a smug smile.

My heart sank. "You have the Cross already?"

"We do not." Her eyes blazed blue. "But we've had it before, twice, to no gain. And we've had other bits of that damnable wood. We sacrificed men, women, children, and vampires in its presence and failed enough to realize that it was not the Cross that transformed us, or at least not the Cross *alone*. It was Nicolas and what he did in the name of that *holy* scrap. This time, another weak man will change the world."

Hayden ripped off his mask as he charged into the hallway with his own long knife. He spun when the twin vampires in red followed him with a pair of three-pointed sai in their hands. They stood across from each other, poised to attack.

"God tested Nicolas," Ariane continued. "Who knows why, but *we* suffered until Nicolas failed his test. After Massimo died and his famous son confidently embraced the night, we sent one of ours to see what the boy was up to. Once we found out, we did nothing but protect David from you, so we could watch *him* fail *his* test."

"You're evil," I said, stopping myself from screaming that it was wrong to condemn the earth based on the actions of one horribly misguided man. Those screams would have fallen on deaf ears, and as much as I hated it, God seemed to be the one testing, and David, the man failing.

The twins in red spun their sai. Hayden glanced back and forth between them.

"You're lucky," Ariane said. "I would like to watch the world go to Hell, and I'd like to do so with my sister. Considering our present situation, that means you three also get to watch." She shifted her eyes to Caleb. "And maybe him, too, if he survives."

I looked at him. "Survives?"

One of the red twins stopped her sai spinning and pushed her thumb down on the bottom of a handle. Ariane smiled.

Boom! Boom! Balls of fire enveloped the wall in front of me. Ariane let me go while everything shook. Victoria stabbed forward, but the explosion had cost her the split second that Caterine needed to escape. I shielded my face from the fire with my arm, then peeked under my elbow when Caleb grabbed me. The vampires in red went through the flames, out to the ballroom. Caterine and Ariane rushed down the hall to the open iron gate, with Hayden and Victoria in pursuit.

BOOM! An explosion near the gate sent Victoria and Hayden flying backward. I crouched low, pulling Caleb close. Victoria landed, then disappeared into the flames blocking the way to the main room.

She returned to the hallway a moment later. "This way!"

All the fire… so much fire.

Victoria spoke calmly, "Go fast, Erin. You'll be fine if you go fast."

Vwooosh! The flames surrounding us intensified, consuming the walls and ceiling for fuel.

I let out a long breath, then folded in my knife and put it back under my gown. I stood up with Caleb close and threw my mask and wig to the ground. "Don't let go."

He wrapped his arms around my neck.

I lifted him a little higher. "And don't drag your feet."

He buried his head into my neck. I stared at the fire for a long second, tightened my grip on Caleb, and darted ahead.

Woosh! I was through to the ballroom, with hot flames all around and Hayden beside me. Bodies had been blown apart or had pieces of wall, chandelier, or art on top of them. Some must have fled; a few on the ground struggled.

Boom! Fire burst at the top of the wall to my right. One after another, a series of gold columns crashed to the floor.

Victoria and Hayden darted for the entrance, and holding Caleb close, I followed. When I was almost there—*BOOM!*—a wave of heat lifted me into the air and out of the building. I landed with one knee on the asphalt. A discord of rapid, high-pitched sirens sounded from arriving police cars, ambulances, and fire trucks.

Caleb's eyes met mine. I still clutched him tightly. His clothes had been charred—like my gown—but he appeared otherwise all right. Most vampires were long gone, but people continued to run from the burning building. Victoria, phone at her ear, and Hayden came over to us. Finally, I stood and let Caleb go.

"'However you speak, come find the peak,'" I announced. "The last clue."

"What were the other two?" Hayden asked.

Boom! Another explosion behind us.

Victoria put down her phone. "Helicopter's on its way to get us out of here." She threw her wig to the ground and let down her long hair.

I recited the clues in order. "'Come to the meadow, to the forest.' 'Come to my home from the north… no, come from the east.' 'However you speak, come find the peak.'"

"It's on a mountaintop," Caleb said. "The peak."

"Could be," Hayden agreed. "But there are lots of mountains."

Caleb crossed his arms. "'Come from the north, no, come from the east.' It doesn't make sense now, by air, but if it's been hidden for centuries, maybe it only used to be approachable from those directions?"

I finished typing the combined parts into Google on my phone, but the results didn't help. "'However you speak' has to mean something."

"Different languages," Victoria concluded confidently. "For meadow, forest, north, east, maybe even peak, though that's clearly a reference to a mountain. North is nord, norte, norden, east is est, este, osten." She shook her head. "I could go on, and everywhere has a northern-most or eastern-most mountain."

"Monte Cervino comes to mind," Hayden said thoughtfully. "Cervino is a misspelling in Italian, which is why it stands out. The C should be an S. It's from a word meaning wood or forest. Nearly fifteen thousand feet high. I've been, but haven't climbed—"

"That's it," Victoria said. "It's Matterhorn in German. Matte comes from a word for meadow. It's the same mountain, meadow, and forest, in two different languages."

"'However you speak!'" We had it. Switzerland made sense based on the country's recent history of neutrality. "How far away is it?"

"Sixty, seventy miles, on the Swiss-Italian border."

"That's all?" I looked down the road, past the arriving emergency vehicles—too far to run. "How long by helicopter?"

"Half an hour. But it's pointless, Erin," Victoria said. "It would be better if it were farther so we had more time to catch up to David. With an hour head start, he likely already has the Cross."

Her attitude shocked me. "What if he couldn't figure out the clues? Or can't get to the top of the mountain?"

She didn't answer.

"We can't just give up!" I pleaded.

"You heard Ariane." Victoria sounded defeated. "David failed his test."

Caleb's heavy eyes looked to me. I answered them with resolve. "If we don't try, then we fail ours."

Caleb nodded.

Woosh-woosh-woosh-woosh. A wide military helicopter with a pair of Spectavi pilots up front and banks of rockets on each side landed twenty feet away. I ran to the chopper slowly enough for Caleb to keep up with me. Hayden followed, and then, so did Victoria.

19

Twenty-five minutes into the flight, I sat on the flat metal floor, searching on my phone and trying to think over the noise of the helicopter. Victoria and Hayden sat across from me and Caleb beside me. I glanced at the clear, moonlit sky while a page loaded, then I tapped on a link to an image.

I called over the whooshing of the rotors, "I don't think it's at the top of the mountain."

"Where, then?" Victoria asked.

"Matterhorn's first summit by humans wasn't until 1865. Sometime after that seems kind of recent for the Cross to have been brought there. It struck me as odd, so I thought about the north and east clue. The word 'no' in it is peculiar. 'Come to my home from the north… *no*, come from the east.' Matterhorn's peak has been reached from all directions. Some are more difficult than others, but they're all doable. But it says 'Come to my home.' 'My home' might mean a building, and then a church seemed like a reasonable bet. There's a small chapel in Blatten that had its original, north-facing entranceway walled up in 1704. It's still clearly visible in the pictures. The new entrance is from the east."

"Wow," Caleb said.

Hayden nodded.

Victoria called to the pilot on the left, "Head for Blatten."

Caleb asked, "What do you think will happen if he beats us to the Cross?"

Pure red flashed to mind, and then the mixture of reds, oranges, and blacks I had seen when drinking from Ariane. I imagined D.C. burning first, then my neighborhood and up the hill to Zhilan's.

The copilot turned to us. "That's it down there. We'll be on the ground in a minute."

I stood and squinted through the front windshield to find the narrow white building with an arched front entrance below a brown triangular roof. Patches of rock and high grass surrounded the modest chapel.

WoooOOOSH. The helicopter's nose tilted up high, sending me falling against the back of the cabin. As we leveled out, the pilot halted our approach, and I saw a bright red beam out the front windshield. I stood and traced the red down to a hole in the roof of the chapel. Our helicopter made the only noise.

"Keep going!" I yelled.

The pilots looked at Victoria. She nodded. "Go."

The beam turned orange as we got closer. It became black for a moment, blacker than the rest of the night, and then it was red. Waves of orange and black mixed in. Glowing flames flared beyond the constraints of the beam.

The furious blaze rose high, ending in a raging fireball.

Low wailing sounded, followed by long moans and piercing shrieks. On the ball's rolling, bubbling surface, screaming faces with horns, flapping reptilian wings, and sharp talons morphed from one state to another, and again to flame. Chained bodies, dark stallions, deformed skulls—the images oozed over and into the ball. We were too late. Red would rain.

We began our descent to the chapel yard, and the beam and fireball disappeared and silenced, all at once. I blinked, and they were still gone. The only evidence they had ever existed was the hole in the roof.

Caleb rushed to the helicopter door. He slid it open and leapt out when we were still ten feet off the ground. "David!"

Victoria, Hayden, and I raced ahead of Caleb. Inside, David lay motionless, his body facedown over the simple altar. A small scrap of wood hung around a statue of Mary carrying the child Jesus.

"David!" Caleb called again, running past us. He stopped when he got to his brother's body.

Hayden joined him at the altar and put his hand on Caleb's shoulder. "He's gone. I'm sorry."

Caleb wiped tears from his face. He pointed at the statue. "Is that it?"

"I think so," I said.

While Caleb lifted the string over Mary's head, I inspected the scene at the altar. A bowl of water—possibly holy—was deep red. David's cut wrists hung inches from it. I looked at the ceiling; the red beam had probably shone from the bowl.

Victoria stood in the far corner of the chapel, pointing down. "It was here."

We surrounded a hole in the broken floor of the northeast corner of the building. Inside an opened, thick iron box, the glass of a wood-framed case had been shattered.

Caleb handed me the Cross. "What do we do with it?"

My first instinct was not to touch it, but I would have regretted missing the chance, so I took it from him. It was such a little thing—physically. A few inches of old wood. "I think we should destroy it." I handed it to Hayden.

He studied it for a moment, tilting his head to the side. "Fine with me." He held it out for Victoria.

Her reluctance surprised me, but she eventually took the relic. "Jesus was nailed to this wood, unless it is a fake. We could run tests to try to find out. No matter what, it holds some special power." She looked up at us. "Or it doesn't, and Nicolas and David were all that mattered."

Victoria slowly exited the chapel. I almost ran after her, but held my ground as she stopped and stared skyward. After a few moments, she called to the pilots, then walked back to us. "Come. They will build a fire. We'll burn it right here."

The helicopter blades stopped, and the two Spectavi got out and went into the brush to collect sticks for kindling.

We all joined them, and a minute later, with the help of a Spectavi lighter and tinder, we had a small fire on the dirt path. No one spoke while we stood in a circle, watching flames consume the first twigs. One pilot added larger pieces of wood. The fire didn't strike the same terror as the blaze in Lausanne, but I found myself scooting closer to Caleb regardless.

With loud crackling and popping, the bigger logs caught. Victoria handed Caleb the Cross. "I cannot bring myself to do it."

He took it and stepped forward. "I'm sorry for what my brother did." He shook his head. "If it matters." He chucked the Cross into the fire.

Caleb came back to stand beside me and watched with the rest of us as the ancient shard of wood lit. Flame engulfed the relic, and it shrank for a few seconds until it was gone.

"When will it rain?" Caleb asked. "And what will happen?"

"I do not know," Victoria answered.

With his eyes on the fire, Caleb took my hand. I squeezed his. Spectavi, Sanguan, human, none of us knew what was to come.

20

At a little after ten the next night, I stepped off the last stair in my basement, threw my backpack to the floor, and leaned my sword against my desk. My coffin lay exactly where I had left it. I wasn't physically weary from traveling—my body didn't work that way anymore—but mentally, I was exhausted. I was also quite thirsty, and thirsty for someone in particular.

I hadn't seen or heard of any red-colored rain. No blood had fallen from the sky. Caleb hadn't noticed anything, nor had Hayden, Zhilan, Grant, or Houjin on the west coast. I had been in close contact with Victoria, who was helping organize a cover up that would blame Sanguans in Europe for David's death and his murders. With all the resources of the Spectavi at her disposal, she had found no red rain either. We didn't know exactly what we were looking for, but it hadn't seemed to have happened yet.

In San Francisco, instead of reporting to work, ten Spectavi—office workers and guards—assembled half of a mile from the Golden Gate Bridge. Five drove their own cars, two took motorcycles, and three stole cars to make the trip. When the last arrived, they marched to the bridge, where confused motorists slowed to avoid them. Halfway across, the Spectavi stopped two cars and forcibly removed the passengers. The vampires pushed the vehicles to the side of the bridge and, using small explosives, set them ablaze. One at a time, ignoring the shouts of horrified onlookers, the Spectavi walked into the fires. Each took only a few seconds to burn to ash before another followed to die.

The Spectavi denied all claims that their synthetic blood could have been responsible for the events and blamed a small group of dissidents in their ranks. As expected, from the oldest to the youngest, no Spectavi furor arose over the incident—at least not a public one. Thankfully, Victoria never asked me about it.

But people *were* asking the President and leaders all over the world. Roughly half of Americans didn't believe the Sanguan explanation for what had happened. Those that did were sharply divided between being outraged at the Spectavi and accepting their tactics as necessary. If change was going to be forced upon the Spectavi, it would have to come from the top.

———————

Jonathan answered the door and turned around. "It's for you." He returned to the couch and the TV, and I entered the apartment.

Luke got up. "Hey, baby."

I hadn't told him I was back. "Hey."

We met halfway, embraced, and kissed. My fang nicked

his tongue. Luke's blood! Oh, how I had missed it.

"Ahhem," came from the couch. "You have a room."

I didn't bother acknowledging Jonathan while shoving my rock star toward his room. I threw Luke onto his bed and shut the door behind me with no intention of opening it anytime soon.

With no hint of red rain by the following night, I sat on a bench at the large park near my house, waiting for Caleb. A pickup basketball game went into sudden death under the lights across the field.

Footsteps came from behind me, and I turned.

"How are you?" Caleb asked.

"Fine, you?" I motioned to the bench. The fang marks above his dress shirt collar had begun to fade.

"Fine." He sat very straight next to me.

"I'm nervous," I admitted.

"So am I." He relaxed some. "I hate just waiting, knowing we failed and not knowing what's coming, or if there's anything we should be doing to stop it."

"I don't think there's more we can do." I loved that spirit, though. "Waiting's awful, but I think Victoria's right that we're lucky to even know what we do."

"Any chance what's done is done and that David's life is the end of it?"

I liked his optimism, too. "We both saw that fireball. I don't know, but I feel like *something* is going to happen."

"Yeah." He put his hand over mine. "You know what I

thought when David dragged me from Paris, had his Sanguans drink from me, and made me watch him kill that last man?"

I shook my head and shifted my fingers so they interlocked with his.

"I thought since you were responding to my messages and had shown up on the rooftop in Paris that I would be okay. You're different from all the others. I knew it right away. I figured you wouldn't stop until you won. You'd get your way and accomplish what you set out to do, so I'd live." He leaned to within inches of me. "It kept me going."

"I didn't win. I hate it."

"Well, at least we're here to hate it together." He kissed me... and it was the best kiss of my life.

We stopped, and he moved his neck toward me. I gently leaned him back and brought his wrist between us. "Let those heal first. We'll start here."

———————

I met Caleb the next night at his downtown loft apartment. We spent the time between sips searching online for red rain and other updates. Media sentiment sided heavily with the Spectavi, but scientists confirming the feasibility of altering the synthetic garnered a bit of attention. Advocacy organizations demanded change, and pressure was building for the President to make a statement, one way or another, about the synthetic.

The night after, I visited June and Zack. June practically leapt into my arms at the restaurant. Even Zack wore a wide smile. The first drink got me caught up on all I had missed in June's life while away. Sipping from Zack provided the deep understanding of their relationship that I treasured.

I left them for Luke's show in D.C., and afterward, he and I spent the remaining hours before sunrise at his place.

The following night, I met Blaine at a club for an hour. He wanted to dance. I insisted we sit instead, and while I was a little distracted, it relaxed me to calmly people watch, talk, and drink.

———————

The next sunset, I rose and went to my computer. My news alerts were filled with announcements of a presidential address concerning the events surrounding the Spectavi synthetic blood. It was scheduled for nine p.m.

Zhilan texted, telling me to meet at her place for the speech.

———————

In a side room, similarly neat, but filled with more modern furniture than the rest of Zhilan's home, I sat on the edge of an L-shaped, white leather couch. A flat-screen television on the wall showed the closing moments of a sitcom. Grant sat to my right with Max—a short vampire who often worked with us—Zhilan, and Renshu on the longest portion of the sofa. Renshu's skin had lightened, and if he was still in any pain, he hid it completely. Out a side window, the Capitol and Washington monument were perfectly visible on the clear night.

The screen went dark, and the oval office faded into view with President Hughes at his desk. He was flanked by an American flag and the navy blue flag of the President, as usual. We all quieted as he began to speak.

"Good evening. The Spectavi demonstration in San Francisco came as a shock to us all."

It shouldn't have. Zhilan and others had been warning people of Spectavi lies for years.

"In the aftermath, my administration has been in contact with Spectavi leadership on a daily basis. For decades as close partners and for centuries on their own, the Spectavi have been reliable allies in humanity's struggle against Sanguan vampires. With their help, we've maintained a civilized, lawful society in the face of a powerful, inhuman evil. I know nighttime would be far more dangerous without the Spectavi, and after consulting with other government leaders, I know that sentiment is shared around the world.

"For that reason, it heartens me to report that after a thorough review, my science advisors have concluded that synthetic blood was not responsible for what happened in San Francisco. Instead, the blame rests wholly with a small group of rebellious Spectavi, urged on by Sanguans."

Lies, lies, lies. We had published the science for the world to see.

"Make no mistake, the news is still troubling. Sanguans cannot be allowed to terrorize our society. That is why, on behalf of the hundred and fifty-eight countries who have signed a joint pledge, I am announcing our continued commitment to working with the Spectavi as close allies."

Grant slapped the couch. I shook my head. Zhilan slouched slightly.

"This is our world—men and women's. Yet an inhuman evil wakes to join us in it each night. Should we cower and hide with the setting sun? Americans and people all over the world must never do that.

"The Spectavi offer their assistance and seek nothing but our cooperation, trust, and support as they do their work. It is a small price to pay to safeguard our nights, and continuing to work with them is in the best interest of all mankind. I look forward to new victories against those Sanguan vampires who insist on living outside the law. Safer nights lie ahead. Thank you, God bless you, and may God bless the United States of America."

Tink. We all looked toward the window.

Tink-tink-tunk—more rain drops hit. Max went over to look outside. I ran through Zhilan's living room to the kitchen and stopped at the sliding glass door to her deck.

Tunk-tunk-tink-tunk-tunk-tunk. Large drops hit the wood and gutter. Thick fog and clouds obstructed the view of downtown. I slid open the door, and the others bunched up behind me. I extended my hand.

Plunk. A heavy drop, mostly clear, but undeniably red-tinted, hit my hand, and then many did, as the rain intensified. I turned to the group of worried faces.

Grant stuck his hand out past me, then licked it. "It's not blood. It doesn't taste like it, anyway."

I stepped out onto the deck, into the steady, red downpour. I licked my wet hand and tasted only the usual nothingness of water. Grant and Max came out with me. While we got soaked, I closed my eyes, tilted my head back, and opened my mouth. I collected nothing but tasteless liquid.

"What will happen?" Grant asked.

The ground had not ignited in flame. Demons had not sprung forth from the falling drops. The water didn't wash me away. I looked at Zhilan and Renshu, still standing inside the doorway.

"I do not know," Zhilan said.

I sat at her round table and laid my head down in my folded arms. Max went inside, but Grant sat with me. I watched the rain fall while drops pelted my back and face, then dripped off.

I lifted my head and said, "It wasn't one man's failure."

"What wasn't?" Grant asked.

"This. So many failed. David played his part, but judgment didn't come until all those countries lined up behind the President. We still had a chance until tonight."

Grant nodded, and we sat for another fifteen minutes in steady, unstoppable rain.

I went home. Red ran off of me in the shower, and for a change, it wasn't human or vampire blood from a fight. Or maybe Grant had been wrong, and it was blood in some unknown form. I had no idea what had risen from the chapel in Switzerland or what fell from the sky that night.

I brought my laptop to my living room and put the news on TV. Weather maps showed blobs of rainclouds scattered over half the country, appearing off the West Coast and marching steadily eastward. The same rain had cropped up all over the world. Most of it hadn't been forecast, and all of it was red. Theories on the news and online included a rare atmospheric occurrence, algae in the air, extraterrestrials, and a reaction by a higher power to the President's address.

While drops pelted down outside, I thought it over. The Spectavi *did* make nighttime more livable for humans. That was undeniable. But they had done so for centuries *without* synthetic blood. Was the world safer with the synthetic and with their decision to use it as they did? Almost certainly. But the cost was great, and apparently, too great.

Caleb called, and we talked for a while, sharing no relief that the red rain had finally fallen. All we did was speculate about the hell that seemed certain to follow.

21

I pushed open my coffin lid and took a moment to summon the energy to rise. News of the prior night's events filled my RSS reader.

Red Rains Down on America and the World

President, Spectavi Have No Explanation for Red Rain

Red Rain! More on the Way?

I trudged upstairs and out back to a clear sky. My concrete patio—dry. My green grass—damp.

Down in my basement, a little research told me that the rain had continued into the day across America, then stopped mid-afternoon.

My phone chimed with a text from Grant:

Some human blood isn't right. Finding news on Twitter.

I had heard of Twitter, but never used it. I thanked him and searched the site for "blood red rain." My heart sank at the first result.

Was told my blood tasted like nothing! Is it the damn red rain?

Tweets below referenced the rain in general, until one read:

Just left the bar. Three Sanguans said my blood was worthless. It's getting crowded, and Sanguans are getting angry. Red rain?

Oh, my God. My aching to feed hit me and lingered.

It didn't make sense. With no blood, we'd all starve. What Hell would a world with no Sanguans be? I couldn't drink that synthetic, but would I rather die?

I threw on some clothes and called Caleb. No answer, so I tried Luke.

He picked up. "Hey."

"You home?" I asked.

"Yeah."

"Don't go anywhere. I'm coming over."

"Sure thing, baby."

During my half-mile run to the Fourteenth Street Bridge, a man on a bicycle pedaled toward me.

I got in his way and called, "Stop!" I had to know.

He turned left, crouched low, and pedaled harder. I raced in front of him and grabbed him in one hand and his bike in the other.

"Help!" he screamed.

While he struggled, I laid the bike on the ground and bit into his neck.

"Ah!" he yelled, unaffected by my fangs inside him.

I tasted nothing.

"Help!"

My sucking produced water—or it might as well have been. I pulled more. No heat accompanied his blood, no fire was stoked inside me, no memories came. The cavernous void inside me persisted, unfulfilled.

I released the man. "Go."

After tripping over his bike, he picked it up, got on, and pedaled away.

My lips were parched. My head hurt. At least I still had my strength and speed. I ran north over the bridge, block after block for three miles, weaving between people, cars, and buses. I turned west and sprinted to Luke's building. Out of breath, I pushed the buzzer, and the door clicked open.

I ran up three flights of stairs and down his hall, then pounded on his door.

He swung it open and found me gasping for air. "What's wrong?"

I froze. My plan had been to launch myself at him and bite him to know for sure. But what if I didn't want to know? Was uncertainty preferable to crushing disappointment?

"Erin?"

I wrapped my arms around him, my fangs touched the familiar skin of his neck, and then… the familiar warmth. I squeezed him tight and sucked. Waves of heat and power launched out from my core, one after another. His blood made me whole.

I withdrew my fangs and kept hugging him.

"What is it, Erin?"

I wiped tears away. "Something's happened. After that red rain, people's blood isn't… working… like it used to. I don't know why, but yours is fine."

"What do you mean?"

"You'll see in the news later. I have to go." I gave him a long kiss. "Bye, Luke."

Blaine worked nearby, so he was next. What was going on?

Down six blocks and over four, I ran to the restaurant. Inside, I ignored the hostess and made my way between tables toward the back, where Blaine was taking a group's order. I headed for the computer near the kitchen, figuring he would go there next.

"Erin?" he asked when he arrived.

"Got a minute?"

"Uh, sure."

"Come on." I pushed through the swinging door to the kitchen, and he followed.

"What's up?" he asked.

I grabbed his wrist. He smiled. I bit. He winced. Nothingness.

I held off tears while pulling out more useless liquid.

Blaine looked terrified. "What happened? Are you okay?"

I let him go. "The rain. I *think* I'm okay, but you've changed."

"What do you mean?"

"I don't know. Something changed in some people. But not all. Your blood is like water to me now." I shook my head. "I have to go."

"How long will it last?"

"I don't know."

"Will you be back?"

"Not tonight."

I pushed open the door to the dining room.

"Ever?"

My face went blank. "I hope so." I left.

Caleb lived closer, but still didn't pick up, so I called June from outside the restaurant.

"Can you and Zack meet me?" I asked as soon as she answered the phone.

"Sure! When?"

"Now."

"Um. Zack's studying for a test tomorrow. I don't know if he'll want to. But I will."

"I need to see you both. It's important."

"Oh, well, okay." Concern filled her voice.

"That dive bar a few blocks from campus?" I suggested.

"Sure. Is everything all right?"

"Maybe. I'll see you there." I hung up, and a Sanguan darted into view at a bus stop across the street where a man and a woman waited.

The Sanguan bit into the man, and the woman screamed. The vampire let the guy go and took hold of the woman. While the man ran, the Sanguan drank on and on, until eventually letting his victim's limp body fall to the ground. "Finally!" he roared to the sky.

A vision of a future came to mind—Sanguans everywhere, starved to the point of attacking humans in plain sight, without regard for laws or Spectavi retaliation.

I raced to meet June and Zack, past cars and crowds, block after block for over a mile. I waited in a booth up front. That future sounded grim, but it didn't make complete sense. Surely, the Spectavi deserved to be affected by the rain, too.

I texted Victoria, being intentionally vague: *Do you know what's going on?*

June came in first and spotted me immediately. Zack was only a few steps behind her.

She sat down next to me. "What's wrong?"

Zack sat across the table.

I explained, "Some people's blood has become like water to us. It doesn't satisfy our thirst."

June appeared sickened. "Who?"

"I don't know. It'll be in the news soon. Maybe there's a way to predict who's affected."

"Can you tell?" Zack asked.

June slid closer to me.

I leaned across her and bit the far side of her neck. She flinched and grimaced. Blood trickled from where I withdrew my fangs.

"Try again!" she shoved her wrist at my face.

Talking her out of it would have taken longer, so I bit— nothing.

"I have to go," I said.

Stunned, June didn't budge at her end of the bench. "What about him?"

"It doesn't matter." I couldn't be so cruel as to continue drinking from Zack, but not her.

"I have to know." She looked so pitiful.

He extended his arm. Again, biting was simpler than arguing.

I took his wrist, broke the skin, and after he winced, Zack didn't react because his blood was dead to me.

I stopped and let go. "I'm sorry."

"Is it permanent?" he asked.

"I have no idea," I said. "That red rain probably caused it, I guess, and I don't know how long it will last. I don't know much, but I do have to go."

June's eyes watered. "When will you be back?"

"I don't know." Scenes from their lives raced through my mind, the fascinating lives that were suddenly hidden from me.

"Can you fix it?" she asked.

I hadn't begun to think about that. "I don't know."

"You have to come back," she pleaded. "No matter what."

"I will." It was both the simplest answer and the truth. I couldn't imagine never seeing those two again. I nudged her toward the end of the booth.

With a huff, she slid out and got up. After I stood, she gave me a hug. She must have been crushed, but I had expected her to break down completely. For all I knew of her, from each drop of her life I had drunk in, she turned out to be stronger than I had estimated.

I checked my phone on the way out and found a missed call from Caleb and a response from Victoria. I read her message outside.

We're all affected. Our synthetic is half water, and the machines we use to produce it are suddenly breaking. Our scientists are baffled, but the only thing that's changed is the water from the red rain. I'm not optimistic they'll find a solution. We have reserve synthetic and can use bottled water to produce more, but unless something changes, we'll run out in two months. Some places, sooner.

So things would get worse. Our plan to push the Spectavi out of favor with governments had failed, yet our fears of a whole crop of newly hungry vampires would be realized. The few people whose blood would satisfy them would be in even higher demand.

I wrote back, *Any idea why not all humans are affected?*

I called Caleb and told him I had to meet him. He was in Virginia, so the park near my house was convenient for us both.

While I was on my way, Victoria responded, *No.*

I paced on the sidewalk in front of the park. Caleb's black Mercedes pulled into a space.

He turned off the engine and stepped out. "You've heard the news, I'm sure."

I stopped at his car. "I have."

"I just did." He shut the door. "And I heard there are some—not many, but some—whose blood is unaffected."

"There are."

He came near. "How cruel would it be to have found you, only to become worthless to you?"

I tried to sound confident. "You wouldn't be worthless." I took his wrist.

He tilted his head. "Why not here?" Only the faintest traces of the other marks remained on his neck. "If it's the last time you ever drink from me, I'd like it to be from there."

I thought of reassuring him, but he was no fool. I reached for the back of his neck and gently pulled him close. I had expected my first bite there to be special.

My fangs rested on his skin. I sniffled.

"Do it," he said.

I bit down, and the warmth I craved so badly, the warmth my heart cried from its depths for, poured into me. I sucked and melted as he did. We burned in each other's arms.

"Thank God," he said.

We kissed and kept kissing, until I needed another drink.

22

I spent most of the next week with Caleb, Luke, or Zhilan. When Zhilan and I sparred, landing solid blows against her was no longer a rare occurrence. She congratulated me on the tournament victory and continuously pushed me to fight faster, smarter, and harder.

I visited my grandfather in Manassas for a few hours and explained all that had happened. He said he wasn't scared and urged me not to be. His blood brought me no taste, warmth, or memories. I hated the absence of my lost past, but had seen enough on previous visits, that little, if anything, would have been new. Besides, I had more pressing things to worry about.

No more red rain had fallen, but its effects persisted. Humans whose blood satisfied a vampire's thirst were extremely rare, and no one had found a common thread that tied the group together.

Rumors were spreading that the Spectavi would soon run out of synthetic. While the Spectavi denied the allegations, Victoria had no update for me, except that production remained impossible with anything but previously procured water.

Even without the Spectavi being added to the number of

hungry blood drinkers, nighttime had already grown more dangerous. Vampire attacks were way up, with Sanguans drinking from person after person until they found useful blood. As many of those whose blood could feed Sanguans stopped going outside after sundown, gruesome attacks in homes became increasingly common. Killing those who couldn't feed them was a release of rage for some hungry Sanguans, and also held a certain logic—why leave those around who wouldn't satisfy them?

I called Zack, who said June missed my visits, but that they were fine. Hearing his voice evoked a flood of memories. I missed them so much. I urged him and June to stay indoors after sundown and told Blaine the same. They were all scared, but I didn't have any better advice to offer.

There had been no sign or word from the twins. The pair seemed content to watch the world slip into the chaos—the hell—they had been so eager to see. Some people blamed them for what had happened, but most found it unfathomable that two vampires could have been responsible for something so big. Many faulted government leaders for ignoring the truth and accepting the Spectavi's ways, in spite of what had happened in San Francisco. Most ultimately blamed God to varying degrees.

That I had killed Louis upset me less and less. Compared to what appeared imminent, one life seemed trivial. I would do my best not to let it happen again.

I hated that Nate was gone forever, but he had made his choice. Even after the fighting began, he might have been able to outrun Caterine. Whenever I thought of him, I wished he would have tried.

In the face of the hell on the horizon, it was nevertheless satisfying to have found Ahmose and to have discovered how it all started with Nicolas. David Sartori added the final chapter to the story of that True Cross fragment, but if I hadn't made it to Seorsum, we wouldn't have known the beginning. I took pride in my success, while dwelling on what we could have done differently at the end.

Haunted by how suddenly my other mortal friends had changed, I cherished my time with Luke and Caleb. They both asked who else I drank from and claimed not to mind when I told them, but their blood revealed otherwise. Because I was only seeing one other person regularly, they did care. The two men were so different, yet I could never have chosen between them. Their blood also told me that neither would ask me to choose and risk losing me entirely.

Our hours together were filled with a passion born from fear that each embrace, each kiss, or each bite would be our last. Returning to my coffin alone before each sunrise was harder than it had ever been for me.

───────────

Grant followed me out to the deck, where Zhilan, Renshu, and Max were sitting.

"When they run out, it's going to get far worse," Zhilan was saying, while Grant and I sat down.

The United States and most of the other countries the President had spoken for refused to acknowledge that their decision had anything to do with what had happened. They stubbornly stuck to their claim that the synthetic hadn't been responsible for San Francisco. The President reiterated his confidence in the Spectavi to keep the peace, seemingly blind to how much worse things had already become.

Grant stood and began to pace. "For the first time in decades, the Spectavi are going to have to hunt for their drinks."

"What do we do?" Max asked.

"Take advantage of the opportunity to crush them," Renshu suggested.

Grant nodded.

Zhilan shook her head. "They may not become as weak as you think. *They* may take advantage of the opportunity to attack us more ruthlessly than before. We presumed the twins' freedom would change everything, and it has. Things are far worse."

"Maybe," I said. "But there is hope."

Renshu asked, "Didn't you say 'hope' is what caused this?"

Grant stopped pacing.

I shook my head. "Hope twisted *them*." I looked around the group. "Things got real bad for Nicolas and David—truly horrible, in their minds. And when they were tested, they failed. But would you let that kind of hope twist you? Or would you be stronger?"

I didn't expect anyone to answer, and no one did. "I thought my test was beating the twins and David to the True Cross. I no longer think it was. I think we were meant to bear witness to what David did."

"I think my test—our test—is yet to come." I made eye

contact with Grant and thought of Alice. "Caleb's and Luke's blood is every bit as wondrous as it has always been. If none could feed us, I might see things differently."

Renshu argued, "The existence of a scarce number who can sustain us is necessary for this hell to function. Our kind is to tear the world apart fighting over the few like your friends."

"You might be right," I admitted. "The night is dark and soon to be far darker. It's only a matter of time. But Luke and Caleb... I know those like them will play the role you describe, but there *has* to be more to it. We *can't* be at the beginning of an inevitable end."

I took a deep breath. "When I look at Luke and Caleb, I see hope."

THE END OF BOOK IV

Connect Online

Thanks for reading. If you enjoyed the story, please leave a review at your favorite online retailer.

Get the latest updates about S.M. Perlow's works by signing up for his newsletter:

smperlow.com/newsletter

Find him online at:

smperlow.com

twitter.com/smperlow

facebook.com/smperlow

WORKS BY S.M. PERLOW

Vampires and the Life of Erin Rose

Novels

Choosing a Master

Alone

Lion

Hope

War

Short Stories

Alice Stood Up

—

The Grand Crucible

Novels

Golden Dragons, Gilded Age

—

Other Works

Short Stories

The Girl Who Was Always Single

www.ingramcontent.com/pod-product-compliance
Lightning Source LLC
Chambersburg PA
CBHW031023120726
47905CB00007B/2017